RELUCTANT HOPE

Acclaim for Erin Dutton's Work

"*Designed for Love* is…rich in love, romance, and sex. Dutton gives her readers a roller coaster ride filled with sexual thrills and chills. *Designed for Love* is the perfect book to curl up with on a cold winter's day."—*Just About Write*

"*Sequestered Hearts* is packed with raw emotion, but filled with tender moments too. The author writes with sophistication that one would expect from a veteran author. …A romance is about more than just plot and character development. It's about passion, physical intimacy, and connection between the characters. The reader should have a visceral reaction to what is going on within the pages for the novel to succeed. Dutton's words match perfectly with the emotion she has created. *Sequestered Hearts* is one book that cannot be overlooked. It is romance at its finest."—*L-word Literature.com*

"*Sequestered Hearts* by first time novelist, Erin Dutton, is everything a romance should be. It is teeming with longing, heartbreak, and of course, love. …as pure romances go, it is one of the best in print today."—*Just About Write*

In *Fully Involved* "…Dutton's studied evocation of the macho world of firefighting gives the story extra oomph—and happily ever after is what a good romance is all about, right?"—*Q Syndicate*

With *Point of Ignition* "…Erin Dutton has given her fans another fast paced story of fire, with both buildings and emotions burning hotly. …Dutton has done an excellent job of portraying two women who are each fighting for their own dignity and learning to trust again. The delicate tug of war between the characters is well done as is the dichotomy of boredom and drama faced daily by the firefighters. *Point of Ignition* is a story told well that will touch its readers." —*Just About Write*

Visit us at www.boldstrokesbooks.com

By the Author

RELUCTANT HOPE

by

Erin Dutton

2011

ISBN 10: 1-60282-228-X
ISBN 13: 978-1-60282-228-3

This Trade Paperback Original Is Published By
Bold Strokes Books, Inc.
P.O. Box 249
Valley Falls, NY 12185

First Edition: June 2011

CREDITS
EDITOR: SHELLEY THRASHER
PRODUCTION DESIGN: SUSAN RAMUNDO
COVER DESIGN BY SHERI (GRAPHICARTIST2020@HOTMAIL.COM)

Acknowledgments

During the process of bringing these characters to the page, I was reminded that though they may be fictional, their stories could be very real. Every day, many people face the same challenges as these two women. I am inspired by their strength and grace, and that of the families and friends who walk through this disease with them.

Cancer touches most of us in one way or another. So I decided I wanted the effects of this story to carry through my life off the page as well. In looking for a way to do that, I found many organizations that contribute to research and offer support to people coping with various forms of cancer. In the end, I chose a foundation that offers support and assistance with treatment options.

A portion of my royalties from this novel will be donated to The Minnie Pearl Cancer Foundation. The foundation was started right here in Nashville by two local doctors. They continue to help families dealing with cancer, not only in my community but across the country.

For more information visit: www.minniepearl.org

CHAPTER ONE

Brooke Donahue hadn't considered the afterlife since her childhood Sunday-school classes, and she didn't have any more idea what she believed now than she had then. It wasn't as if she were feeling philosophical. She wouldn't be contemplating it now if she hadn't been forced to.

She negotiated down the tree-lined neighborhood street and pulled to the curb more out of habit than intention. Today would likely be the last time she drove the familiar route—the last time she visited the home of her best friend since high school. She remembered when Diane had bought the house, shortly after her divorce. After spending nearly ten years with her husband, Diane had been nervous about starting over on her own. She'd regretted her failed marriage but been optimistic about her new beginning.

We're so sorry for your loss, but at least she's in a better place. That's what people had been telling Brooke for three days now. But she was convinced they didn't know what else to say. No words could make up for losing your closest friend or express no longer having the only person in the world you could rely on.

Instead, well-meaning folks told her how Diane was no longer suffering. Brooke didn't know if people actually *went* anywhere when they died. But, if so, how could anyone be certain that it was a better place?

The sentiment didn't provide any more comfort than the countless unwanted hugs that Brooke had endured in the past few hours. Somehow she'd made it through Diane's funeral, steadfastly ignoring the tears that trickled down her cheeks. Thank God, at the burial she'd had the afternoon sunshine as an excuse to hide behind her sunglasses.

She shook away the memory, reminding herself that her next task would be just as difficult. Instead of getting out of the car, she sat and watched a lone woman go up the walk to Diane's house. Brooke had seen her at the funeral and thought then that she seemed familiar, but she couldn't place her. The woman stepped carefully onto the uneven porch like someone treading on unfamiliar ground. After glancing at the numbers on the column, she crossed to the front door and rang the doorbell. Then, instead of dropping her hand she raised it to smooth the length of her auburn hair. Brooke had time to register the woman's black pencil skirt and loosely draped charcoal blouse before someone opened the door and the woman disappeared inside.

With her convenient distraction gone, Brooke forced herself to get out of the car. At the cemetery, Diane's mother had made her promise to come back to the house afterward. Brooke couldn't say no when she looked into those eyes so much like Diane's. So instead of fleeing she pushed open the door.

As she entered, she dropped her keys on the table to her right and glanced in the ornate mirror hanging over it. She looked nearly as haggard as she felt. The smudges under her eyes testified to her restless sleep lately. Instead of her usual purposely careless tousle, her dark hair hung limply against her forehead, and she didn't bother to push it out of her eyes.

Brooke wove through the people gathering in the living room. Diane would have laughed at the rotund man perched carefully on the edge of the dainty settee. She'd raved over the antique piece when they'd discovered it at an auction, but to Brooke it still looked like a silly little sofa. Brooke's taste tended as far toward simplicity as Diane's did toward opulence. Even from the beginning, when they met in junior high, their differences had somehow made their bond stronger. Diane was flamboyant and impulsive, and she often pushed Brooke outside her comfort zone. But when Diane could have gone over the top, Brooke's practical side pulled her back.

Diane's tiny kitchen was the one drawback of the house, but Diane hadn't minded since she so rarely cooked. Now, the small space was filled well beyond capacity, and Diane's mother stood at the center of the crowd. Brooke had seen pictures of her when she was Diane's age and often teased Diane that she had a living snapshot of how she would age. Brooke swallowed against a ball of grief in her throat. What had become a running joke between them every time her mother was around was now a sad reminder that Diane would never reach this age. The hair that had been graying around Diane's temple for years would never go completely white like her mother's.

Despite the other people in the kitchen urging Diane's mother to sit down and let them handle things, she bent to pull a casserole out of the oven.

"I prefer to keep busy," she said as she set the dish among the patchwork of other food lining the counter.

"Someone else can do all this." A well-meaning woman in a paisley frock patted her shoulder.

"Brooke," Diane's mother said when she saw Brooke hovering just inside the room. "I'm glad you stopped by."

Brooke dutifully wound her way into the room and allowed Diane's mother to embrace her. She breathed in the heavy scent of perfume and wondered if she would ever be able to smell flowers without thinking of the funeral home.

"It's so hard being here, in her house," Diane's mother whispered in her ear.

"I know," Brooke said, forcing the words through the thick emotion climbing up her throat. Growing up, Diane's mother had been as close to Brooke as her own, and it cut deep to hear the pain in her voice. Brooke gathered her closer and led her into the adjacent laundry room and away from the chattering women around them.

"You cared so much for my Diane."

"She was my best friend."

"She was more than that. And you were more to her." She smiled sadly. "She was your sister. And you're still a daughter to me." She grasped Brooke's hand desperately.

Brooke squeezed back, amazed that Diane's mother offered such comfort in the midst of her own pain.

"I just want everyone to leave, so I can be alone with her." The shaking voice echoed Brooke's own feelings. Her heart broke at the anguish in those words, but before she could say anything, Diane's mother pulled away and swiped at her tears. "So many people who loved her are here. I suppose they need to grieve just like I do."

She returned to the kitchen and dove back into the busywork of adding to the mountain of food already set out. Brooke worked her way around the outside of the kitchen, then paused in the archway leading to the living room and looked back. Diane's meticulously decorated kitchen faded into the homey, comfortable room where they'd eaten chocolate-chip cookies fresh from the oven. She erased the memory before it could penetrate her heart.

She stood there awkwardly for several more minutes, then spun toward the living room and nearly ran into the redhead she'd seen outside.

"Excuse me," the woman murmured as she turned sideways to slip between Brooke and the door casing.

"I'm sorry. I seem to be right in the way here." Brooke tried to step back quickly, but almost lost her balance. The woman grabbed Brooke's flailing hand and steadied her. Suddenly Brooke was looking into eyes nearly the same shade of cool charcoal as the woman's blouse.

"You're Diane's friend, Brooke, right?"

"Yes."

She nodded. "I saw you at the funeral. Your eulogy was beautiful." She squeezed Brooke's hand before releasing it.

"Thank you," Brooke muttered, feeling strange about accepting compliments on such a speech. She'd been nervous enough, addressing a room full of people about something so personal as her relationship with Diane, and her struggle to contain her grief had made things worse. Her recollection of the eulogy was a myriad of discomfort and pain.

"You must have been very close to her. By the way, I'm Addison Hunt. I hadn't known Diane long, only a year or so since she joined our group. She was a wonderful woman."

Brooke nodded, unsure what she should say in response. She didn't necessarily doubt Addison's sincerity, but she'd been listening to how wonderful Diane was all day. Did anyone go to a funeral and mention the deceased person's faults? Did anyone say she was a stubborn woman who always had to have things her way? Or that she loved to gossip? Or that she spent entirely too much money on uncomfortable furniture?

Brooke wouldn't have tolerated such remarks anyway. Much like siblings, they were allowed to talk badly about the other, but would fiercely defend them against anyone else doing the same.

Diane's illness was probably the only thing she'd ever tried to keep from Brooke. She had first battled bladder cancer two years ago and endured treatment for several weeks before she broke down and told Brooke what was going on. Diane had been resistant to treatment, both psychologically and physically. She had fought her diagnosis and her doctors with every new step, convinced she could will the disease out of her body. The radiation, then chemotherapy made her extremely sick. But as far as Brooke was concerned, it was all worth it when she was finally declared cancer-free.

Then, a year ago, the cancer was back, and this time the prognosis was worse. After the second diagnosis, Diane's attitude had changed. She immersed herself in an aggressive treatment plan and attended a cancer support group. And though Brooke had never understood why, Diane had taken immediately to the group. Brooke couldn't imagine that being around a bunch of other sick people could make anyone feel better. Weren't they all just waiting to see who would die first? Brooke wasn't surprised that she resented even the mention of the group, but she hadn't expected to be disappointed when she discovered Addison was a member.

"…such a positive attitude even when things were difficult. We're planning a special tribute to her at our next meeting, and we'd love it if you would come."

Addison hadn't stopped talking and Brooke had missed most of what she said.

"I—um…" Brooke searched for a polite way to tell Addison she wouldn't attend. And that she didn't think some cluster of strangers who had only been acquainted with Diane as a cancer patient knew her well enough to honor her. Really, this woman thought Diane had a positive attitude, but Brooke had seen Diane's agony and darkness when things got bad.

"I'm sorry. I'm rambling."

"No, you're not."

"Yes, I am. I do that when I'm uncomfortable." The shy way Addison smiled contradicted the outward confidence Brooke had sensed in her.

"Well, maybe you were. But it's okay."

The beginning strains of a sad melody drifted from the other side of the living room, and the crowd fell silent. Someone had turned on the television and Diane's face filled the screen. Brooke vaguely remembered glimpsing the slide-show DVD earlier at the service, and had even provided some of her own personal photos to Diane's family to be included. But in her effort to keep enough control to give her speech, she had purposely not watched the progression of pictures. Now, the crush of people coming from the kitchen to see the screen penned her in and she couldn't escape.

So she gathered her defenses and inwardly promised herself she could break down later if she could just get through the next couple of hours. As Diane's childhood played out on the television in front of them, the expected chorus of "awww" and "how cute" didn't drown out the unrestrained sobs of Diane's mother.

As the photos reflected Diane's teenage years, Brooke began to appear in them as well. During high school, they had been inseparable. Brooke cringed at their over-teased hair and the stretch pants and oversized T-shirts they wore. When Diane's brother made a teasing remark, Brooke ignored him, and even though she didn't look, she sensed Addison's eyes on her.

The images flashing on the screen chronicled Diane's life, but so much was missing. These snapshots in time left glaring gaps that laughter, anger, sadness, strength, and sometimes frivolity had filled. Pieces of Diane were absent now, and Brooke struggled to ensnare them in her mind so she wouldn't lose them.

In the next slide, Diane smiled and held up a plastic cup as if toasting. Despite her wide grin, an ashen pallor dusted her skin like too much makeup. Five months ago, after finding out that her bladder surgery hadn't been successful and her cancer had spread, Diane had thrown herself a party—to celebrate her life, she'd said.

She didn't want to wait until her funeral to hear all the nice things people would say about her. She'd called together all her friends and, as they reminisced about good times, she seemed the happiest Brooke had seen her since her diagnosis. But despite Diane's repeated appeals, and a good deal of pouting, Brooke had refused to—as Diane put it—do a dry run of her eulogy.

"That was the first time I'd ever been to a party quite like that," Addison murmured.

"You were there?" Brooke didn't remember seeing Addison, but maybe that explained why she seemed familiar.

Addison nodded. "I didn't stay long. But I remember thinking it was actually a good idea."

"A good idea?"

"Yes, to celebrate, instead of feeling sorry for herself."

"Celebrate what?" Brooke bit back. She maintained enough composure to keep her voice down. "Giving up? Deciding not to fight? Dying?"

Addison flinched at the last word. "I think she preferred to think of it as acceptance and appreciation for the time she'd been given."

A renewed flush of anger filled Brooke, but she shut it down before it could surface. "I couldn't see it that way."

"But you were there that day, right?"

"Yes."

"Didn't you see how happy she was to be surrounded by her family and friends?"

"Happy?" Diane had certainly put up a good front that night. But countless other nights Brooke had held Diane while she cried, when pain assaulted her in intense waves and she was hyperaware of her mortality.

"Well, maybe 'happy' isn't the right word, given the circumstances. But not everyone gets the closure of saying good-bye."

Brooke didn't agree that "closure" was a good thing. She'd hated feeling like she was waiting around for Diane to die. She couldn't make herself cherish those moments. But she also didn't feel like debating with Addison. "I suppose whether you see that as positive or negative is a personal opinion."

"You may be right about that." Addison glanced around the room, her gray eyes clouded and serious. "I recognize some of Diane's family and friends from the party. I can't believe I don't remember seeing you."

"A lot of people were there." Brooke recalled being uncomfortable in the crowded room and taking her first opportunity to escape. She didn't think Diane would miss her, but she'd barely gotten down the block when her phone signaled a text message. Diane's gentle admonishment wasn't enough to make her turn the car around though. Now she wished she'd gone back, that time and every other time as well.

"She was well-loved. I don't think I've talked to anyone who didn't like her instantly."

Brooke nodded absently and mumbled, "Excuse me." She couldn't stand to listen to Addison talk about Diane in the past tense any longer. She skirted the people gathered nearby and headed for the hallway.

Addison watched Brooke walk away, caught off guard by the sudden change in Brooke's demeanor. Their entire exchange had been odd, beginning with the jolt of awareness Addison felt when she'd inadvertently brushed against Brooke's breasts in the doorway. Taken by itself, that feeling wasn't foreign; Addison had been in touch with her sexuality since high school. But she'd barely felt anything for anyone in over eight years because she'd been focused on other things.

She turned back to the slideshow in time to see a quick succession of photos flash on the screen like the rapid-fire finale of a fireworks display. A series of shots of Diane and Brooke on a beach flickered by. They both seemed happy, but Addison could tell Diane was nearing the end. Her illness was even more apparent next to Brooke's obvious vitality. The thick hair falling across Brooke's forehead was dark and shiny. Her skin glowed beneath the bright sunlight and her cheeks were slightly flushed, unlike Diane's pasty complexion. The photo was gone before Addison could figure out the expression in Brooke's dark eyes, and a shot of Diane standing alone at the edge of the surf replaced it.

The last picture lingered for a moment. Diane seemed small against the vast expanse of water behind her. She smiled down at her feet, where foamy water swirled around her ankles. The image faded with the final strains of the music, and Diane disappeared in an eerie flicker of white light before the screen went black.

Around the room, conversations resumed, but Addison couldn't shake the memory of a time when she had feared her own friends and family might gather this way to mourn her passing. She'd approached her own diagnosis in the same manner as she did everything else. After allowing herself less than a day to succumb to the fear, she shoved it aside and began to think practically. She hit the Internet to research and attended her next doctor's appointment armed and ready for war.

But there the similarity to her and Diane's situations ended. Addison's treatment had given her back her life, and Diane's had failed. She didn't know if she could have handled the end with as much grace as Diane had. Would she have known when it was time to stop fighting?

❖

Addison left the noise of the living room behind and walked down the darkened hallway. She opened the first door on her left and didn't realize she'd chosen the wrong room until she'd already stepped inside. She'd entered what appeared to be the master bedroom. Brooke sat on the edge of the bed, her fists balled in the plush red comforter as if that were the only way she could keep from bolting from the room. She'd looked up when Addison came in, and fresh tears clung to her eyelashes.

"I'm sorry, I was looking for the bathroom."

Brooke swiped at her eyes. "It was the second door on the left."

"Are you okay?" Addison hovered in the doorway, unsure if she should leave.

"Not really."

"Of course, stupid question. I'm sorry. Do you want to talk?"

"We just did, out in the living room."

"Yes, but—"

"I can't talk about Diane anymore right now."

"Okay." She hadn't said she didn't want to talk at all. Addison sat on the bed beside Brooke. "Pick another subject."

"I don't—I can't—" Brooke appeared frustrated and her fists tightened even more. Addison reached to cover the one closest to her, but Brooke snatched it away. "What about you? What's your story?"

"My story?"

"Your cancer? Doesn't everyone in your little group have one?"

The rancor in Brooke's tone confused Addison. She'd never seen anyone react so negatively to their support group. She wanted to snap back at Brooke, but friends and family members had all kinds of reasons to be angry, and those feelings sometimes got misdirected.

"Breast cancer. I was diagnosed eight years ago."

"Eight years? Weren't you too young?"

"There's no such thing as *too young*." Addison was surprised to still hear the bitter edge in her own words after so long. At first she too had believed she wasn't at risk. She'd known women her age who found lumps and had them removed, then discovered they were benign, and she fully expected that would be the case with hers.

"Well, I meant statistically—"

"I was thirty-three when I was diagnosed. And, yes, it's less common at that age, but it happens."

Brooke had studied bladder cancer after Diane's diagnosis, but her education on breast cancer consisted only of the publicity found on television or in magazines. She'd seen the ads about the importance of mammograms and self-exams, and she tried to visit her gynecologist once a year. But until Diane's first diagnosis, cancer always seemed like something that happened to other people.

Brooke felt bad for Addison. Surely her ordeal was difficult, but she was still alive. Diane was gone, and Brooke couldn't seem to put aside her grief to find true empathy for Addison. She didn't want to accept that she would never talk to Diane again.

Reminders of her filled every room in this house, both when she was well and, worse, when she was sick. Brooke had sat on this bed and commiserated with Diane through her divorce. She'd also lain next to her when, ravaged by both cancer and chemo, she couldn't go to sleep, and they had talked until one of them drifted off. She couldn't escape the painful memories while in this house. Maybe she could somehow shake the ghost in her own apartment.

"I'm sorry. I can't do this." Brooke jerked to her feet. "I needed a moment in here alone, but now I've got to go."

"I can go. Leave you by yourself." Addison stood quickly as well, her knees bumping Brooke's as they stumbled into the same space next to the bed.

When Addison grasped Brooke's shoulders, Brooke cupped her hands around Addison's elbows for as long as it took to regain her footing. Again Brooke looked into gray eyes now softened with more sympathy than she could bear. Her desire to hold Addison for a moment longer, to cling to the comfort of her touch, surprised her. She summoned her usual need for physical distance and eased Addison away from her.

"No, you stay. I have to get out of here." She waved at the room around them, which smelled like Diane, an annoying combination of vanilla and lilac. She hadn't eaten since yesterday and the heavy scent turned her stomach, but she drew it in and engraved it deep in her memory.

CHAPTER TWO

"Damn it." Brooke shoved her guitar out of her lap and onto the sofa beside her. Sighing, she struggled to extricate herself from the overstuffed cushions, then crossed the room. "Stupid sofa," she muttered, aware of how irrational she sounded blaming the furniture for her frustration.

She glared at her guitar, though she knew the instrument didn't deserve her anger either. After all, her current lack of focus or her inability to compose even a simple verse wasn't her guitar's fault. It only lay there on the couch, innocently, mocking her. *Come on, play me. You'll feel better.* She'd been struggling with her latest song for over an hour—well, butchering her latest song was more like it— and she didn't feel any better.

Every day she went through the same routine. She forced herself to work and felt absolutely no inspiration. She couldn't quiet her mind enough to focus and usually gave up after a token attempt at writing. More times than she wanted to admit, she ended up watching true-crime television. But she was determined to keep trying. She couldn't hide out in her little apartment forever, and after three months she should be productive again.

She wandered over to the bookcase and lifted a framed picture from a middle shelf. Diane smiled back at her and Brooke's eyes welled. Through her loneliness, she imagined she could feel the judgment in Diane's expression. Shortly before Diane's cancer returned, she had sold a couple of songs, one of which had finally made it to radio as a single. She'd been living off that check and her savings ever since. In the beginning, she did so out of necessity, as Diane's treatment left her weak and ill and needing a lot of help. But later, Brooke sought to remain in her misery. She couldn't summon the passion for songwriting that she'd set aside so many months ago.

After staring at her guitar for several more seconds, she accepted that inspiration wouldn't strike right now. *Weak, Donahue.* She should force herself to work on the new song. When the phone rang, she opted for the lesser punishment and answered it.

"Ms. Donahue?"

"Yes."

"My name is Stacey Tanner. I'm calling to let you know we'll be having our first meeting Monday night at seven."

"Meeting?"

"Yes, I know the event is still several months away, but the earlier we start planning the better. At this first gathering, I'll split everyone into various committees, then you'll meet in your smaller groups. I mainly wanted to call and make sure you'll be there Monday and also to ask if you have any special skills that might steer you toward a specific committee."

"Special skills?" Since Brooke still didn't know what they were talking about, she didn't have a clue what skills she might have that this woman would be interested in.

"Yes. For example, Diane mentioned that you were a songwriter. Does that mean you have contacts in the music business and maybe could help plan the entertainment for the concert?"

Diane. Brooke had completely forgotten that she'd told Diane she would help plan a benefit event to raise money for cancer research. At the time they hadn't known if Diane would be around to see it through, but she'd made Brooke promise to get involved either way.

"I could make some calls." Maybe if she tossed a few moderately famous acts in Ms. Tanner's direction that would be enough to fulfill her obligation.

"Great. Hang on to those names, and after you've met with the rest of your committee you can start lining people up. I'll put you on the entertainment committee."

"Well, actually I have a lot of—"

"I'll see you on Monday." She hung up before Brooke could argue.

❖

"Ramsey, five minutes." Addison stuffed a peanut-butter-and-jelly sandwich into a plastic Baggie.

"I can't find my hat."

"Your dad will be here soon."

"We're going on a field trip to the park today, Mom. I need my hat."

Addison smiled. Ramsey had Addison's practical side, but the pink-and-brown striped cap she waved in the air as she entered the kitchen perfectly matched her sweater and showed a glimpse of her father's appreciation for fashion.

"Well, since you found it, make sure you wear it." Addison tugged the brim of the hat low over Ramsey's forehead and brushed her hand down one of Ramsey's pigtails. "I don't want this beautiful face sunburned." Ramsey had her father's golden complexion and didn't burn immediately, like Addison. But, hypervigilant against skin cancer, Addison still insisted that Ramsey slather on sunscreen often.

As Addison finished packing Ramsey's lunch in an insulated bag, the chime of the alarm sensor signaled the front door opening. Charles was predictably punctual, especially when it concerned Ramsey. Addison couldn't recall a single time that he'd been late picking her up.

"Daddy," Ramsey exclaimed.

"Hello, gorgeous girls," Charles said as he entered the kitchen.

He caught Ramsey when she flung herself against his legs and swung her into his arms. He didn't flinch when she grabbed his silk tie and tugged.

"Ready for school?"

"Yep. We're having a picnic."

"I know. You're going to have fun. And all I get to do today is work." He pressed his cheek against Ramsey's for a moment.

"You can take vacation and come on my picnic."

He smiled. "Vacation? I wish I could, sweetie. But I have a very important meeting."

"Closing the deal today?" Addison asked. She crossed to them and touched Ramsey's shoulder.

"Let's hope so." Charles swept fashionably shaggy blond hair off his forehead. "I've been wooing these people for months. I think we've finally found a hook they'll love." Charles had been leading his team on a proposed advertising campaign for a national sporting-goods chain.

Though Nashville wasn't known for advertising, twelve years ago, Charles's college roommate had opened a small but aggressive agency, and Charles had followed to work with him. Since then, they'd built a great reputation locally, but still had to fight hard against agencies in Chicago, New York, and L.A. for the big jobs.

"Well, good luck. I know you'll be great." She smoothed a hand over the impeccably pressed shoulder of his shirt.

"I'd better be. We need this campaign."

"Is everything okay?" He hadn't mentioned a problem, but Addison knew he'd been stressed about this pitch.

"Oh, yes. Everything's fine. It's just that this could be the step into the larger markets that we've been waiting for. And my bonus would put a nice deposit in baby girl's college account."

"Well, she won't get into college by being late for school. So, off you go," Addison said as she handed him Ramsey's lunch, then kissed Ramsey's cheek. "Have a good day, baby."

"Bye, Mommy."

As Charles walked to the front door, Ramsey talked excitedly about her school picnic once more. Addison watched them for only a few seconds before heading down the hallway toward her bedroom. She had fifteen minutes before she should be leaving for work, and she still needed to change and put on makeup.

The mortgage firm Addison worked for had been struggling lately, and rumors were swirling that cuts were coming high up in the ranks. Her boss, one of the brokers, hadn't been producing and wasn't very good at hiding his fear that he was at risk of being let go. As his administrative assistant, Addison was under nearly as much stress. On mornings like this, she wondered if she should look for another job. But she'd been with the company for fifteen years, and with her salary and benefits she couldn't afford to start over someplace else.

So, just like every other day, she'd suck it up and hope the housing market turned around soon enough to take the pressure off. She lived in the real world and no one was ever happy with their job all of the time. She couldn't daydream about doing something different; after all, she had a four-year-old to consider.

❖

Brooke studied the scrap of paper where she'd written down the address Stacey Tanner had given her over the phone. She checked the numbers against those carved into the cornerstone over the door of the old church. The handwritten sign on the front door read: A Community for Hope meeting in basement. Entrance in the back.

As she walked around the building, Brooke considered her last chance to back out of participating in the committee. If Stacey Tanner noticed she wasn't there, she would just explain that she was too busy—no, too distraught. Still in mourning, that sounded more pathetic. She immediately felt guilty for even thinking of using Diane's memory as an excuse to get out of her obligation.

She'd promised Diane, but Diane wasn't here to know whether she kept her word. Remembering the day they'd talked about the event, Brooke forced herself to continue toward the back of the church. Diane had always been the type to get involved. When they were in college she'd been on every committee and in many social clubs, but, knowing Brooke's dislike of crowds, she never pressured her to join in. Since she'd been adamant that they both participate in this fund-raiser, it must have been important to her. Honoring her promise made her feel closer to Diane.

She rounded the corner and descended the steps to the basement. A musty odor reminded her of junior high when she used to spend her lunch break hiding out in the music library because that was better than sitting alone in the cafeteria. She ate her sandwich while leafing through old, yellowed pieces of sheet music and memorizing chord progressions. She didn't return to the cafeteria until high school, after she met Diane.

Someone bumped Brooke from behind as she paused in the doorway and jolted her from a remembered wisp of loneliness. Without looking at the offender, she moved aside and nodded in response to the mumbled apology.

Several rows of folding chairs faced a large dry-erase board hanging on the opposite wall. Brooke chose a seat toward the back, but as she sat down, the chair shifted and groaned, and she immediately stood back up.

"Okay, everyone, let's get started." A tall blonde strode to the front of the room. She tossed her head as she walked, making her ponytail swing from side to side.

Brooke stepped back against the wall as several people eased past her and sat down. As the row closest to her filled, several chairs creaked, but they all seemed to be holding up. Brooke counted heads—ten others besides herself and Ms. Tanner. She had no idea how much planning went into an event like this, but she hoped that meant her responsibilities would be limited.

"For anyone I haven't met yet, my name is Stacey Tanner. Let me thank you for generously volunteering your time. Cancer has touched many of you in this room very intimately. If not you personally, then someone close to you. And by being here, by helping to organize this fund-raiser, you're letting cancer know you refuse to give up. We're here to fight, for ourselves and for those who are no longer strong enough to fight for themselves."

When the heavy door at the back of the room inched open, Stacey looked up and smiled in greeting, then continued talking. Brooke vaguely registered more of the same speech, strong words meant to inspire them to give until it hurt. But her attention wavered as Addison Hunt snuck in the back door, followed by two other stragglers.

Addison quickly took the seat on the end of the row nearest the door, and Brooke couldn't help watching her cross her long, stocking-clad legs with surprising agility in the cramped space. Addison wore a navy-blue suit and her skirt pulled tightly across her thigh, just above the knee. She'd probably come to the meeting directly from work. Used to spending her work days in jeans and a T-shirt, Brooke didn't envy her having the kind of job that required her to dress so formally. Lately, some days Brooke didn't make it out of her cotton pajama pants.

Addison looked good—comfortable in the suit and probably in the business world that went along with it. From her upswept hair down to the tips of her stylish heels, Addison exuded the kind of confidence that had always escaped Brooke. Oh, she'd done her best to fake it and had gotten pretty good at it, but inside she was still the scared, shy girl she'd always been.

Brooke was still considering her own insecurities when Addison glanced up and met her eyes. Addison smiled and gave a small wave. Brooke forced herself not to jerk her eyes away. Instead, she casually lifted her chin in greeting, then slowly slid her eyes back to the front of the room.

"So I've broken you up into teams to work on each facet of the event based either on your areas of expertise or where we need extra help," Stacey said as she passed around a stack of stapled papers. "In this packet you will find a list of each team, including contact numbers and some tips on getting started. Of course, my number is in there as well, and you may call me at any time."

Addison took the stack of papers from the person in front of her, then passed it along. She kept one for herself and held one out for Brooke. When Brooke leaned forward to take it, Addison slid one chair to her right, leaving a vacant one beside her. Brooke took the packet and settled in the empty chair as quietly as she could.

"If you flip to the last page of your packet, you'll see a map of the park we'll be using. Those of you working on the picnic and entertainment committees, please stay within your allotted areas because space will be limited once the park is filled with attendees."

"She's the most organized woman I know," Addison whispered as she leafed through the bundle of papers.

Brooke flipped through the pages until she saw her name listed under the heading for entertainment, just where Stacey had said it would be. But she paused when she saw the name listed next to hers: Addison Hunt.

"Looks like we'll be working together. Small world, huh?"

"Yeah," Brooke whispered. *Too small.* Of the dozen or so other people in the room, how had she been paired with Addison?

"Honestly, Stacey told me you'd signed up to help out. She said you're a songwriter."

"That's right."

"I asked Stacey to put me on entertainment with you. I've worked on this project every year for a while now, and I figured since you don't know anyone in the group you might want to see a familiar face. Oh, I know we only met the one time, but we already have Diane in common."

Brooke nodded, not trusting herself to speak. Hearing Diane's name still sent a shaft of pain through her chest. And the way Addison so casually compared their respective relationships with Diane irritated her.

Stacey Tanner was winding down and Brooke couldn't wait to get out of there. Stacey reminded them about the next meeting and asked each group to have a status report ready at that time.

"Would you like to meet later this week to brainstorm about the concert?" Addison asked after Stacey had finished.

"Sure, whenever," Brooke said as she stood.

"Really? Whenever?"

"Yeah. My schedule is flexible."

"Wow. I can't remember the last time I could say that and really mean it. Well, I'm pretty booked until this weekend. How's Saturday afternoon for you?"

"Saturday it is."

"Good." Addison pulled a pen and notepad out of her purse. "Here's my address. Come over any time after three."

"Addison, it's good to see you again," Stacey called as she made her way down the aisle.

She smiled and revealed teeth so straight and white they didn't seem real.

"Hello, Stacey. How are you?" Addison greeted her in the socially polite way that Brooke never felt comfortable with.

"I can't complain."

"Good. And the twins? I haven't seen them in so long, how old are they now?"

"Almost nine."

"That's right. You were pregnant when I—when we met." Addison touched Brooke's arm as if trying to draw her into the conversation. "Stacey, this is Brooke Donahue."

"Of course, we spoke on the phone. It's nice to meet you." Stacey grasped Brooke's hand and shook it before releasing it just as quickly.

"Excuse me for a moment, I want to go say hello to Virginia and Tessa." Addison slipped away, leaving Brooke awkwardly standing with Stacey.

"Addison told me you were close to Diane. I'm so sorry for your loss. She was a wonderful woman."

Brooke clenched her teeth and nodded.

"I met her in our support group. I wasn't sick, it was my husband. He had testicular cancer."

How did one respond to such a statement? Brooke actually wasn't surprised at how willing Stacey was to share her personal history or, more accurately, her husband's medical history. She'd experienced the same thing while sitting with Diane in the hospital during her treatments. Bonded by a similar disease, and possibly shared fear, the patients there often talked openly about their diagnoses.

"I'm the one who convinced her to help out with the fundraiser this year. I'd hoped she would be..." After a few seconds of tense silence that felt like an hour, Stacey said, "I'm sorry, I—"

"It's okay."

Maybe it wasn't, but Brooke was sick of hearing people apologize, and she didn't want pity from someone she didn't know.

In fact, she didn't want anything except to escape from this whole situation. Brooke scanned the room and paused when she spotted Addison. She stood with several other women, all of whom listened intently to whatever Addison was saying. She gestured while she spoke and her hands punctuated the air sharply.

"I think you'll find Addison very easy to work with," Stacey said, tossing her head.

Brooke saw her opening. "Well, I was planning to talk to you about that. If she could be more helpful someplace else, lining up a few music acts is probably just a one-person job anyway."

"Oh, no, it's more than just the closing concert. The entertainment committee is responsible for several blocks of time throughout the day. It's a lot of work, and while I don't doubt you could handle it on your own, I wouldn't want to burn you out your first time with us. Addison is experienced and I'm sure she'll prove very helpful."

CHAPTER THREE

Saturday afternoon, Brooke stood on Addison's porch, apprehensive about the number of cars parked in the driveway and on the street in front of the house. Had she gotten the time wrong or had Addison forgotten they agreed to meet? This whole project had already been more trouble than it was worth, and now she'd have to deal with this flighty stranger in order to get through it. Deciding not to delay any further, she pressed the doorbell.

The door swung open, but instead of finding Addison on the other side, Brooke had to drop her eyes several feet until they rested on a little girl. She looked like a china doll in a frilly blue dress the exact color of her eyes.

"Hi. Are you here for my birthday?" The girl's smile lit up her tiny features.

"Um—"

"Ramsey, what have I told you about opening the door? Always let Mommy get it," Addison called as she crossed to the door.

"She's here for my birthday," Ramsey said, still gazing up at Brooke.

"No, baby, this is my friend, Brooke." Addison met Brooke's eyes and tilted her head toward the girl. "My daughter, Ramsey." She rubbed a hand over the girl's blond curls, then steered her back toward the living room. "Why don't you go see if Daddy is ready to cut the cake?"

"Cake!" Ramsey hurried across the room.

"Come on in." Addison stepped back and let Brooke enter before closing the door.

"You said after three. If now's not a good time, I can come back later."

"No, I'm sorry. The party's running longer than I expected. I thought they'd be done by the time you got here. Do you mind waiting until I can herd all the guests out?"

"Of course not." Brooke wanted to leave. "Did I hear something about cake?"

"Yeah, follow me."

Brooke followed Addison through the kitchen, out a set of French doors, and into a small fenced yard. More kids than Brooke could count ran around, weaving among the legs of a handful of adults.

"Ramsey had to invite every kid in her preschool class. Who knew they would all come."

"How many are here?"

"I don't know. They won't stand still long enough for me to count them," Addison said with a smile. "Seriously, there are twelve, including mine. Do you want something to drink?" Addison gestured to an open cooler filled with juice boxes and bottles of water.

"I'll have a fruit punch."

"The other cooler has sodas for the grown-ups. But if you really want a juice box, you're welcome to one."

"Yeah, sure. It's been a while."

"They're a staple in our house." Addison picked up a fruit punch, opened the straw, and pushed it through the hole. When she looked up and saw Brooke watching her, she glanced back down as if she hadn't realized what she'd been doing. "Sorry, habit."

"Actually, that's good. I can never get the straw in without mangling it," Brooke joked, taking the offered drink. "So, you have a daughter."

"Yes. She's five today. But I guess the big number five on the cake kind of gives that away, doesn't it?"

"I wouldn't have guessed you had a kid." *And a husband?* She'd said "Daddy" was cutting the cake. But Addison didn't wear a ring. And though Addison hadn't said or done anything to outright confirm her sexual preference, Brooke hadn't gotten a "straight" vibe from her.

"Why not?"

"The couple of times I've seen you, you seem so...put together, I guess."

"And by that you mean I don't have Cheerios in my hair. A mom can't be put together?" Addison smiled. "Being organized and efficient is a necessary part of being a mother."

"It's not that. I don't know. You were wearing more formal clothing the other times I've seen you, and maybe that threw me off. For whatever reason, I just didn't expect it."

"This is my 'mom' uniform." Addison gestured down at her light-pink T-shirt, which clung to her breasts and followed the plane of her stomach and the curve of her waist. Perfectly manicured, rose-tinted toes stuck out of leather sandals beneath the frayed hem of her worn jeans. "Do you like it?"

Brooke liked it—probably too much. She cleared her throat, hoping she could keep the warmth that was suddenly spreading through her out of her eyes. "Yes. It's very—matronly."

"Nice. Thanks." Addison laughed and swatted Brooke's shoulder. For a second she'd thought Brooke might be flirting with her, but she must have been mistaken. Now, Brooke didn't make eye contact and her expression gave nothing away. Apparently, Addison was sorely out of practice when it came to flirting. Brooke was probably just being nice. After all, what choice did she have after she'd shown up expecting to work on the project, only to find a child's birthday party going on?

"Mommy, it's time for cake." Ramsey returned and tugged Addison's hand. She looked up at Brooke for only a second before grabbing her hand as well. "You can come, too."

As Addison followed Brooke and Ramsey across the yard, Ramsey chattered about her cake. She asked Brooke if she liked chocolate, and Brooke only had time to nod before Ramsey began raving about the butterfly theme on her cake and how much she loved butterflies, and didn't Brooke think they were pretty.

"Birthday girl, it's time to make a wish," Charles called as Ramsey ran up to the table that held her cake. He'd just finished lighting the candles and was trying desperately to keep one of the dozen kids running around from blowing them out prematurely.

"I know exactly what I want to wish for."

"What?"

"I can't tell you or it won't come true." Ramsey squeezed her eyes shut and her forehead wrinkled in concentration. Then she opened her eyes, sucked in a big breath, and blew out all five candles. She clasped her hands together under her chin, obviously delighted that she would now get her wish.

Charles cut the cake and handed plates to one of the other parents, who then distributed them to the children. Ramsey had now abandoned Brooke in favor of her dessert, and Brooke was left, trapped in the middle of the chaos. She stood rigidly, clearly wanting to dart away from the crowd surrounding her.

Addison grasped Brooke's wrist and pulled her free of the bundle of kids. As she led Brooke to safety, she scooped up a piece of cake as well.

"Share this with me. I don't need all the calories," Addison said as they settled on a pair of folding chairs next to a small card table. She handed Brooke a plastic fork and put the plate between them. "Unless you want your own piece."

"No, this is fine." Brooke took a bite. "Ramsey was right. Butterfly cake is the best."

Addison smiled. "Thanks."

"You made this?"

Addison nodded.

"Well, it's great. So I should add 'baker' to the list of things I wouldn't have expected about you?"

"Not really. It's all part of the mom thing."

"Really? Because my mother couldn't bake at all. She tried—for years—until she finally gave up and got store-bought desserts."

"Ah, well, not all moms are blessed with the same talents. For example, I can't sew worth a damn."

"It's good to know you have weaknesses," Brooke said before taking another bite.

"Please, I have plenty. And fears, too."

"Yeah? Like what?"

"When Ramsey was a baby, I was petrified. I guess I figured because I waited until later in life to have her, I would have everything together by then. But I worried about little things like what was the best formula for her, or the best sleeping position. And the big stuff, too."

"Big stuff?"

Addison nodded, and a flash of remembered fear created a thick ball in the back of her throat. "Like would I be around to watch her grow up."

"I'm sorry. I didn't mean to make you remember all that."

Addison shook her head, reminding herself of her pledge to take things one day at a time. "It's okay. I've mostly made my peace with my reality. But when I was trying to get pregnant I sometimes felt I was being selfish to want her."

"Is it—I mean, is there still—do you think you need to worry?"

"I have no guarantees."

"Of course not. But—well, you don't have to tell me if you don't want to."

"My prognosis?"

"Yes."

"Maybe we should save that for another time."

"Absolutely. I'm sorry."

Brooke probably assumed her past was too difficult to talk about. Enough time had passed that Addison could usually discuss her cancer without getting emotional. But her daughter's birthday party wasn't the place to do so. Today she was celebrating.

"The kids are all full of sugar. It's time to send them home," Charles said as he joined them. He wrapped an arm around Addison's waist.

"I agree." A few of the other parents had been checking their watches earlier, and Addison expected them to start corralling their children soon. "Brooke this is Charles, Ramsey's father."

"Hi, Brooke. Addison has told me a little bit about you." Charles stuck out his hand.

Since she'd said Brooke was moody and distant, Addison hoped he wouldn't elaborate.

"Nice to meet you," Brooke said.

"I'm looking forward to the fund-raiser. I wanted to be involved in the planning, but work has had me swamped lately. So I'll have to be content with attending."

"What do you do?"

"I'm in advertising."

"That sounds interesting."

"Sometimes. But it can be a headache, too." Charles squeezed Addison's waist and kissed her cheek before releasing her. "I'm going to start cleaning up so you two can get to work once everyone clears out."

"Thanks, Charles. I see a couple of parents gathering their gift bags already." Addison had spent yesterday morning stuffing goodie bags for all the kids. She turned to Brooke. "Make yourself at home, out here or inside, whichever you prefer. I need to see Ramsey's guests out."

❖

Brooke stepped inside the house as Addison closed the front door for the last time. The guests had all left and, though evidence of the party remained, cleanup efforts had begun. Brooke lingered at the back door as Addison walked through the open living room, picking up party favors, streamers, and empty plastic cups. By the time she reached the kitchen she had an armload of debris.

"Let me help," Brooke said as she followed Addison around the counter.

"Thanks, but it's a delicate balance. If you move one piece, I may lose it all." Addison crossed to the trash can and stepped on the pedal that lifted the lid. She dropped everything in and brushed her hands together. "I'll get to the rest of it later. Have a seat." She indicated the dinette table in front of the bay window.

Brooke sat facing the window, taking in the view of the backyard. The crowd of people out there had distracted her earlier so she hadn't noticed how nicely the area was landscaped. Two large trees sprinkled shade across the lush grass, and a tire swing hung from one of them. A hammock on a stained teak stand stood under the other, and Brooke imagined Addison lying in it while watching Ramsey play nearby.

Where's Ramsey?" she asked.

"She went home with Charles for a while. He'll bring her back before bedtime." Addison retrieved a notebook and a pen from a small secretary desk in the adjacent alcove and sat across from Brooke.

"He doesn't live here? So, you're divorced?" Brooke didn't want to examine the hint of excitement she heard in her own voice.

"Divorced? God, no, we weren't married."

"Oh." She'd assumed they were a couple, given the comfortable way he'd put his arm around her and the obvious affection between them. She couldn't imagine Addison having a baby with someone casually.

"Brooke, Charles is gay."

"Oh, I wouldn't have guessed." In the few minutes Brooke had spoken with him, she hadn't picked up any clues about his orientation. Apparently her gaydar was off. Perhaps she was wrong about Addison as well.

"He'll be happy to hear that. He prides himself on being butch."

"So you guys—I mean, he's Ramsey's—never mind, it's none of my business." Brooke seldom asked such personal questions of someone she barely knew. Actually, she rarely had conversations with strangers that didn't concern her work.

Addison shrugged. "It's not a secret. I always wanted kids, but I didn't want to do it on my own. Charles is my closest friend, and I was confident our friendship could withstand raising a child together."

"So you guys just—oh, my God, I'm sorry. This is really not—um—congratulations." Brooke felt her face flush with embarrassment. She'd pretty much just asked Addison, someone she barely knew, about her sex life."

Addison laughed. "It's okay. No, we didn't do it the old-fashioned way. I'm used to people asking about it."

"You shouldn't have to be. It's private and none of my business."

"When I was diagnosed, my doctor told me the treatment could create problems with my fertility. So we froze some of my eggs, just in case. After treatment, I had them implanted."

"Was it safe?"

"Relatively. My doctor recommended I be two years cancer-free. I waited two and a half, then tried a couple of times before it worked."

"Wow. You're braver than I am."

"I don't know about brave. My future was still questionable, but I was done waiting for things to happen for me. I'd just been given a very big lesson in how short life can be. Charles provided a good sounding board, and at some point during our discussions, we came up with the idea of him being the father. He wanted kids, too. This way Ramsey gets a mom and a dad. And if anything happens to me, she'll be in good hands."

"And she's cool with the whole gay-parent thing? Or does it even matter to her at that age?"

"We both agreed not to bring dates around her unless it was serious. But that hasn't really come up. Charles is so in love with her, when he has her, it's all about her. If he's going to see someone, he does so when I have her. And I—" Addison stood and crossed to the refrigerator. "Would you like something to drink?"

"No, thank you." Brooke waited to see if Addison would pick up that thread of conversation again. Though she really wanted to hear more, she wasn't sure she should ask. They were assigned to a project together, that was all. And Brooke had been here for over an hour and they hadn't even started yet.

"So, I have all the paperwork Stacey put together for us," Addison said as she returned to the table with a glass of orange juice. She opened a folder and leafed through several pages. "Here's the map of the park she made." She flipped that page out and laid it on the table between them. "She's also blocked out the time periods that we're responsible for filling."

Stacey's plan involved breaking up the day with various activities in different areas of the park. The fund-raising walk would take place early in the morning, right after the opening ceremonies, in order to avoid the hottest part of the day. Brooke and Addison needed to line up a couple of acts to provide music during the walk. Stacey had simply specified that they come up with a creative form of entertainment or contest for the spectators to participate in at several times later in the day. The event would close with a concert and fireworks.

"I was thinking, we need a good band for the evening concert, maybe a big name to draw in a crowd. Do you know anyone?"

"Let me make some calls. I'll get back to you."

Addison nodded and made a note on her copy of the schedule next to the appropriate time slot. "Any ideas for 'creative entertainment'?"

"How about an open-mic portion? I could put out the word to some songwriters here in town. A charity event like this is sure to bring in some of the music business community. It would be a good opportunity to showcase local talent."

"That sounds like a great idea. Will you play?"

Brooke shrugged. "I'm sure we'll be very busy that day."

"But you just said it would be a good opportunity."

"Yeah, but—"

"So it's decided. You'll play." Addison leaned forward, meeting Brooke's eyes.

"Yes. I'll play." Brooke had no idea why she'd agreed so easily, except that suddenly she wanted to satisfy the expectation in Addison's expression.

"Good. I can't wait to see what you've got."

Brooke couldn't speak and she couldn't tear her eyes away from Addison's. The innocently spoken sentence had caused a twitch low in Brooke's belly. Her quick and intense response to Addison's words surprised her.

"Have you written anything I might know?" Addison carried on with the conversation, apparently oblivious to the reaction she'd caused.

Brooke reined in her overactive mind and forced her focus back to Addison's question. "I doubt it."

"Why not?"

"Are you a fan of obscure country music?"

"Um, I'm not really a fan of country music at all."

"None? Reba? George? Martina? Tim and Faith?" Brooke had grown up in Nashville, and though she appreciated other musical styles, country music was in her blood.

"I've heard of them, of course. But, no, I don't listen to it."

"What? How can you live in Nashville and not listen to country music? Not even accidentally?"

Addison laughed. "Accidentally? How do you accidentally listen to something?"

"Country outweighs all other markets on local radio. Haven't you ever been flipping the dial and stopped on one?"

"I guess I probably have. But nothing stands out as memorable. So, I guess I don't know if I have listened to any of your songs. I'm sorry."

"Don't worry about it." Brooke waved off the apology, feeling a bit foolish. She could almost certainly say that Addison hadn't heard any of her stuff. She'd had only a few songs released as radio singles, and they didn't exactly climb the charts. She'd made a name for herself writing solid songs often used to fill out an album and had been waiting for her chance to sell a breakthrough single. But she'd allowed her career to stall when Diane got sick.

"I'll get to hear at least one at the event, I guess." Addison picked up her pen. "Okay. Anything else?"

"I have a friend who does karaoke at a bar downtown. He would probably help us out. Maybe a little audience participation will break up the day."

"Sure, but let's not put it too close to the songwriters. We want to distinguish between the crowd and the pros so no one feels self-conscious."

"Put the karaoke in the afternoon so people have plenty of time to sign up and choose their songs," Brooke said.

"Good idea. Well, that gives us a good start."

"Yes." Brooke glanced at her watch and was surprised at how much time had passed. Outside, the shadows of dusk were giving way to darkness. "It's getting late, I should get going."

"I wasn't trying to run you off. You're welcome to stay and chat. I just figured we could work on these things, then meet again to check in."

"Absolutely. And you're not running me off. I have some things to do at home and you'll probably be ready to tuck Ramsey in when she gets home." When Brooke stood, Addison rose as well.

"Well, thank you for coming over, and for being so patient about the party."

"No problem. Just give me a call when you're ready to get together again." Brooke already anticipated their next meeting far too much. She hoped she could get a bit of distance by letting Addison schedule it.

❖

"Today was my best birthday ever," Ramsey said as she climbed into bed.

"I'm glad, sweetheart." She'd said the same thing the year before. Addison tucked the covers around her and bent to kiss her cheek.

"Next year, I want a ladybug cake."

"We've got plenty of time to decide about next year, love." Addison was certain she would change her mind several times before then. She would be in kindergarten and following whatever fad was popular among her peers at the time.

As Ramsey talked about her plans for next year, her voice sounded increasingly drowsy and eventually she drifted off to sleep. Addison remained perched on the side of her bed, softly stroking her hair back from her forehead. Thinking about her little girl going off to school caused a knot in Addison's stomach. Being separated from

Ramsey didn't make her anxious. They'd spent time apart. From infancy, Charles had taken Ramsey regularly, and she also went to preschool or daycare when they were both at work. But Addison had been having mixed feelings about Ramsey's fifth birthday all day.

She was proud of the way Ramsey was growing up. She was smart, funny, and kind-hearted; even at her young age she seemed sensitive to the feelings of those around her. Yet at the same time Addison still remembered clearly her decision to have a baby, despite all her worries about potentially getting sick again and leaving her child without a mother. Having Charles around eased some of her concerns, but even the wonder of pregnancy couldn't completely eradicate them. Before Ramsey was born, Addison secretly wished she could hold a part of herself back from her daughter, but the minute she saw her, she fell completely in love.

However, the day she sent her off to school marked the beginning of a new stage in Ramsey's life. She would become increasingly independent, and Addison would miss the days when she and Charles were Ramsey's whole life. Though it was an important part of Ramsey's development, she dreaded when Ramsey would prefer time with her friends over time with her mom and dad.

For now, she would try to cherish days like today, when she and Charles were still Ramsey's heroes. She kissed Ramsey's forehead, then folded the blanket tighter around her shoulders.

"Good night, my sweet girl," she whispered. Ramsey mumbled softly and rolled over, curling her knees toward her chest and pressing her fist under her chin.

Addison eased out of Ramsey's room and closed the door. She crossed the hall to her own bedroom and felt the beginnings of fatigue when she saw her bed. She had made this room her sanctuary and often could slough off hours of stress from work just by walking in here. The walls were painted a pale lavender that matched the pinstripes in her Egyptian-cotton sheets. A white duvet and a soft heather-gray blanket made up the layers of bed linens that Addison loved to bury herself between. She liked to be cozy when she fell asleep, until the middle of the night when she cast off all but the sheet.

A house full of four- and five-year-olds could turn a long day into a marathon. She longed to crawl between the sheets and close her eyes. But her to-do list was overflowing with things she'd been putting off. In the end, she compromised and took the notes she'd jotted during her meeting with Brooke into bed with her and sat propped against the headboard while she went over them.

She'd sensed Brooke's reluctance the other night at the fundraiser meeting. She'd also seen Brooke's discomfort in dealing with Stacey and at first thought she was just shy around new people. But Addison sensed something more—something in the edge of bitterness when Brooke talked about cancer. Of course, it had been only a few months since Diane's death and naturally she was still grieving. Addison wondered if she had gotten any counseling to help her deal with the loss, but, though they'd made some progress that afternoon, they weren't at a point where she could ask such a personal question.

Addison could usually read people well, but Brooke was a proverbial closed book. She didn't volunteer much information about herself, and what she did offer only confused Addison further. She'd always thought artist types were dedicated and full of emotions that they poured into their work. For a songwriter, Brooke seemed to have very little passion about what she did.

CHAPTER FOUR

"D id you bring me a new song?"

Brooke had barely made it through the door at Poppi's Cabaret before the owner and namesake of the bar accosted her. Despite her cutesy name, Poppi was no pixie. She topped six feet easily. Enfolding Brooke in long arms, she pressed her close to her large breasts. Brooke endured the hug until Poppi released her with nearly as much force as she had swept her up.

"Sorry, Poppi, I haven't finished anything."

Poppi had been after her for weeks to put together a set for one of her famous monthly showcases.

"What's going on, chick?" Poppi's question was actually an accusation, delivered with a bob of her head that set her thick dark curls in motion.

"It's just been a rough few months."

"Aw, baby girl, I know. But you've got to keep on going. And that means getting up on that stage." She gestured to the darkened platform at the far end of the room. Then she rounded the bar and smacked a hand on its scarred surface. "But first, what are you drinking?"

"Just water."

"Water?"

"Please." Brooke slid onto a barstool. Poppi had laminated signed pictures of country stars who had played there onto the bar's surface. She also had several rows of photos hanging on the wall behind the bar and added new ones every time a rising star became famous.

Poppi slapped a napkin on the bar in front of Brooke and put a bottle of water on it. "So if you didn't bring me a new song, what are you doing here on a Monday afternoon?"

"Diane roped me into helping plan this benefit to raise money for cancer research. I'm working with another woman on organizing the entertainment. I was hoping Keith might host the karaoke for us."

"He's not here yet, but I'll ask him." Poppi propped her forearms on the bar and settled over them. "As a matter of fact, I'll make you a deal. Keith will DJ your karaoke, no charge, if you play in my next showcase."

"Shouldn't you ask him first?" Brooke backpedaled. Getting on stage was her least-favorite part of the job to begin with, and she'd already committed to playing at the benefit. She'd much rather stay at home and write the songs and leave the performing to someone else. But playing one of these showcases every now and then was a good way to keep her name in the right circles, and she'd seen the budget Stacey had given them. If they wanted to pack in the entertainment, they'd have to take donations wherever they could.

"I don't have to ask him. He'll do what I tell him."

Brooke smiled at the image. Keith was a big guy and no one would dare tell him what to do—no one but his wife. Keith and Poppi made an imposing pair, but Brooke had rarely seen two people more in love or happier with how they spent their time together. Keith had worked two jobs to support them when Poppi opened this bar. Then when the bar was doing well, he came to work for her. And anyone who'd seen them together knew that Poppi was definitely the boss and Keith had no problem with it.

"So, do we have a deal?"

"Damn it, okay. But I need time to come up with some new stuff."

"You concentrate on your event. After it's over, will you agree to play the next showcase?" Poppi stuck her hand across the bar.

"Fine." Brooke shook Poppi's hand.

"So tell me about this benefit. What else can I do to help?"

"It's a whole day of activities, kind of like a community-picnic setting with a 5k walk around the trail at the park. We're setting up a stage and doing a full day of musical entertainment, which the other woman, Addison, and I are planning. There'll also be a kids' zone with all kinds of games and an inflatable play castle or something."

"Sounds great. If you need anything else from us, let me know." Poppi smiled. "I probably would have helped out even if you hadn't agreed to the deal."

"Thanks a lot. So you just bullied me into that promise to torture me."

"No, I did it for your own good."

"Same thing. But I'll hold up my end of the bargain, and I may take you up on the offer of more help." Brooke slid a stack of her business cards across the bar. "I need to line up some acts. I've got some contacts, but you know everyone. And I trust you. If you say they're good, they are. Would you mind passing along my number?"

"Will do." As Poppi tucked the cards in the breast pocket of her gray button-down shirt, Brooke noticed the name "Larry" sewn on the shirt and a patch on the other side advertising Larry's Custom Chrome.

"Who's Larry?"

Poppi glanced down at her shirt. "Old boyfriend. Don't tell Keith. He thinks I bought it at a flea market. What? Don't look at me like that. We have some secrets. That's the key to a healthy marriage."

Brooke laughed. "I wouldn't know."

"That's because you don't try. You're a songwriter in Nashville. You could hook up with new people every night if you got yourself booked in the right bars."

"I'm not interested in finding someone that way." She'd met a few women in bars over the years and it never worked out. Typically, Brooke was there for business, not pleasure, so when she came across a woman who was there hanging out, in the end, they had very little in common.

"Don't worry. When it's right, you'll know."

"People say that a lot. But I'm not sure it always works out that way." She'd been waiting for magic. Hell, she'd even settle for a tiny spark, but she'd never felt that connected to anyone. Her strongest bond ever had been with Diane, and knowing how that turned out, she wasn't sure she wanted to love anyone.

❖

The shrill blast of a whistle cut through the giggling of the dozen four- and five-year-olds sitting on the edge of the pool. From her lounge chair nearby, Addison glanced up from her romance novel long enough to make sure Ramsey was obeying her swim instructor. The children had completed their required lessons early and, as a reward, they now waited in line for their chance to jump off the diving board into the deep end and, later, to swim races. One instructor was treading water below to help them get back to the side, and the other stood by the board. Though the kids were excited and restless, the threat of losing this privilege calmed them down.

One at a time, they plunged into the water, trying to outdo each other with the creativity of their jumps. As Ramsey approached the diving board, Addison laid her book aside. Ramsey was fearless, and her goal often seemed not just to impress her friends but to scare her mother. She looked over at Addison and grinned. Addison smiled back, knowing Ramsey loved the attention.

Ramsey stood at the back of the board. After a running start she flung herself off the end, tucked her chin, and kicked her legs in the air. She didn't get enough rotation for the flip and landed flat on her back in the water. Addison held her breath until Ramsey surfaced. Her worries were soothed when Ramsey came up smiling and shoving her hair out of her face. Her dive wasn't pretty, but it was enough to earn a round of applause and laughter from her friends. Ramsey pulled herself up the ladder and hurried over to Addison.

"Don't run," Addison warned her. Charles said she babied Ramsey and joked that it was his job to toughen her up. Admittedly at times she had to remind herself that Ramsey wasn't a fragile child and that she shouldn't be raised in a bubble because of Addison's fears. But, as a mother, she had a right to worry occasionally about her daughter.

"Did you see, Mom?"

"I did. That was great. I give it an eight and a half." Addison never gave tens, wanting Ramsey to always strive for more.

"I need to practice."

"Did it hurt?"

Ramsey shook her head, but Addison didn't think she would admit if it'd stung even a bit.

"Do you think Daddy will take me swimming tomorrow, too?"

"You can ask him. But for now, go back to your class."

Ramsey rejoined them just as the instructor was separating them into groups for races swimming across the pool.

Addison smiled and picked up her book again but had trouble concentrating on the story. Ever since her meeting with Brooke on Saturday, she had wondered when they would get together again. Brooke had left things up to her. Certainly, two days wasn't enough time for either of them to have accomplished anything worth talking about. But maybe by the weekend she would feel okay calling Brooke.

"Daddy!" Ramsey's exclamation drew Addison's attention. Charles waved at Ramsey as he crossed to where Addison sat.

"I'd planned to drop her off at your house," Addison said as he stretched out on the chaise next to hers.

"I know. But I was out running errands and knew you'd be here. It seemed just as easy to stop by and get her. Besides, I like watching her swim."

"She's already planning to ask you to bring her back tomorrow."

"We won't have time tomorrow, but maybe I can make it up to her with a trip to that big playground she likes this weekend. I'll let her invite one of her friends along."

"She'll love that." Addison gave him an exaggerated smile. "You're the coolest daddy ever."

"Yeah, whatever. How was work today?"

"Same as usual. Everyone's hoping the market will turn around while waiting for the next wave of layoffs."

"That's understandable. It's tough all over right now. Are you still solid?" He stretched back and rested his hands behind his head. When he crossed his ankles, he looked every bit the beautiful, arrogant man Addison had thought him to be when they first met.

"I'm good. Even if Evan goes, I'll get moved to another broker. I've been there longer than a lot of the other assistants."

Many of the other administrative assistants had come and gone, leaving for jobs with larger agencies. Addison had stayed put, not because she hadn't had other opportunities, but because the sacrifice for stability in her professional life was worth the gain in her personal life. Her current job allowed her to devote more time to Ramsey. Though she knew plenty of women who juggled motherhood and an advancing career, Addison didn't want to waste a minute that she could spend with her daughter.

"I meant to ask you the other day how things went with that woman who came to Ramsey's party."

"Brooke? Fine." She hoped he wouldn't press further.

"She's hot. Very quiet, though. And a little too butch for you, but if that's what you're into these days—"

"I'm not. Into—that, um, her." Addison shook her head as if she could clear the sudden confusion that thinking about Brooke caused. "We're working on the fund-raiser together, that's all." *Too butch?* Addison hadn't really thought of Brooke that way. Yes, she had strong features, and her cargo shorts and T-shirt were a bit boyish, but her soft brown eyes framed by long lashes and her slender hands were quite feminine.

"Really? I saw the way she looked at you. She's clearly into you. And you seemed a bit more flirty and girly than usual. Are you sure there's nothing between you?"

He was fishing, Addison was certain. He couldn't have gotten anything from the few minutes that he'd spoken to Brooke on Saturday.

"Nope. Nothing. Just working together."

"What did you guys talk about after everyone left? Just work?"

"Yes. Why are you so interested?"

He shrugged. "You haven't dated anyone in almost a decade. You're nearing some kind of Guinness record, and if you get in that book you'll be famous."

"You're an ass." Addison sneered at him. "You're in a bit of a slump yourself. Have you been out with anyone since the golf instructor?"

"No. And I'm still sorry that didn't work out."

"Why?"

"My swing was really starting to come around."

Addison laughed. "So, Mr. Guinness-record-holder, when was the last time *you* got laid?"

"Wow. Who was talking about sex? Your mind goes straight to the gutter."

"That's your influence. Besides, it's been so long since either of us was involved with anyone but each other that talking about relationships means I have to go back to our younger days in the club when nothing mattered beyond the weekend."

He looked wounded. "You don't think I'm looking for something serious?"

"Are you?" He wasn't a playboy. But aside from the time he spent with Ramsey, he was extremely independent, and she'd assumed he was satisfied with his solitary lifestyle.

"Maybe I am. I don't know. We've been us—you, me, and Ramsey—for so long that between that and work it's difficult to think about directing my energy anywhere else."

"Any time you need a break from parenting, you can tell me. That was part of our arrangement."

"I know. And I don't mean to put it all off on Ramsey. I love my time with her and wouldn't trade it for a dream date with a gorgeous man. But that doesn't mean that at times I might not want a partner to share it all with."

"You've never told me any of this." Charles was her closest friend, and she'd thought they shared pretty much everything.

He shrugged. "Once, I thought I might lose you. So I know exactly how blessed I am to have you and Ramsey in my life. I don't want to dwell on what I don't have."

Addison didn't know what to say. He really wasn't the same man she'd met so many years ago. She'd been through a lot since her diagnosis and needed to remember that he'd been at her side every step of the way, so of course it had affected him as well.

"It's really too bad I'm not straight. That little girl is a chick magnet. Moms hit on me at the park all the time." And just that quickly, the Charles she knew and loved was back, breaking up the seriousness with a joke.

"Really? That doesn't happen to me."

"Well, I guess you need to figure out where the single lesbian moms hang out."

"Please." Addison tossed her hair. "Those moms wouldn't be able to handle all of this." She swept her hand down her body in an exaggerated motion. Even as she made the flippant comment, her mind flashed on Brooke's look of discomfort when a dozen five-year-olds surrounded her. Could Brooke be attracted to a woman with a child?

"You're probably right."

Fifteen minutes later, after Ramsey finished her races, Addison retrieved Ramsey's backpack from her trunk and kissed her good-bye. As she sat inside her SUV and watched Charles's car drive away, she suddenly felt lonely but couldn't pinpoint why.

While Ramsey was an infant, Charles had spent his time with her at Addison's house, often sleeping over in the guest room. Since Addison hadn't been able to breastfeed, Charles took turns getting up with Ramsey. But by the time Ramsey was a few months old, he was taking her home overnight, then for several days.

Charles was a very involved father, and since he lived only five minutes away, Addison had watched Ramsey leave with him countless times in the past five years. She loved her daughter and missed her, but they were accustomed to time apart and it didn't seem to affect their bond.

Perhaps her conversation with Charles was responsible for the funk she currently was slipping into. Charles hadn't been far off in his estimation of the time since her last date. She hadn't been in what she would term a relationship since a year before she got sick. For two years after her diagnosis she'd been engrossed in her treatment and the fear that followed. Then Ramsey came along and...Addison could conjure up a list of excuses, but basically, by the time she'd run out of more important things to concentrate on, she didn't want to disturb her comfortable dynamic with Ramsey and Charles.

She'd been single for nearly a decade now, and if that thought alone wasn't enough to deter her from getting involved, the idea of getting naked with someone again terrified her. She hadn't had any qualms about sex when she was younger. She still had a decent body, but, though her plastic surgeon had done a great job on her implants, she had considerable scarring. Surgery had changed her breasts dramatically, not to mention the number that childbirth had done on her once toned and firm stomach.

Brooke Donahue was hot. If Addison were younger and less jaded about life, she might even have a little fun flirting with Brooke. But she'd also felt Brooke withdraw when it came to anything cancer-related. She wouldn't be fending off any advances soon.

CHAPTER FIVE

Sunlight poked through the canopy of trees and warmed Brooke's skin as she stepped out of her car in the north lot of Sycamore Park. Mature woods that faded from dense foliage into well-spaced trees lined the edges of the park.

Addison steered a black SUV into the spot next to hers. Sleek and compact, it wasn't an over-consuming monstrosity, but more like a sports car stretched and blown back into an elegant machine.

"More mom gear?" Brooke asked as Addison got out.

Addison smiled. "I'm not really the minivan type."

"Shall we?" Brooke led her to the beginning of the path.

"This was a good idea. I needed to walk off the stress of my work day before I pick up Ramsey. And what better way to find inspiration than to stroll through the very park where the event will be held."

When Addison had called and asked if they could meet and compare notes, Brooke suggested the park. The weather was gorgeous, and she'd offered an afternoon stroll first.

As they walked quietly side by side, Brooke breathed deeply, enjoying the humid summer air and the teasing scent of Addison's perfume. Brooke slowed and moved behind Addison in order to let a jogger pass. Though she felt like a cad, she couldn't help sneaking a peek at Addison's body. Addison's T-shirt was the perfect length. The hem ended just above the waistline of her athletic pants, leaving a sexy little strip of skin bare.

"The stage will be over there." They had passed through the trees and entered a large open area. Addison pointed to the far end of the grassy expanse. She glanced over her shoulder and, afraid she'd been caught looking, Brooke practically stumbled back to her side of the path. "The concession tents get set up there."

"That leaves plenty of room for people to spread out in front of the stage."

Addison nodded. "We usually get families who stake out a piece of grass with a blanket and use it as home base for the day."

"Will we have someplace the musicians can get organized before going on?"

"We set up an enclosed tent to the left of the stage. It serves as a dressing room, staging area, and whatever else we need." Still following the path, they circled the outer edge of the clearing. "We've gotten a little better at this over the years. The first event was a complete mess. We overestimated attendance and paid the caterers for way too much food. We sent the considerable leftovers to a homeless shelter so it wasn't a total loss, but it hurt our budget. Luckily, we've grown since then and are hitting the attendance numbers we wanted that first year. One year we had a horrible storm and the wind blew several of the tents down on top of attendees."

"Was anyone hurt?"

"Nothing more than minor bumps and bruises, luckily."

"You couldn't be held accountable for the weather, though."

Addison appreciated the reassurance now, but it wouldn't have helped three years ago while she struggled to pull countless yards of wet PVC fabric off the guests. "No, I guess not. But it certainly didn't make the day feel like a success."

As they reached the playground, Brooke veered off the path and headed for the swings. "Let's sit for a minute."

Addison grabbed the chains of Brooke's swing, low, near the seat, pulled her back, then released her.

"I haven't done this in years." Brooke pumped her legs and propelled herself higher.

"The swings are Ramsey's favorite. She loves going as high as she can and usually wants me to race her." Addison sat next to

Brooke. The feel of the swing hugging her hips and the creaking of the chains always inspired a sense of nostalgia.

Brooke's shorts bunched higher on her thighs, and beneath the edge of her sleeves, her arms tightened as she pulled on the chains. Competitiveness surged in Addison, so she planted her feet and pushed off. She'd almost caught up when Brooke started pumping faster, rocking back and forth as if trying to gain more momentum. Brooke glanced over to check Addison's progress and Addison saw challenge in her eyes. Addison picked up her pace as well. They both worked furiously until they reached that height where the chains got slack and the ride became jerky.

"Not bad." Brooke grinned. "Want to see who can jump off and land farther?"

"Lord, no. I'd break something for sure. I'm not as young and flexible as I used to be."

Brooke lay back, stretching her arms out to hold herself up, and straightened her legs. "You almost beat me."

"What? Almost? I passed you easily."

"I don't think so."

"I do. Do you want to go again?"

Brooke hooked her elbows around the chains and rubbed her thighs. "No. I don't think I have it in me."

Addison coasted to a stop and put her feet down. She wandered over to the play area, running her hand over the sun-warmed surface of a slide. A thick plastic, padded apparatus had replaced the metal monkey bars of her youth. She'd watched Ramsey run around with the same abandon she used to. But when Ramsey fell, she landed in a thick layer of rubber mulch instead of the hard-packed sand Addison remembered.

While Addison could look back fondly on her childhood, she would also do anything to spare Ramsey the experience of slipping from wet metal bars and hitting the ground so hard it took her breath away. She would save Ramsey from pain at every stage of life, even though she'd known since she decided to gamble on pregnancy that she could never promise her child a pain-free life.

"Hey, what happened?" Brooke crossed to her. "You spaced out on me."

"Sorry. I got lost in childhood playground memories. Don't you ever miss being that carefree?" Addison returned to the path and Brooke fell into step beside her.

"I haven't thought about those days in a very long time."

"I became extremely reflective while I was sick, and I guess I hung onto a little of that."

"Diane was the same way. She got in these moods and wanted to talk about the good old days, but I refused."

"Why?"

"I told her that she shouldn't spend her energy wallowing in the past, but instead should focus on getting better."

"That's what you told her. But what was the real reason?"

Confusion flashed across Brooke's expression and she hesitated for a second before answering. "Diane was my closest friend—at times my only friend. She and I shared so much. I didn't want to think about a time when she was gone and no one remained to share those memories with."

Instinctively, Addison sided with Diane because they'd been in nearly the same place. Brooke's perspective was interesting, and Addison wondered if her own friends and family felt something similar.

"She needed to revisit those memories for herself, to try to recollect that happiness and warmth. But she probably wanted to make sure they were fresh for you as well."

"What difference is that supposed to make? She's still gone." The hard edge of anger crept into Brooke's tone.

Addison searched her memory for the feelings she'd had to sort through when she was sick. Her stomach clenched as she immersed herself once more in the stark fear of dying. "That's complicated. When we love someone, we want to spare them pain—to know they will be comforted and not hurt too much if we die. But a selfish part of us wants to know that we'll be missed when we're gone, that we've left some kind of legacy. Reminding loved ones how much we meant to them is a step toward both of those things."

"That's just mean. So you're saying she wanted me to miss her more."

"Unconsciously, maybe. I don't know, Brooke. It's what I did. And a lot of people from our support group have talked about doing the same thing. You should come to a meeting with me sometime."

"No, thanks," Brooke answered immediately. She walked faster and Addison lengthened her stride to keep up.

"You might find some closure—"

"I doubt it."

"Why do you become so angry when I talk about our group?"

"Because I don't get it," Brooke snapped back. "You keep talking about what a positive person Diane was and how she embraced treatment, but that's all bullshit. You didn't know her the first time she was diagnosed. She was an angry mess. She fought her doctors, she fought me, she hated all of it."

"She wasn't that different from the rest of us."

"She is." Brooke stopped walking. "She was. She was different because she was my friend. You can't lump her in with some group and say you're all the same because you've all had cancer."

"I'm not trying to take anything away from her individually. And I'm not trying to force you into something you don't want to do." Addison took a step closer and touched Brooke's shoulder. Brooke's eyes were dark pools of agony and Addison wanted to pull her into her arms. But so much tension was vibrating through Brooke's body she would most likely fight the embrace. "I didn't know Diane then, but I do know that, in the end, she found a degree of comfort in our support group. That's all we try to offer, not only to those battling cancer, but their family and friends also."

"Yeah, well. I don't need any comfort." Brooke stepped back, severing their physical connection. She held Addison's gaze for a moment longer and reconstructed an almost-visible wall around her raw pain before she turned and began walking again.

Addison quelled the urge to argue. Brooke wouldn't gain anything from a meeting unless *she* was ready to attend. She clearly didn't think much of support groups, or perhaps just this particular one. From what little she knew of Brooke, trying to push her into attending wouldn't make her more likely to go.

They continued without speaking, the only sound the slight panting of Brooke's breath. Addison had several inches of height over Brooke and didn't have to work as hard to maintain their pace, but she didn't slow down. Brooke was the one who had sped up and Addison took a tiny bit of pleasure in forcing her to keep going, then in pushing it a little faster. Brooke pumped her arms as she struggled to stay with Addison.

They followed the path silently for about another quarter mile before Brooke finally slowed. "Okay, okay. You've proven you're in better shape than I am." She stopped, bent, and braced her hands on her knees.

"What do you mean?"

"Cut the innocent act. I know what you were doing. A little competitive, huh?"

"A little," Addison said.

"Have you always been?"

"In school I played several sports and remained active into adulthood. When I got sick, I had to take a break, then another when I got pregnant. But I've tried to continue returning to an exercise routine each time."

"It sounds like you're a lot more dedicated than I am, even with everything you have going on." Brooke patted her stomach. "I've gotten sedentary and pudgy."

"Please, you look great." Addison didn't see a thing wrong with Brooke's body. Maybe she didn't have the stick-thin figure women seemed to sweat for in the gym, but she was soft and curvy in all the right places.

"Seriously, I wasn't fishing for a compliment. I'm just being honest. I've been slacking in every area of my life recently. Maybe that's why Diane bullied me into this fund-raiser, to get me moving."

"She bullied you?"

"I certainly didn't volunteer."

"Well, we aren't so desperate for help that we have to drag people in against their will." She'd endured Brooke's disdain for the support group, but she'd worked on the fund-raiser for years and wouldn't let Brooke disrespect their efforts.

"Really? Because I saw how few people were in that meeting. Seems like you can't afford to turn anyone away."

Addison stopped walking. Brooke was probably trying to cover up the wounds she'd revealed a short time ago, but Addison wouldn't let her use that as an excuse to be rude. Not only had cancer personally affected her over the years, but she'd also become friends with many others in her situation. Brooke's apparent inability to see the importance of this event irritated her. "If you want to just forget the whole deal, I can handle the planning myself."

Still walking, Brooke slowed, turned backward, and faced Addison. "I didn't say I wouldn't do it."

"No, you didn't. But clearly you don't want to." Yes, Addison felt defensive of the project, but a part of her took Brooke's rejection even more personally.

"It's fine. I've already put feelers out to get some names for the concert."

"We've managed with our mediocre talent for years. I'm sure we could again."

"I merely said Diane had to convince me to work on the fund-raiser."

Addison took a deep breath and resumed walking. Was she getting unnecessarily aggravated? She wasn't sure, but she didn't want to let Brooke turn this around on her. "It seems like you think I'm—we're supposed to be grateful that you've made time in your *busy* schedule for us."

Brooke's mouth tightened and Addison knew she'd touched a nerve. Addison usually had no problem controlling her temper, and even now she could have reined it in, but she really didn't want to. From the first time they'd met she'd felt like she had to tread carefully, and she was tired of it. Brooke had refused every offer of help. If she wanted to deal with everything alone, why should Addison care?

"I get that you're angry, Brooke, I really do. You're grieving. Fine. But I don't understand your obvious disdain for a committee whose sole purpose is to raise money for a good cause, or your hostility toward our support group, which comforted your friend when she was ill."

"You weren't more than an acquaintance and you don't know what I'm feeling. You don't know what I've lost."

"I have an idea." Addison wanted to reach out to Brooke, but the tight fold of Brooke's arms over her chest didn't invite affection.

Brooke bit her lower lip. "It's not the same. Being left behind is—Diane got out easy."

"Dying isn't the easy way, Brooke." The flash of acute anxiety surprised Addison. She was accustomed to ghosts of fear, but usually she could shake them off. Today, they clung to her, sending her heartbeat into overdrive and stealing her breath. "There's nothing easy about any of it. Someday, you'll be able to see that."

"Not today," Brooke said matter-of-factly.

"Okay." Addison wanted to be sympathetic, but Brooke was shutting down her every effort. "Maybe you should just give me a call when you're ready to discuss plans for the fund-raiser."

"Damn it. Addison, wait."

Addison didn't look back.

CHAPTER SIX

B rooke heard the distant peal of the doorbell inside and still couldn't decide if she wanted Addison to answer the door. She rarely felt the need to grovel, but in this case it was necessary.

Addison opened the door and walked away, leaving Brooke wondering if she should follow. She stepped inside, inwardly preparing her apology. Addison continued into the kitchen where Ramsey sat at the table with an array of construction paper spread out in front of her. Addison brushed her hand over Ramsey's hair as she passed. She went to the sink and submerged her hands in soapy water, clanging a pan against the side of the sink as she scrubbed it vigorously.

After Addison had left Brooke in the park two days ago, Brooke tried to call but Addison didn't answer and hadn't returned her messages. She knew she would see her Wednesday night at the next fund-raiser meeting, but she didn't want things to be awkward between them then. So, while out running errands this morning, Brooke decided to take a chance and apologize in person. She had no idea what Addison's Saturday mornings usually consisted of, but she hoped Addison wouldn't consider her visit an intrusion.

"Hi, Ramsey," Brooke said.

"Hi." She raised her head, then returned her attention to the paper and safety scissors in her hands. The tip of her tongue poked out and curled around her top lip as she concentrated on cutting the paper.

"What are you making?"

"A card for Mommy."

"Yeah? Is it her birthday?" Brooke glanced at Addison, but her back was still turned.

Ramsey shook her head.

"What's the card for, then?"

"Just because."

"Is it okay if I make one, too?"

"Sure." Ramsey opened a plastic pencil box next to her and passed Brooke a pair of scissors.

"What color do you think?" In the mirror hanging on the opposite wall, Brooke caught Addison peeking over her shoulder.

"Mommy likes purple."

"Then purple it is." Brooke chose a lavender piece of paper and a darker purple crayon. She folded the paper in half and drew a large flower on the front.

Ramsey rose on her knees and peered closer, resting her hand on Brooke's shoulder for balance. "Yellow flowers, too."

"Yellow?" When Brooke glanced at her, Ramsey nodded and handed Brooke the appropriate crayon.

Under Ramsey's watchful gaze, Brooke added smaller yellow and white flowers. She drew green stems resting in a red vase. "What do you think?"

"Pretty." Ramsey smiled.

"We'll see what your mommy thinks," Brooke whispered. She reclaimed the dark purple crayon and added a message to the inside.

Brooke stood and Addison turned, wiping her hands on a towel, but her expression provided no clues about what she was thinking. Without a word, Brooke held out the card. Addison took it and flipped it open as if she didn't care about what was inside. She took much longer than was necessary to read the two words "I'm sorry," followed by a smiley face. Brooke would have been concerned if she hadn't seen the corner of Addison's mouth twitch.

"A word of warning." Addison held up her index finger and waved the card in the other hand. "I'm letting this pass as an apology this time, because it's cute. But if you screw up any bigger, this won't suffice."

"Real flowers?" Brooke teased her, enjoying the flirtation. "Candy? Bigger, huh? Jewelry."

"Diamonds. Big, big diamonds. For sure."

"I'll keep that in mind."

"Mommy, I want diamonds, too." Ramsey jumped down from her chair and stood between them. She grabbed Addison's hand and looked up at Brooke, touching her knee shyly.

"That's right, baby. And don't settle for less." Addison shrugged and laughed. "I may as well teach her to expect the best."

"Of course, start her young."

"Look at my card." Ramsey held up her creation.

Addison bent and admired her work. Ramsey beamed as Addison gushed over the card, then swept her up in an exuberant embrace and deposited her back in the chair.

"Since you're here, would you like to discuss our progress on the project?"

"Did you have plans that I'm disrupting? I just wanted to stop by and apologize for the way I acted the other day."

Addison glanced at Ramsey, who had begun work on a new drawing. "I know this is a difficult time for you."

Brooke shook her head, attempting to ward off the sympathy in Addison's voice. "I shouldn't take my issues out on you."

"Give yourself a break, Brooke. Healing takes a while."

"Stop being so nice. I was rude and you didn't deserve that."

"Okay. Agreed."

"Good. Well, I'll get out of your way."

When Brooke looked like she wanted to bolt from the room, Addison touched her arm. Brooke's apology, and the adorable way she'd interacted with Ramsey, had charmed her. "You're not disrupting anything. Ramsey and I were planning a lazy day anyway. Coffee?"

"No, thank you."

"It's a beautiful day. Let's sit outside." Addison picked up a mug and crossed to the French doors. "Leave it open a crack so I can hear Ramsey."

Brooke followed her out and they settled into the chairs at a table under the shade of a large umbrella.

"So, at Ramsey's birthday you asked about my prognosis."

"You don't have to—"

"I don't mind talking about it." Addison took a deep breath and rested her forearms on the table. She'd been involved in awareness and fund-raising since her diagnosis and had told her story countless times. But something about meeting Brooke's dark eyes made her nervous. "A little over eight years ago I found a lump in my right breast. I put off going to the doctor, thinking, like many people do, that it was nothing. I knew I should make an appointment but convinced myself that I didn't have time. When I finally did go, the doctor found stage-three breast cancer. There's a bit more to it than that, but you get the idea."

"I can guess, based on what I know about Diane's cancer."

"My oncologist gave me just about even odds of surviving five years. After that point my chances got increasingly better. But first we had to get rid of the cancer. I had a mastectomy and radiation, then later reconstructive surgery."

"What does that entail? The reconstructive part, I mean. Is that question too personal?" Brooke looked uncomfortable with the conversation.

"It's okay. I brought it up. I have implants. Saline, specifically."

"Implants? Both?" Addison smiled as Brooke's gaze dipped to her breasts.

"Yes. I've always been small-chested, so I convinced the doc to pump them up a bit. Does that make me sound too shallow?"

"I—uh—"

Addison laughed. "You don't have to answer, I was kidding. Actually, in order to make sure they were as symmetrical as possible, my surgeon put a small one in on the left side as well. You want to touch them, don't you?" Brooke shifted in her chair and Addison almost felt guilty for teasing her. But it was worth it to see the flush of red creep higher up Brooke's neck and into her cheeks.

"God, I'm sorry. I'm sitting here staring at your breasts."

"It's okay. Everyone wants to touch them. Sometimes, on a whim, I'll just let strangers feel me up."

Brooke planted her hands on the table and began to stand. Addison reached across and covered her hand. Brooke flinched but didn't pull away.

"Please, wait. I'm kidding. Your curiosity is a natural reaction. My boobs never got this much attention when they were real. Cancer has some advantages."

"How can you joke about something like that?"

Addison shrugged. "It's habit. Sometimes it was the only way to get through the bad days." Even so many years later, Addison could remember how alone she felt lying in that hospital bed after her surgery. She'd had plenty of visitors; Charles had been there often, and her friends and family stopped by as well. But she'd known, as she'd smoothed her hand lightly over her heavily bandaged chest, that none of them could truly understand what she was going through.

"Were you scared?"

"Yes."

Though Brooke had been afraid when she'd learned of Diane's diagnosis, she had resolved to be strong for Diane. She hid her tears and kept her concerns from Diane until the very end. During that last week, she'd finally allowed herself to break down at Diane's bedside. But she had no idea how she would have coped had she been in Diane's place.

"How did you handle it?"

"What was my alternative? Not fighting was never an option. I'd read somewhere that frame of mind could affect your treatment. I don't know if it's true, but I wasn't taking any chances so I tried to be as positive as I could about every step. Trust me, that wasn't always easy."

"I don't know how you can be so matter-of-fact."

"Time. I went through the anger and fear, first during treatment, then, later, during my pregnancy. And the shadows of those feelings are still there. But these days, I'm trying to live every moment and hold onto hope that my cancer will never come back. You were right about one thing, though. I didn't know Diane as much more than an acquaintance. I saw her in group and we talked over coffee after group a few times."

"I shouldn't have said—"

"I've already accepted your apology. I didn't know her well, Brooke. But she seemed to possess remarkable poise, and though her grace could be perceived as weakness, actually she was a strong woman."

"You didn't know her during her first diagnosis. She was stubborn and selfish and secretive. Does that sound like a graceful woman to you?"

"No. It sounds like one who's afraid—of being sick, of the challenges she's about to face, and of that dark force that until then was simply a word to her: cancer. Those can be rather daunting and isolating fears, Brooke. You've got to cut her some slack." Addison stroked her thumb in soothing circles over the back of Brooke's hand.

Brooke didn't trust her voice to hold up against the emotion surging into her throat. Tears burned her eyes and she wished for once she could just let them go. With Addison, she wanted to. As crazy as it felt, she wished Addison would take her hand and lead her to the hammock nearby, then hold her while she let it all go. But though a small part of her could admit that's what she wanted, she couldn't possibly ask for it. Instead, she drew her hand out of Addison's grasp and back to her side of the table.

"Okay, that's enough of the depressing stuff." Addison clapped her hands together, as if she could dismiss the heavy mood that easily. "Let's talk about our progress on the fund-raiser. Stacey will want an update when we meet with the committee Wednesday night." Addison picked up a notebook from the coffee table. "I've been looking at the rough schedule we talked about, trying to tighten it."

Brooke cleared her throat, grateful for a new topic. "I've got confirmation on the karaoke."

"Great. How much?" Addison clicked her pen and held it over the page she'd been keeping their budget on.

"Nothing."

"Really?"

"Yeah, I know the guy who hosts it."

"And he said he'd do it for free?" Addison put a check mark and a zero next to karaoke on the budget.

"Yes. Well, his wife did. It's not exactly free. But it won't cost the committee anything."

"What do you mean?"

Brooke sighed. "Keith's wife owns Poppi's Cabaret on Broadway. I had to promise I would play a new song at one of her talent showcases, and she bartered her husband's karaoke business in return."

"When is the showcase?"

"I don't know." Brooke waved a hand dismissively. She still hoped she could find a way out of the commitment. "I have to set it up with her after our event."

"Do you have a new song?"

"Not yet."

"Will you let me know when it is? I'd like to hear you play." Addison sounded tentative, and when Brooke met her eyes they were soft and filled with uncertainty.

"Sure." Brooke forced a casual tone, but the idea of Addison in the audience made her nervous. Perhaps she'd be okay in a bar full of people. But her stomach fluttered with excitement when she imagined a more intimate setting, playing only for Addison. What would she see in Addison's eyes after the final strains of music? Admiration or interest? Would she see the same warm awareness she felt now, sitting here across from her?

Just inside the partially open door, Ramsey scraped her chair against the floor and jarred Brooke from the sensual haze she'd created for herself. Ramsey ran out the door and leapt into Addison's lap. Addison caught her without hesitation; clearly she hadn't experienced the same fantasy as Brooke. That was just as well, since Brooke shouldn't be daydreaming about Addison. She needed to keep things all business between them until the fundraiser was over and she could return to her solitary life.

CHAPTER SEVEN

Addison scooted her chair back and stared at her computer screen. The numbers in front of her were starting to blur, and she rubbed her eyes in an effort to ward off fatigue. The offices around her had dimmed over an hour ago when most of her coworkers left. Addison, her boss, one other broker, and his assistant were the only ones left in the building. Her boss had spent most of the day on the phone with lenders while Addison had orchestrated the faxing back and forth of the necessary forms.

They'd been working with a local real-estate company on a new high-rise in the trendy South-of-Broadway area. They were handling the mortgages on over 60 percent of the units, all of which were scheduled to close soon after the ribbon-cutting next week. Addison's boss needed the boost that success on this project would give his career, which meant Addison would work late for as long as necessary to meet their deadline.

In order to take some of the pressure off Addison, Charles had arranged his schedule so he could have Ramsey this week. She missed Ramsey, but so far she had arrived home in time to eat dinner, get in a quick run on the treadmill, and fall into bed for five hours, then get up the next morning to do it again.

Tonight, she had to leave soon if she hoped to make it to the fund-raiser committee meeting, though she could probably use work as an excuse to miss. Brooke could update Stacey on their progress. Next week, if her schedule calmed down, she would find time to get together with Brooke. She'd probably been thinking about Brooke all day only because they'd forged a truce on Saturday.

She stretched her arms over her head and felt tightness between her shoulder blades. If she didn't get out of this chair, she might end up with a permanent knot in her spine. Maybe she should go to the meeting and start fresh tomorrow. She'd made a commitment to this fund-raiser and—she shook her head. Now she was finding excuses to see Brooke. The thought of waiting five or six days to be with her again left Addison feeling hollow.

She saved the document on her computer and closed it down. As she transferred a pile of papers from her desk to her laptop bag, she vowed to work on them after the meeting. Then she gathered the Chinese take-out cartons from their late lunch. Since she wouldn't have time to eat before the meeting, she hoped the meal would stick with her.

Addison poked her head into her boss's office long enough to tell him she was leaving, then headed directly for the elevator.

❖

Brooke glanced at the door, then at her watch for about the tenth time in fifteen minutes. Stacey Tanner was making the rounds of the room, encouraging everyone to get some coffee and pastries before taking a seat.

Brooke had arrived early after spending her day finding reasons not to work. Her guitar stood silently in the corner, but her apartment was spotless—hell, it was nearly surgical. The laundry was done, as was her shopping list. She'd left her apartment thirty minutes before the meeting was scheduled to start and had driven through downtown before reaching the church and had still arrived in plenty of time to help Stacey arrange the chairs.

Stacey wanted everyone sitting in a circle in the center of the room. She said it would promote a more cooperative atmosphere than if she stood in front of them in an audience-type arrangement. Brooke wasn't sure that was true and didn't think Stacey could help but exude a leadership vibe, but she kept her mouth shut and moved the chairs as directed.

"Everyone, let's get started. We have a lot to cover." Stacey waved her hands in the air as she strode across the room.

Brooke chose a chair as far away from the door and the cluster of people gathered there as possible. But as the crowd spread out to claim their own seats, those around her filled up. An older woman nearly dropped her entire armload of folders and notebooks as she practically fell into the chair next to Brooke. Instinctively, Brooke stuck out a hand to steady her, but she managed to right herself on her own. She chuckled and smoothed a hand over the nape of her neck, brushing her white, hot-rolled curls.

"Hello there, young lady." The man sitting on her left crowded closer than she liked. Brooke tried not to wrinkle her nose against the sting of too much aftershave and the pungent odor of cigarette smoke.

She smiled tightly and nodded.

"What are you working on?" Judging from the way he squinted at her through his thick black-rimmed glasses, he hadn't changed the frame style or the prescription in decades.

"Entertainment."

He held up a handful of crumpled receipts. "I have food vendors. But I'm almost done. You're new this year, aren't you?"

"Yes."

"I could help you. You know, show you how we do things." He smiled, revealing tobacco stains and tooth decay.

Brooke bit back her first response and was formulating a more polite one when she heard the door open across the room. Addison hurried in, mouthing a silent apology to Stacey, and took the closest empty chair. She scanned the circle of chairs until she met Brooke's eyes, then smiled and raised her chin slightly.

Brooke nodded in return. "Actually, I'm working with someone," she replied, inching away from the man and closer to the woman on the right.

"Ah, Miss Addison. Well, then, you're in very capable hands already." He winked at her in a way that made her want to shiver.

She didn't like the idea of this strange man thinking about Addison's hands, capable or otherwise.

Brooke was saved from answering when Stacey took control of the meeting. Consulting a thick notebook open on her lap, she ran down the list of subcommittees and asked each one for an update. Brooke only half listened as members of each group detailed their progress, relying on Addison to give their report.

Her attention kept drifting to Addison and she snuck glances across the circle. Addison had clearly come directly from work again. Today she wore a rust-colored blouse and chocolate-brown pantsuit. The jacket and pants appeared to be well-cut. And though the swath of brown argyle socks made Brooke smile, Addison's ankles were not what she wanted to see. She retrieved the memory of Addison's firm calves and the hint of thigh her pencil skirt revealed, and her libido rose in response.

Brooke imagined herself helping Addison strip off the jacket. She wasn't close enough to determine if the fabric of her blouse would rest stiffly against her body or if it would be soft and pliable, caressing her breasts. Inevitably, Brooke thought next of sliding her own hand inside that jacket and cupping it over Addison's breast. Would Addison's nipple grow hard against her palm?

Brooke caught herself angling forward to try to get a better look and realized that anyone in the circle could easily see her leering at Addison. She jerked her eyes up and found Addison watching her. Judging from Addison's intent stare, Brooke had been found out. But even from across the room she could see her desire mirrored in Addison's eyes. Knowing that Brooke was looking at her had turned Addison on.

So instead of pulling her gaze away, Brooke let her mind wander back to its previous path. She had her hand inside Addison's jacket and felt the firm press of Addison's nipple against her fingertips, but this time instead of passively resting it there, she imagined closing her fingers over the pebbled tip. A steady throb began between Brooke's thighs, and she barely contained a groan when Addison pulled one side of her lower lip between her teeth. Brooke stared at her, pushing herself as deeply into her arousal as she could stand.

She wanted Addison—wanted those teeth closing against her own flesh. The throb intensified, matching the increased pounding of Brooke's heart.

Brooke jerked her eyes from Addison's and shook her head. She looked around, but the meeting appeared to have gone on as normal. *What just happened?* She'd never lost control of her thoughts so quickly. Her body still hummed with need and her face felt flushed. Her own nipples felt impossibly tight and sensitive when they rubbed against the cotton of her T-shirt. She crossed her arms over her chest and took a slow breath, attempting to calm her system.

Focus on other things. The woman to Brooke's right shifted and her chair creaked in response. Around the circle, a man hunched over a notebook, apparently taking extensive notes on everything Stacey discussed. He scribbled quickly, as if in a hurry to get down every word. What in the world could Stacey be saying that was that important? Brooke hadn't heard a word in several minutes. The young woman next to him tapped her foot impatiently and snapped her gum every few seconds. The man glanced at her in annoyance after a particularly loud snap.

Brooke's pulse felt slower and she risked another glance at Addison to test her reaction. She still registered a trickle of awareness, but her body didn't immediately go into overdrive.

She'd been relieved to see Addison walk in, partly so she wouldn't have to talk in front of the group, but also because she wanted to see her. They were stuck together until the fund-raiser, so though she couldn't date Addison, she could still enjoy looking. Addison was smart and interesting, and Brooke liked talking to her. She also had cancer, Brooke reminded herself. People like Addison tacked that word "survivor" on the end, and maybe that made them feel better. But the fact remained, there was no cure. Despite what doctors said about odds and survival rates and clear margins, they had very little control over the disease, which could inflict its damage again indiscriminately and without warning.

Despite what had just happened, Brooke couldn't allow anything to develop between them. In spite of their obvious attraction, she certainly didn't have to give in to it.

The beginning of a headache blossomed behind her eyes and, rather than the thoughts in her head, she blamed creepy-aftershave guy. She took as few shallow breaths as absolutely necessary. If she thought she could scoot her chair closer to the older woman without making that loud scraping noise, she would have.

Finally, Stacey reached the end of her list. She talked for several more minutes, about her expectations for the next meeting, before dismissing everyone. Steeling herself, Brooke left her chair and headed across the room.

"Hey," she said as she reached Addison's side.

"Hi. I'm sorry I was late. Work has been insane this week." Addison apparently intended to act like the sultry exchange hadn't happened, and Brooke was content to do the same.

"I'm glad you could make it."

"You could have saved me a seat." Addison's grin let on that she was teasing.

"I was going to say, you should have been on time so I wouldn't have had to sit over there." Brooke lowered her voice so no one would overhear, though most of the crowd had begun to file out the door toward the parking lot. "That guy's weird."

"Mr. Poole?"

"Friend of yours?"

"He came to our group once—"

"Is everyone in that damn group?"

Addison continued as if Brooke hadn't spoken. "But never came back. He lost his wife a few years ago."

"I'm sorry for that. Although it clearly hasn't stopped him from smoking. He's still creepy."

"Brooke Donahue." Addison chastised her, swatting Brooke's arm lightly. Then she smiled, deciding not to examine how just talking to Brooke could make her feel so good. "Yes, he is. I've caught him leering at me more than once." *Not quite in the way you leered at me earlier,* she wanted to add. Mid-meeting, she'd glanced at Brooke and found Brooke looking at her with clear intention in her eyes. She'd had little doubt what Brooke was thinking about.

Though she wasn't surprised that her body had reacted, how quickly it did so was unexpected.

"He's probably looking for his next wife," Brooke said.

"Stop."

"What, you don't want to be Mrs. Aftershave? Maybe he has a fortune stashed under his mattress and would someday leave you a very rich widow."

"Brooke."

"Okay." Brooke held up her hands in surrender. "So why is your job so crazy right now?" Brooke asked as she and Addison fell in with the last of the stragglers and exited the church.

Addison shook her head. "I don't want to talk about work right now. Tell me what you did today."

"Nothing."

Addison laughed.

"Really. Not much productive, anyway—some cleaning and errands."

"No writing?"

"I've been having a bit of trouble in that department lately."

They had reached Addison's car and Brooke opened the driver's door for her. Addison got in and rolled the window down before swinging the door shut.

"Would you like to get a drink?" Addison had no idea why she'd blurted the invitation, but if Brooke accepted, she could easily ignore the pile of papers in her computer bag.

"Sure."

"Okay. Where should we go?"

"Well, I'm not far from here. I've got a decent bottle of Riesling in the fridge if you're interested."

"Absolutely. Riesling is my favorite. I'll follow you." Addison didn't hesitate. She'd recalled the arousal in Brooke's eyes, but rather than feeling apprehensive, she was intrigued. Brooke's gaze had lingered on her chest, but she doubted Brooke could accurately conjure up the image of what Addison's breasts really looked like. And since Addison hadn't let any woman see them since her surgery, she was certain she had enough self-control to keep Brooke from becoming the first.

❖

Brooke pushed open the door and flipped switches as she led Addison inside. Recessed lighting illuminated spots on the honeyed hardwood floors.

"Make yourself at home. I'll get the wine." Brooke headed for the kitchen.

Addison stepped into the open living area. "You have a beautiful loft." The outer walls were adorned with large, vibrantly colored abstracts. A few pieces of furniture, made of leather, metal, and glass, were scattered around the room.

"A musician I've worked with a few times owns the place. The décor is mostly his. He spends most of the year on the road. But it's a great building in a prime location, and he doesn't want to part with it. I take care of it for him and pay a very reasonable rent." Brooke handed Addison a glass of wine, set the bottle on the coffee table, and settled into the plush leather sofa.

Addison continued to walk around the outside of the large space. The furniture and the artwork weren't Brooke's, but surely something here would provide a clue about who Brooke was. Maybe she just needed to look a little harder. She found promise in an acoustic guitar perched on a stand in the corner.

She reached out to touch the guitar, but drew her hand back before making contact. "May I?"

"Yes. Do you play?"

"No." Though she couldn't play any type of instrument, Addison had always admired creative people. The ability to inspire a mood with music was amazing on its own, but some artists possessed such talent that she was convinced it must be a gift from God.

Carefully, she curled her fingers over the head of the guitar, tracing the scrolled letters that identified the manufacturer with her thumb. She ran her index finger down one of the larger strings, and the texture of the metal made a zinging noise as it rubbed against her skin. "It's beautiful."

"It's a '71 Martin. Diane got it for me for Christmas about seven years ago."

"That's an incredible gift."

"I know. It was perfect and I've never been able to match it."

"Gifts aren't supposed to be competitive."

"That's what she said." Brooke stood and crossed the room, her socks whispering on the hardwood floors. She stopped close enough for Addison to smell the woodsy scent of her perfume.

"She was right. I bet she really enjoyed giving you this, and that was enough of a gift in return."

Brooke touched the guitar, her fingers resting next to Addison's. "I hope it was." The shadows in the corner warred with the glow of the streetlight streaming through the window and enhanced the angles of Brooke's face. Sadness filled her eyes, and the smudges under them made Addison wonder when she'd last had an undisturbed night's sleep.

"I'm sure it was." Addison covered Brooke's hand and stroked the back of it with her thumb. Brooke's skin was warm and soft. She'd intended to comfort Brooke, but she also liked the light-headed feeling she got when she touched her. She caressed the back of Brooke's hand and touched the tender inside of her wrist.

Brooke slipped her hand free, but Addison wasn't sure if she did so in reaction to her touch, because she immediately picked up the guitar. She cradled it against her body, wrapped her fingers around the neck, and rested her other hand against the strings.

"Now I want to hear you play even more." Watching Brooke handle her guitar was sexy, and Addison was dying to know what she could do with it. Her hands were capable and confident, and they seemed to be meant to hold the instrument.

"Yeah, well, I haven't had much luck with it lately. Maybe I'll snap out of it soon." Brooke put the guitar back on the stand, and Addison sensed a perceptible difference in her as the connection was severed. Whether it was any guitar or particularly this one, something in Brooke transformed when she held it. She became confident and more centered.

Brooke returned to the couch, picked up her wine, and took a sip. She appeared calm, but Addison thought she noticed a tiny tremor in the hand that held the glass.

Addison wandered across the room and stopped in front of a bookshelf that reminded her of a ladder leaning against the wall. The shelf at eye-level held framed photographs of Brooke and Diane, as well as one of Brooke wearing a graduation cap, flanked by an older couple.

"Your parents?" she asked, picking up the frame.

Brooke shared similar features with the man in the photo—the shape of their eyes and the uneven lift of the mouth when they smiled.

"Yes."

"Do you see them often?"

Brooke shook her head. "They've both passed away."

"I'm sorry."

"That picture is at my high-school graduation. You can probably tell they had me late in life. Mom had just turned forty and had pretty much given up on having children when she found out she was pregnant with me."

Addison returned the picture to the shelf and continued her search of the bookshelf. She passed up a collection of vases she could already tell weren't Brooke's, but paused when she found a small sound system and a collection of CDs.

"Are these yours?"

"Yes."

"You have eclectic taste. Not alphabetized?" Pink resided next to Chris Botti.

"Nope."

"How do you find what you're looking for?"

"I know where they are."

Addison ran her fingers along a row of jewel cases. "I don't think I even know where my CDs are. They're all packed in boxes somewhere. Everything I want to listen to is on my iPod. And these days I just download the individual songs I want."

"But then you miss out on the joy of finding an unexpected gem of a song that may never make it to radio."

"Like one of yours?"

"Maybe." Brooke laughed. "I never thought anyone would consider me old-fashioned for having CDs."

"What's this?" Addison slid out one of the thin plastic cases and flipped it over. "Donahue's Greatest Hits?" she read off the cover. "Are these yours?"

"Yeah. It's all the stuff I've written that other artists have recorded. Diane made it for me."

"Do you mind if I listen to it?"

"Take it." Brooke forced a bit of disinterest even though the idea of Addison hearing her music made her jittery. She hadn't worried about anyone's opinion of it since early in her career, but she wanted to impress Addison.

"Thanks." Addison sighed as she sank into the sofa. She plucked something from the back of her head and her hair tumbled free. "I hope you don't mind. I've had an excruciatingly long day and I need just a bit of comfort."

"Make yourself comfortable." Brooke kept her own hair short so she wouldn't have to figure out how to make it defy gravity with just a pin or two. She clenched her fists quickly then forced them open, trying to hide the urge to bury her hands in Addison's shiny auburn strands.

Addison kicked off her shoes and propped her sock-feet up next to Brooke's on the glass edge of the coffee table. She rolled her head and reached up to grab the back of her neck. Brooke wished she could help knead the tension away, but she wasn't sure she could control herself if she touched Addison.

"Tell me why you're not working. Are you not feeling inspired?" Addison asked.

"Not especially."

"What do you usually do when that happens?"

"It's never been a big problem—at least not for this long. Usually, if I take a break, then go back to it fresh, I can produce something."

"That's not helping this time?"

"No." Brooke was growing uncomfortable with the direction of the conversation. She didn't want to discuss her shortcomings.

"What are you supposed to be working on?"

"It's not a matter of a certain project. If I don't write, I have nothing to sell, and I don't get paid."

Addison sat up and rubbed her palms together. She angled in her corner of the sofa, facing Brooke more squarely. "So, let's get you paid. Do you have an idea for a topic?"

"Not yet."

"Maybe I can be of use. Let's see, there are the obvious breakup and makeup songs, right? But maybe you should do something different. What about—"

"I don't need you to fix this, Addison." Brooke sounded angrier than she'd intended.

"I was just trying to help."

"I know." Brooke drew a deep breath. "I'm sorry. I know. You can't do anything about this. I need to work it out myself."

"Ah, so you're the I-can-do-everything-on-my-own type. Don't even bother trying to deny it. I've met your kind before."

"My kind?"

Addison smiled. "I guess that sounded bad, huh."

"You weren't wrong. Stereotyping, maybe, but not wrong. I guess I am pretty independent."

"Okay. But will you promise to let me know if I can do anything?"

"Yes." Brooke didn't expect to be making that call soon. But she did realize she'd been rude again. She shoved a hand through her hair in frustration. "I'm sorry. I know I'm being a bitch but I can't seem to stop myself." She'd been short-tempered lately. Just when she thought she was doing better, something would remind her of Diane and the wound felt fresh all over again. She didn't have any other friends and had been floundering without Diane to talk to and spend time with.

"You know, it's difficult to get mad at you when you're calling *yourself* a bitch."

"Do I need to make you another apology card?"

Addison smiled. Brooke's puppy-dog look absolutely charmed her. "I told you I wasn't letting you get away with that again."

"That's right. Am I up to expensive gifts now?"

"Not yet. I'll let you know." Addison stretched her arm across the back of the sofa and let her fingers rest inches from the back of Brooke's neck. She could easily close the gap and find out if her hair was as soft as it looked.

"Yeah, be sure to, because I'll need some time to save up for the diamonds."

"How much time?"

"What?"

"In a relationship. How quickly do you get serious?"

"Is this a personal inquiry, because I have to say—"

"No, of course not." Though Addison had sensed the distance Brooke purposely put between them, she didn't want to hear Brooke say she wasn't interested in her. She hadn't meant that *she* wanted to be involved with her anyway. "It was just a general question, a conversation starter."

"Oh, well, I don't know. I've never been in what I'd call a serious relationship."

"Never?"

"No. I suppose you have."

"A few. Before I got sick."

"So what happened?"

"Oh, no, you're not turning this around on me. I asked about your past." Addison shoved Brooke's shoulder gently.

"I don't really have a past. I've dated a little, but nothing serious."

"So you're a serial dater, never committing."

"It doesn't sound like a good thing when you say it like that." Brooke shook her head. "I don't know that I can't commit. Maybe I just haven't met the right woman yet."

"That sounds like a line. Next you'll be telling me that I'm the right woman."

"Ha. You couldn't be further from the right woman."

"Wow. Okay, now I'm insulted."

"I just mean, I'm not looking to get involved."

"That's not what you said."

Brooke sighed. "You're right. I don't think you and I should get involved."

"You don't think we'd be compatible?" Addison knew she was inching closer to danger, even as she inched closer to Brooke on the sofa. She touched Brooke's neck, her fingers light against the downy edge of her hairline.

"I don't think we would—I don't think—it's not a good idea."

"Well, I know that. Between work and Charles and Ramsey, I've got my life on a good schedule and don't need anything disrupting it. And you're too afraid—"

"I'm not afraid."

"Yes, you are."

"Of what?"

"Of caring for someone and losing them. And you want to get as far away from cancer as possible. You certainly couldn't accomplish that with me."

Addison waited for a denial but none came. She hadn't realized how true the statement was until she said it. If it weren't for Brooke's promise to Diane, she would have run from everything cancer-related months ago. And Addison had very visible reminders of her history in the scars that lined her breasts.

Brooke stared at her hands, clenched into fists and resting on her thighs. Addison could feel Brooke withdrawing from her, and suddenly she was desperate to keep that from happening. Hoping a physical connection would help, she stroked along the collar of Brooke's shirt and up the side of her neck. She toyed with Brooke's earlobe, and Brooke tilted her head almost imperceptibly toward her. "And I must be crazy because knowing all of that doesn't keep me from wanting to kiss you right now." Addison's own frankness stunned her, but she couldn't have held the words back.

"Addison. Don't." Brooke's words seemed to scrape through her throat, tight and rough.

"You don't feel it?"

Brooke hesitated, then said, "I'm sorry, I don't."

"No, I'm sorry." Brooke's words broke through and Addison jerked her hand back. Had she imagined the entire scenario? No, she hadn't. There was something between them, and because she could barely restrain herself from kissing Brooke, she was shocked that Brooke could so easily dismiss whatever this connection was. "Maybe the wine is going to my head."

Brooke looked down at Addison's still-full glass but didn't call her out on the obvious lie. Addison slid back to her end of the sofa, hoping some space between them would clear her mind. Grabbing her thighs, she squeezed them, trying to press away the feel of Brooke's skin. She hadn't been thinking and probably could have been okay with being that impulsive, but apparently Brooke wasn't.

CHAPTER EIGHT

I was a little surprised to get your invite," Addison said as Brooke got out of her car and approached the bench Addison occupied at the edge of the parking lot.

"Why?" Brooke carried a large brown paper bag in one hand and two bottles of water in the other.

"I wasn't sure how we left things last night." Addison had gone home with the uneasy feeling that they'd crossed a line that might make things awkward between them. She'd been surprised to get Brooke's mid-morning text inviting her to have lunch in the park.

"Things got a little intense last night. But I like spending time with you and I don't want a small misunderstanding to stand in the way of that."

"A misunderstanding?" Addison thought they'd understood each other a little too well.

"Addison, I'm attracted to you. If I tried to claim otherwise I'd be lying. But I meant what I said, I don't want to get involved."

"You don't want to get involved *with me*."

"However you want to put it."

"It's an important distinction. You aren't necessarily against relationships, just those that involve people who've had cancer or might someday have cancer. You're really cutting into your dating pool, you know."

"Let's sit down." Brooke nodded toward a nearby picnic table. "How about over here in the shade?"

Addison took the bottles of water from Brooke and followed her to the table. "At least with me you'd know the risks. There's no guarantee anyone will remain healthy."

"All the more reason to avoid relationships altogether. Why are we even talking about this? You said you don't want to be with me either."

"I said that I didn't think it was a good idea, not that I didn't want to."

Brooke set down the bag and stared at her. "Well, do you?"

"I don't—not want to."

"What the hell does that mean?"

"It's complicated. I'm attracted to you, more than anyone I've met in so long. But it really has been *so long* since I've been with anyone. I'm comfortable with my life and you make me decidedly *un*comfortable. Then I always have to consider how my actions will affect Ramsey, and I'm not sure this is a good time for her to have two mommies, and—"

"Two mommies? Whoa, Addison, slow down. You're rambling again. God, I hope you are."

Addison took a deep breath. "Yes, I am. I was trying to say that I didn't expect to feel like this. But it doesn't matter that much how I feel, because you're still grieving for Diane. And if you ever do let another woman in, it won't be right now."

"Addison—"

"Brooke, we'll be spending time working together on this project. After that we can go back to our separate lives if we want to. Or not. Can we please leave it at that?"

Brooke looked like she wanted to say something else, but in the end she simply nodded and sat down at one side of the picnic table.

Addison sat across from her and switched to a more neutral topic. "Have you found any bands for the local-talent portion?"

"Actually, I may have. I'm waiting to hear back from a couple of acts. And there's another one I'm not sure about." Brooke unpacked clear plastic containers of tossed salad loaded with vegetables. She also set out two wrapped sandwiches and a Styrofoam cup of soup. "I wasn't sure what you wanted," she said in response to Addison's curious look.

"Salad's fine." Addison took the offered container. "Why aren't you sure about the band?"

"I've never heard of them. Poppi says they're going to be big, though, and I trust her judgment. They just signed a record deal. She booked them in her bar this weekend, and she wouldn't do that unless they were good."

"Maybe you should go check them out."

Brooke passed Addison a handful of various dressing packets and unwrapped one of the sandwiches. "That's a good idea. Let's go down to Poppi's Friday night."

"Actually, I said maybe *you* should go."

"Come with me. What if I need a second opinion?"

"You already said Poppi likes them. You *are* the second opinion. I appreciate the invite, but I'm not into the bar scene."

"Neither am I. Come on, Mama. When was the last time you had an evening out, just for fun, that didn't involve kids?"

"I get out all the time. And don't ever call me *Mama* again."

"Fund-raisers and support groups don't count."

Brooke looked at her expectantly, but she didn't have an answer. By the time she focused on work, Ramsey, and her charitable efforts, she didn't have a lot of time left for herself. But she wouldn't change a thing about her life.

"It's okay to have a few hours of fun every now and then," Brooke said, as if reading Addison's mind.

"I happen to enjoy my fund-raisers and the support group."

"I'm not judging. Okay, maybe it sounded like I was, but a night out might be a good change of pace. Besides, we're checking out a band for the fund-raiser, so it's business, not pleasure. Come to the bar with me, please?"

"Okay." Brooke had a sound argument, but ultimately the way she said "pleasure" had made Addison give in. Maybe she'd imagined that Brooke's voice got softer as it caressed the word, as if implying a promise.

She was also curious to see the private, reserved Brooke there. Would she act differently in a bar? Somehow she couldn't imagine Brooke as the center of the party, wherever she was.

❖

Brooke stepped inside Poppi's Cabaret and immediately wished she'd asked the band for a private audition. But, in addition to her and Addison's opinion, she wanted to gauge the crowd's reaction to the music. And tonight she'd have plenty of opportunity to do that. Every table was occupied, as well as nearly every inch of floor space. A Friday night at Poppi's guaranteed a good time, good music, and drink specials that beat every other bar on Broadway.

The din of conversation overtook the music that had spilled out the open door as Brooke wove toward the back of the room, stopping several times to select a new route around a particularly tight bunch of people. Brooke wedged between two patrons and propped her elbows on the bar. Poppi waved from behind the bar, then dodged two bartenders as she made her way to Brooke's end of the counter.

"I'm glad you could make it," Poppi said as she set a longneck bottle in front of Brooke.

"I just had to see this hot new sensation you've been bragging about."

"Good. Get comfortable, they're on in ten."

Brooke nodded and Poppi hurried away to help another customer. Brooke scanned the eclectic mix of people around her. Poppi's Cabaret enticed the tourists in from the crowded street outside, but it also drew a good number of locals. Among the trendy T-shirts and worn jeans, Brooke recognized several Music Row execs obviously trying to blend in. None of them wanted aspiring artists to approach them. Instead, they probably hoped to evaluate some up-and-coming talent, then escape quietly.

Scanning the crowd again, Brooke saw that Addison had just stepped inside. She wore a crisp white button-down and dark slacks that made Brooke feel sloppy in her T-shirt and loose-fit blue jeans. Addison had nearly as much trouble crossing the room as Brooke had, but she finally squeezed between the two people closest to Brooke.

"You didn't think I bailed on you, did you?" Addison raised her voice over the noise of the crowd.

"I wondered. What can I get you to drink?"

"Rum and Diet Coke, please."

Brooke nodded and signaled the bartender. Someone bumped Addison from behind, and she slammed her hand against the bar next to Brooke to steady herself.

"If I'd known it would be like this I might have stood you up," Addison said.

"Ouch. I guess I'm not charming enough to be worth braving a mob for." Flirting with Addison was so easy, and seeing Addison smile in response warmed Brooke from the inside out.

When the bartender set Addison's drink on the bar, Brooke picked it up and handed it to her, then replaced it with a few bills. Addison reached for her purse, but Brooke waved her off.

"You can get the next round, if it makes you feel better."

"This place is crazy. I haven't been downtown for an evening out in a long time."

"I don't do it often either."

"Isn't it necessary, given your profession?" Addison asked.

"Not anymore. When I started out, yeah, I had to play a lot of writers' nights and open mics. But I've sold enough songs now that I just go to the studio and do the demo. That's the extent of my performance these days, thank goodness."

"Don't you want to be onstage?"

"Contrary to what Hollywood movies portray, not all songwriters want to be country stars. I'm happy writing and leaving the rest to someone else. I only perform when I need to."

Addison had assumed Brooke wanted stardom and just hadn't attained it, yet. But maybe she'd been wrong. Now that she'd gotten to know Brooke better, "fame-seeking" didn't fit anyway.

"So this is where you'll be performing after the fund-raiser."

Brooke pressed her lips together and nodded.

Addison was beginning to remember why she avoided downtown whenever possible. Parking was far too expensive, the bars were too packed, and, judging by the bills Brooke had thrown on the bar and the taste of the rum and Coke in her hand, the drinks weren't worth what they charged for them. She got bumped again and stumbled forward, nearly spilling her drink all over Brooke. She looked over her shoulder and shook her head in exasperation as the offender continued on her way unfazed.

"Come here." Brooke grabbed her arm. She pulled her close and spun her around, in one smooth motion, then tucked her tightly against her.

"Brooke—" Rebelling against the arousal building at the feel of Brooke's breasts against her back, Addison tried to step away but Brooke held on.

"Shh. Be still, there's barely any room in here." Brooke spoke in Addison's ear, her breath brushing Addison's heated skin. She pointed at the stage, which was really just a platform raised less than a foot off the floor. "They're about to start."

A sandy-haired man, wearing a pearl-buttoned cowboy shirt and tight jeans, stepped up to the microphone and introduced his band as Grove Tree Road. He thanked everyone for coming out, then immediately launched into the first song. They had a great sound, clean and not too complicated. The man's steady tenor carried along the lively pace of the country-rock song. Soon the crowd was cheering and clapping along.

"They're good," Addison said over her shoulder.

"Yeah. Poppi was right."

"Do you think we can get them?" Addison turned her head and found her face very close to Brooke's. So close that, even in the dim light of the bar, she could make out the golden flecks in Brooke's dark-brown irises.

"We'll find out later. For now, let's enjoy the music."

Addison tried to focus on the band as they segued into the next song, another quick number that featured a solo by the female lead guitarist. The woman swayed with the music while her fingers flew over the strings. She closed her eyes and rocked her hips against her guitar.

Addison was increasingly aware of Brooke against her backside and just how little effort it would take to thrust back against Brooke. When she moved to let someone pass in front of her, Brooke's thighs pressed into hers. Her pulse quickened and a throb began between her own thighs. She tightened her muscles against the ache and silently chastised herself for getting so turned on. Brooke probably had no idea the effect she was having, but Addison wished she had more control given she was in a crowded public place.

❖

"Thanks for coming out, folks. We sure do appreciate you spending your Friday night with us." Poppi took the stage, her voice carrying easily over the crowd without a microphone. "Now, I'd love it if y'all could help me convince a friend of mine to come up and treat us to a song."

Addison heard Brooke groan and felt the vibration against her back. Brooke stiffened and Addison suspected she was looking for the door and plotting an escape.

"Brooke, where are you?"

"Any chance you could hide me?" Brooke asked.

"Come on, Brooke," Poppi called from the stage. "Maybe a little applause will persuade her. What about it, folks, do you want to hear from a local songwriter?" Poppi waved her arms dramatically and the audience clapped and whistled. "Brooke Donahue, your public awaits."

"I don't think you're going to get out of it," Addison said.

"Damn it." Brooke moved toward the stage, the previously uncooperative crowd now parting to make an aisle. Brooke stepped up and turned to the Grove Tree Road guitarist. "Can I borrow an ax?"

The woman plugged in a guitar, then handed it over. Brooke thanked her as she slipped the strap over her head and made a quick adjustment.

"How about another hand for Grove Tree Road?" Brooke said into the microphone. She waited a second for the applause to wane. "You guys are great." She looked at the band gathered by the edge of the stage. "And I really don't want to follow you."

She strummed the strings experimentally, then took a deep breath and laid her fingers confidently against them. Addison could almost see her drawing on a reserve of strength to put on a front.

When she introduced the song, Addison almost didn't recognize her. Brooke actually seemed outgoing as she talked about the process of writing the song with two guys Addison had never heard of. Judging from the murmurs around Addison, their names were known in these circles. Addison recognized the song from the CD she'd borrowed from Brooke earlier in the week.

Trying to get a closer look, Addison worked her way toward the stage. Brooke's fingers moved competently over the strings, deftly picking out the rhythm. Her voice was strong and a little raspy. The sexy, rough-around-the-edges quality that Addison had occasionally noticed in her speaking voice was amplified when she sang. If Brooke was nervous, she hid it well. Addison didn't detect any tension in her posture. As Addison reached the edge of the stage, Brooke made eye contact with her. Brooke's expression was dark and unreadable, lacking the passion Addison had sensed from the band before her.

Minutes later, as Brooke strummed the final chord and acknowledged the applause with a raised hand before turning away from the microphone, Addison slipped past the few people who separated her from Brooke.

"Thanks," Brooke said as she handed the guitar back to the woman still waiting there.

"No problem."

"Playing it safe, kid?" Poppi asked as Brooke stepped down.

"We had a deal. I told you I didn't have anything new, yet." Brooke's words didn't contain a hint of apology.

Poppi looked like she wanted to say more, but instead she made an excuse about being needed across the bar and walked away.

Brooke turned to the members of Grove Tree Road. "Great job, guys." She shook hands with the lead singer.

"You, too." He smiled.

"I actually came down here to see you play." She touched Addison's arm, drawing her into the circle of their conversation. "This is Addison Hunt. We're organizing the entertainment for a local fund-raiser to benefit cancer awareness. Who can we talk to about potentially booking you?"

"You can talk to me." He pulled a card from his pocket and handed it to her.

"Tyler Cason," Brooke read. "No booking agent?"

"He's a control freak," the guitarist interjected.

"Whatever. It works for us," Tyler shot back. "E-mail me the information about the benefit and I'll check our schedule. We'll help out if we can."

❖

"How about a walk along Broadway?" Addison asked as she followed Brooke toward the door to the street.

Brooke shook her head. She'd spent the last three hours cramped into this bar and was ready to go home. "It's almost as packed out there as it is in here. I'll kill someone if I don't get away from these crowds."

Brooke had barely taken two more steps when a tall, curvaceous brunette stepped boldly in front of her. "Hi there."

"Hello."

"Brooke, was it?" The woman stuck out a manicured hand, her skin unexpectedly cool when Brooke grasped it.

"Yes."

"I saw you onstage. You were incredible." She pushed her shoulders back and stuck her chest out, as if she needed to make sure Brooke saw the ample cleavage that her tight black tank top displayed. Brooke could feel Addison watching them over her right shoulder. She didn't want this woman flirting with her in front of Addison, but she was also irritated that she was so aware of Addison and wanted to prove to herself that Addison didn't matter.

"I don't know about incredible, but thank you."

"It was my pleasure." The woman sidled closer, practically purring the word *pleasure*. "We've been here every night this week and this is the first time I've seen you. Don't tell me we came to Nashville and missed another hot-spot in town where you've been hiding out?"

"Ah, no. I don't perform much." Brooke could feel Addison fidgeting behind her. "So you're not a local?"

"No, I'm from Illinois. We're leaving tomorrow." That sentence carried an implicit promise for Brooke. She was gone tomorrow, but they could have tonight if Brooke wanted to. "Can I buy you a drink?"

"Thank you. But I'm on my way out." Brooke couldn't lead this woman on, despite needing to keep Addison out of her head.

"I could be on my way out, too. Do you want to go together?" She moved closer and, blocking her actions from the view of the rest of the bar, she ran her fingertips lightly down the center of Brooke's chest.

Brooke didn't even consider the offer. She was an attractive woman, probably more so when she didn't smell like 100 proof. But Brooke didn't take strangers home from the bar, not even to prove a point.

"Not tonight," Brooke said, brushing off the woman's touch.

"But I want you to serenade me." She wavered, and her eyes rolled back for a second before she regained her balance.

"You're not driving, are you?"

"If I say yes, are you going to take me home with you?"

"I'll make sure you get safely in a cab."

The woman snorted, suddenly seeming much more sober. "Forget it."

She stumbled away toward the bar, and Brooke hoped it wasn't for another drink. She watched long enough to see the woman practically fall into the arms of another woman, and after a moment their interaction made it clear they were friends. Brooke continued toward the door, confident the woman was taken care of.

Brooke almost wished she could wipe away thoughts of Addison with anonymous sex. That sure would make her life easier. But she wasn't the bad-girl type, and if she tried to pretend she was, the way her stomach flipped at the simple feel of Addison tugging lightly at her shirt as she tried not to lose her in the crowd would prove her wrong.

CHAPTER NINE

"Where did you park?" Brooke asked, as they stepped outside and away from the noise of the bar. Without the auditory over-stimulations, Brooke's other senses took in downtown Nashville. Neon and streetlights cast multicolored circles of light through the night. And behind the mixed odors of food from the bars lining Broadway, she could detect the stale smell of the city— sewer and exhaust, made heavy by the humidity trapped within the corridors between high-rise buildings.

"In a lot around the corner on Fourth Avenue."

"I'll go with you." They walked in silence for a moment. Addison's shoes clicked against the sidewalk, making a staccato beat over the sandpaper crunch of Brooke's rubber-soled Doc Martens. Brooke tried to concentrate on that rhythm, rather than that of her heart thumping. Residual nerves from being on stage had adrenaline still leaking through her. An unexpected layer of anxiety rolled over her. She didn't want to ask Addison's opinion of her impromptu performance, but it mattered to her what Addison thought.

"So?" She finally gave in to her desire to hear Addison's reaction.

"What?"

"Well, you wanted to hear me play. What did you think?"

"I recognized the song from your CD. You didn't look nervous at all."

"I'm always a little queasy."

"You fake it well."

"I've had some practice at that."

"Faking?"

"Yeah." Brooke had felt like a fraud before. She'd sold her first song while still in college. As a music major, she spent four years getting pumped up with praise for her talent and her bright future. But in the years since, she'd failed to deliver on either of those possibilities, never quite matching the success of that first song. Should she be relieved that Addison hadn't said she sucked, or worried that she didn't seem impressed? "You listened to my CD?"

"I did."

"What did you think?"

"It was—nice."

Brooke forced a laugh, though disappointment shrouded her. "*Nice*? That's a diplomatic response. What did you really think?"

"Honestly?" Addison drew her keys from her pocket and hit the button for the power locks. She stopped next to her car and faced Brooke.

"Of course."

"I can't put my finger on it exactly, but it left me with the feeling that I was waiting for something more."

"Something more."

"I wish I could be more specific, but I don't know much about music."

"Well, you know what you like. And my CD was apparently not it."

"Brooke—"

"It's okay."

"Something seemed to be missing. But what do I know? I told you, I don't even listen to country music. It's probably very good and I just have no idea what to listen for. I mean, I—"

"Addison."

"Yes."

"You're rambling again."

"Oh."

They stood there for what seemed like several minutes, looking at each other over the hood of Addison's SUV. The sounds of the city filled the silence between them, the distant hum of car tires on asphalt, the clamor of at least two different bands spilling out of bars nearby, and the occasional horn honking.

"Do you want a ride to your car?" Addison asked.

"Sure." Brooke could easily have walked the two blocks to the lot she'd parked in, but she didn't want to say good-bye just yet.

After she got inside, though, she wondered if she'd made a mistake in accepting a ride. The interior of the car was only dimly lit from the streetlights outside, and she could smell Addison's intoxicating perfume. When Addison started the car, the radio came on to a local top-40 station and she touched a button on the steering wheel that silenced it. Brooke wished she'd left it on so the music would buffer the intimacy between them. She liked to study people's hands, and she watched Addison's as she steered into traffic. They were slim and refined, her fingers long and tipped with lightly tinted nails. She held the wheel gently, applying enough pressure to elicit the desired response.

"That girl in the bar seemed to like your music," Addison said suddenly.

"What?" Brooke tore her mind away from Addison's hands and focused on trying to decipher her tone. She had no business thinking about Addison's touch anyway.

"The brunette who stopped you as we were leaving."

"She was drunk."

"She was hitting on you. If you weren't there with me, would you have taken her home?"

"I don't take advantage of drunk women."

Addison sighed. She thought Brooke might be trying to avoid saying yes, but Addison needed to hear it. In the bar, she'd been confused by the way Brooke seemed to be basking in the woman's attention one moment, then completely backing off the next. If she could somehow see Brooke as a playgirl, she might be able to shake her growing attraction to her. "Okay. If she was sober and I wasn't there, would you have left with her?"

"No."

"Why not?"

"I just wouldn't have. What difference does it make?"

"Are you afraid of being outed? Country music has a reputation for being a bit conservative, doesn't it?"

"It does. But things have changed in the past year or so. The men will be slow to come around, but the lesbians in country music are starting to come out. Besides, songwriters aren't as high-profile as artists. Even the award-winning ones are pretty much invisible to the press, and I'm even less on their radar."

"So, if a *sober*, attractive woman hits on you in the bar, why don't you go out with her?"

"That's a different question. I might go out with her, dinner and drinks or something. But I wouldn't take her home, not the first night I met her, despite being a serial dater," Brooke said with a grin.

Addison had witnessed the exchange between Brooke and the other woman with a knot of jealousy growing in her stomach. She'd managed to quell a competitive urge to step between them and attempt to pull Brooke's attention away. The image of Brooke sharing a cozy corner table with the brunette wasn't enough to erase Addison's own thoughts about being with Brooke. Except Addison's visions of them included tucking Ramsey in, then cuddling on the couch for popcorn and a movie. Even her fantasies were boring. Brooke wouldn't be interested in a dull, domestic date-night with Addison when she could be out in bars having groupies adore her.

"Here we are." Addison drew to a stop in front of Brooke's car. *Just in time.*

Brooke shifted in her seat and for a moment Addison wished she could kiss her. But only a few days ago, Brooke had halted a similar advance.

"Thanks for the ride. And for coming down to check out the band tonight."

Brooke was out of the car before Addison could gather herself and mutter "you're welcome." Addison waited until Brooke got in her own car and cranked the engine before she pulled off.

She took the long way through downtown before heading

for the interstate. As she did, she imagined Brooke going home to her loft apartment. It was late. Would Brooke go straight to bed, or did she need time to unwind before going to sleep? Now that she'd been to Brooke's apartment, she could picture her moving around the space. Would Brooke's bedtime routine be as ritualistic as Addison's, doing everything in the same order each night? Or maybe she would simply brush her teeth and fall into bed. That seemed more Brooke's style.

Addison tried to clear Brooke from her mind. She'd been thinking about her more every day since they met and looked forward to the days they planned to get together. She tried to think of ways to engage Brooke in conversations that had nothing to do with the fund-raiser, simply because she wanted to know more about her.

So she wanted to know her better? That was no reason to stress out. They could be friends. Brooke had made it clear she wasn't interested in Addison, so Addison could simply leave it up to Brooke to keep an acceptable distance between them. In the meantime, she would enjoy Brooke's company until after the fund-raiser, when they would no longer have an excuse to see each other.

❖

"Why can't we just watch a movie like normal people do on a Saturday night?" Charles stretched a long strand off a roll of blue painter's tape and pressed it against the molding around the window.

"Because you promised to help me paint and this is the only time we were both free. Besides, it's easier to do stuff like this after Ramsey's in bed." Addison poured beige paint into a tray, coated a roller, and began to apply paint to the living-room wall.

"She would have helped us."

"Yes, then we'd spend half our time trying to clean drops of paint off my hardwood floors."

"You caught me at a moment of weakness. I'd have done anything to get out of having dinner with my father tonight."

"What's going on?"

"My parents are driving me crazy."

"About the divorce?"

"Yes." Charles stopped taping and faced her. "They've been together for almost thirty-five years. At this point I don't know why they don't just stick it out."

"Come on, Charles. They fight all the time. I kind of respect them for being brave enough to start again." Addison glanced over her shoulder at him and pointed at the tape in his hands. "Talk and work. These therapy sessions aren't free."

He applied a strip of tape to the baseboard. "You can say that, your parents are still together. They're not supposed to split up. They're supposed to make each other miserable for the rest of their lives. That's what married couples do."

"I know it's hard. But don't you want them to be happy?"

"No."

"Charles."

"Okay. But why do they each have to call me and complain about the other? I'm trying hard to stay out of it. You're lucky your parents don't live in town. You have a buffer."

Addison shook her head. "It's not so easy having them three states away, especially not for Ramsey. They miss so much of her growing up, and she misses them. She loves spending time with your parents."

"They love her, too. I can't believe how tender Dad is around her. Having two boys, he never got to play with dolls or have tea parties."

"I'm sure you had a tea party or two when you were a kid."

"Maybe. But the difference is, I didn't invite him. Ramsey does."

"Do you think you should talk to your parents about trying not to put you in the middle?"

"It doesn't do any good." Sighing, he set down the tape, then picked up a brush. "I know they're both having a hard time right now, and I really do want to be there for them. It's just weird to think about either of them starting over at their age."

Addison's parents were almost ten years older than Charles's, and she hoped they never decided to split up. She could sympathize with Charles, though. Any couple who had been together as long as either of their parents was likely to flounder when faced with the idea of being alone again.

For Addison, being single was no big deal. She had Ramsey to focus on, and even though she and Charles weren't a couple, he would always be a part of her life. He took some of the pressure off her when it came to raising Ramsey, and he provided a great deal of support as a friend.

Certainly, at times she thought about trying more actively to date. She'd even gone online and filled out a profile at one of those silly dating Web sites. But her mother's warnings about crazy people lurking on the Internet kept her from meeting anyone who contacted her. How could she know for sure that the profiles she read were genuine?

She was better off not seeking out a personal life. If she was meant to be with someone, that person could just come to her. She had plenty to fill her time and enough people around her who loved her.

"Distract me from my misery," Charles said. "What's new with you?"

Brooke. The attraction she felt to Brooke was new. But for some reason she didn't want to share that with Charles. She wanted to keep the exhilaration she felt every time they were together to herself. Despite Brooke's obvious reluctance, Addison's urge to kiss her only seemed to grow stronger. She'd never looked at a woman and wondered so much what her lips felt like. Would Brooke's kiss be aggressive or gentle? Would she tear her lips from Addison's and leave a hot trail across her jaw and down her neck?

"Addison?" Charles waved a hand at her. "I asked what's new?"

"Nothing," she answered quickly.

"Nothing? That far-away look wasn't *nothing*. Spill."

"Really. You know how I like my routine. Same old stuff."

"Okay, then tell me about the same old stuff. How's your support group?"

Addison stopped painting. "I don't know. I've missed the last few meetings." Normally, she had no trouble making the monthly meetings, but lately the weeks had been slipping away quickly.

"On purpose?"

"Not really. Work was making my schedule so unpredictable, then I got involved with the fund-raiser. Everything seems to be overlapping a bit." Addison vowed to make more of an effort to attend a meeting. The support group had gotten her through some tough times, and she tried her best to stay involved and help others.

"Work should calm down again after you close this deal, right?"

"This week. Thank heavens." Addison turned back to the half-painted wall and began rolling again. She reached to get the top of the wall and felt the muscles stretching in the back of her shoulder. The clean, fresh look of this room when they'd finished would justify her soreness tomorrow.

"The fund-raiser shouldn't be a big deal. You can organize those things in your sleep."

"You're right about that." If the fund-raiser were all that occupied her thoughts she'd be in a lot better shape. But even though after an exhausting day catching up on her to-do list around the house she wanted to be able to fall into bed and go right to sleep, she would spend several restless minutes thinking about Brooke's gorgeous dark eyes and how much she wanted to know what hid in their depths.

❖

"Mommy."

Addison stirred and heard the plaintive cry again. Disoriented, she glanced at her alarm clock. Five a.m. was early for a Sunday morning, but even more so considering she and Charles had stayed up late. She threw back the covers and hurried across the hall to Ramsey's bedroom.

"What's wrong, baby?" Addison sat on the side of Ramsey's bed and touched her forehead. Her skin was hot and dry.

"Head hurts." She coughed weakly.

"I'll be right back." Addison went to her bedroom, then returned to Ramsey's bedside. She measured out the approved dose of liquid medication. "Open up. This will make you feel better."

Ramsey took the medicine and scrunched her face up. She'd never liked the taste, even when Addison bought the kind made for kids. Addison gave her a glass of water and she swallowed hesitantly.

"Does your throat hurt?" Addison asked.

She nodded.

"Try to get some sleep, we'll see if the medicine helps. If it doesn't, we'll call the doctor."

"Can I come to bed with you?"

"Of course you can." Addison picked Ramsey up, cradling her like she had when she was a baby. She crossed the hall and laid her in bed. By the time Addison circled the bed Ramsey had crawled closer to her side. Addison slid in next to her and pulled the covers around them. She stayed awake stroking Ramsey's head until she drifted off and started to snore slightly.

Ramsey slept in fits for most of the morning, refusing Addison's offer of soup and every kind of drink she had in the house. In the afternoon, Addison propped her up on the sofa with her favorite quilt and let her watch cartoons. Her fever broke during her afternoon nap, and she finally managed to get down some chicken-noodle soup.

Between tending to Ramsey, Addison returned some e-mails and cleaned the house. Then she settled in with Ramsey and caught up on her Scooby-Doo.

CHAPTER TEN

I'll have the chef salad with balsamic vinaigrette on the side." Brooke closed her menu and handed it to the waiter.

"I'll have the bacon cheeseburger with a side salad." Addison held hers up as well.

"Bacon cheeseburger and a side salad? If you're ordering a burger, the fries are the best part," Brooke said after the waiter left.

"The salad offsets the cheeseburger."

"Maybe. But I don't think the salad offsets the hit to my cholesterol if I ate the bacon burger."

"Well, that's probably true. You have to watch your cholesterol?"

"Yeah. It'll be even more of an issue as I get older, I guess."

"That's right. You're still a young buck. Just wait until you're my age."

"A young buck?" Brooke laughed. "Where did you hear that expression? Besides, you've only got a few years on me."

"A few? You're not even thirty yet, are you?" Addison laughed, too, and Brooke had to force herself to look away. Addison's eyes came alive in a way that Brooke wouldn't have thought possible, given their color. They seemed to shift from charcoal to nearly silver, depending on Addison's mood.

"This year."

"So a few is more like eleven. Oh, God, I've never felt more ancient."

"You're not. Besides, you're only as old as you feel."

"Honey, that's just something old people say to make themselves feel better. Besides, having a child can make you *feel* pretty old at times. Ramsey has been up sick the past two nights."

"Aw, poor kid. What's wrong with her?"

"Sore throat, earache, slight fever. I think we're on the upswing, though. She was feeling better this morning. I wish I could have stayed home, but things are insane at work right now."

"That sucks."

"Yeah, but my sitter is awesome and Ramsey will be okay with her. I only managed to sneak out of work to meet you because this place is so close to the office and my boss knows how cranky I get if I don't eat."

"Well, where's our food? We'll try to make this quick." Brooke looked around and the waiter appeared with their meals as if she'd summoned him.

"Ask and you shall receive. Can you make anything you want materialize?"

"I wish," Brooke said as she picked up her fork and dug into her salad. What would she wish for if she could do so at will? If she were being unselfish right now, she might want to send Addison home to Ramsey. If she were selfish, she'd want to go home with her as well. "Since we're trying to be quick, let me fill you in on what I've been doing while we eat."

"Okay, go ahead."

"I have the names of a couple more local bands for the show. I brought you copies of their CDs." Brooke passed them across the table. When she'd started this project, Brooke's goal was simple— call in enough favors to line up a few recognizable talents. But lately while she considered potential acts, she'd weighed how well the music would fit for the fund-raiser and whether Addison would be pleased.

Addison flipped a CD case over and read the back. "You didn't have to do that. I trust your judgment. You can sign them up without my approval."

"I wanted you to know what to expect. One of these is country and the other is a mainstream group, kind of retro-made-new."

Addison nodded. "Retro is in."

"On another note, Grove Tree Road is coming through big-time."

"Yeah?"

"Yes. We've been exchanging e-mails and they're ready to go on, for free. Their guitarist even offered to donate one of her guitars, signed by the whole band, for a raffle."

"That's great."

"I know. And it gave me an idea. If we can get each one of the acts to donate an item—something as small as a copy of their latest CD or as big as they wish—then we raffle off whatever it is between each type of entertainment. It helps us out and promotes the individual musicians or bands."

"That's a good idea, and the guitar is the perfect start to the collection."

"And I can hit Poppi up for a donation."

"Actually, I've been thinking about that." Addison paused to sip her water. "We need someone to emcee this thing, you know, keep things moving in between acts. I'll do it if I have to, or you're welcome to, if you want. But watching her work the crowd that night in the bar had me thinking she might be perfect."

Brooke nodded. "She probably would. At least one of us needs to be backstage making sure everyone knows where they're supposed to be and when."

"With the number of different acts and types of shows we're planning, it'd be easier if we both could be back there."

"Keith will handle the stage during the karaoke part, but we'll need someone for the rest of it."

"If you've got someone else in mind—"

"No, Poppi would be great. She's kind of a local celebrity and she has the personality for it. I'll ask her."

Addison's phone vibrated on the table and she glanced at the screen. "This is my sitter. Excuse me, I have to get this."

"Absolutely."

She stood and moved toward an unoccupied corner of the dining room. She paced the small area and threw her hands up in an exasperated gesture. The conversation was short and she didn't look pleased as she returned to the table.

"Everything okay?"

"Not really. My sitter has had a family emergency. I'm sorry, can you give me just a minute more while I call my boss and let him know I need to go home."

"Of course."

Addison turned away again and dialed. Addison had already been seated when Brooke arrived for lunch, so now Brooke took the opportunity to study her undetected. The slender cut of her suit exaggerated the breadth of her shoulders and accentuated the flare of her waist. Despite Brooke's aversion to wearing business attire, she found it downright sexy on a woman. Addison's crisp, navy pin-striped jacket and matching pants exuded power and confidence. When she turned around, the hint of white silk inside the deep vee of her jacket collar hinted at the woman beneath. Brooke had no trouble imagining Addison without her jacket, her shirt untucked, the silk draping softly against her breasts.

"Damn it." Addison snapped her phone closed and Brooke jumped, both from the noise and from the sudden lusty turn of her thoughts.

"What's wrong?"

"I called my boss to tell him Ramsey's sick, but he said he can't spare me."

Brooke scowled. "Screw them. She's your kid."

"It's not that simple. We're closing on a major development today and I've done most of the paperwork up until now. He'd be lost without me." Addison shook her head. "Charles is out of town. I need to call my backup sitter."

"I can watch her," Brooke blurted without thinking.

"No, no, I don't want to put you out."

"Please, what else do I have to do?"

"Well, I…" Addison smiled.

"You can say it. I don't do anything all day. It's one of the perks of the job."

"I wasn't—I—are you sure you don't need to work?"

Brooke shrugged. "Probably. But one more afternoon off won't end my career."

"Actually, it'll likely be the evening as well. I'll be late getting home." Addison still seemed hesitant.

"No problem."

"I don't know, Brooke. Don't take this the wrong way, but have you taken care of a sick kid before?"

"No. But I've been sick. It's pretty much just rest and fluids and monitoring her fever, right?"

"Well, yes. I think she just has a bug, so that's about all we can do." Addison dug in her purse and pulled out a small notebook. She navigated through her phone and copied numbers onto a piece of paper. "You have my cell. I'll give you Charles's cell and Ramsey's pediatrician. If she gets worse and you can't get one of us, take her to the emergency room."

"I'm sure we'll be fine."

"You don't have to do this. It's sweet of you to offer, but you're not obligated to—"

"I know I'm not. Go back to work. Don't worry about us, we'll be fine."

Addison finally passed the paper with the numbers across the table and said, "You're a lifesaver. And for that, I'm going to buy you lunch." She placed her debit card on top of their bill. "I'll call the sitter and let her know to expect you. I have plenty of soup and ginger ale at the house. Ramsey doesn't feel well, so she may actually nap. You have all my numbers, if you need anything at all—"

"Don't call you because you'll be terribly busy."

Addison laughed. "Well, yes, actually. But if you really need me, of course you can call."

If I really need you. Brooke liked the sound of that. What would Addison say if Brooke gave free rein to her recently overactive imagination and told her what she really needed?

❖

"Hi, I'm—"

"Please tell me you're Brooke." The young woman answered Addison's door with her coat on and a backpack slung over her shoulder. She seemed a bit harried, and Brooke hoped that was due to whatever her emergency was and not just her personality. Addison had said she liked this sitter and apparently trusted her.

"I am."

"Oh, thank you so much. Addison called and said you were on your way. I'm so sorry, but I have to go."

"Brooke!" Ramsey rushed to the door. Her cheeks were flushed, and, despite her apparent energy, her eyes looked glassy. She grabbed Brooke's hand.

"Do you know where to find everything?" The babysitter gathered her purse and keys from the table by the door.

"I think I can figure it out," Brooke said.

"She was just about to take a nap."

"Go ahead. We'll be fine."

"Tell Addison I'm so sorry and I'll call her later." She was gone and had closed the door behind her before Brooke could respond.

Brooke glanced down at Ramsey, who still held her hand and looked back at her expectantly.

"Well, she had to go, but your mom sent me over here to stay with you until she gets home." Ramsey didn't appear nearly as nervous about the situation as Brooke felt. Addison had been right to call her out, she didn't know much about kids. But at least Ramsey was old enough to let her know what she needed.

Ramsey nodded. "She told me. Her grandma's sick."

"Oh." Brooke slipped off her coat and hung it on a hook behind the door. "So, I hear it's nap time around here."

"I already napped this morning." Ramsey went to the living room and plopped down on the sofa.

"That's what you do when you're sick, lay around and sleep all day. It's the only good part about feeling bad. Let's get you in bed."

"I want to stay here."

"Okay." Brooke piled the pillows at one end, then helped Ramsey lie down and pulled the blanket over her.

Ramsey barely took up half the over-sized sofa, so Brooke settled on the other end and picked up a book from the coffee table, more out of curiosity about what interested Addison than out of an actual desire to read. She glanced at the cover. She wouldn't have guessed Addison would enjoy romance novels. Several pages in, she discovered that this book featured two female characters. Brooke hadn't even known such books existed.

She read for almost two hours, falling easily into the story about the doctor and her police-officer girlfriend. When Ramsey stirred, then sat up and rubbed her eyes, Brooke was actually surprised to find that she didn't want to put the book down.

"I'm hungry," Ramsey said, as she crawled to Brooke's end of the sofa.

Brooke closed the book and set it back on the coffee table in front of her. Ramsey wiggled into her lap. "Would you like some soup?"

"Chicken noodle?"

"Maybe. Let's go see what your mom has in the kitchen." Ramsey wrapped her arms around Brooke's neck, and Brooke stood and carried her to the kitchen. She set her down in one of the dinette chairs and went to the pantry. "Chicken noodle." She held up a can.

She managed to locate a can opener and a pan and had the soup on the stove in a matter of minutes. Then she found some crackers and a couple of bowls. Ramsey talked while Brooke organized their simple dinner, meandering from one subject to the next. When Brooke set a bowl of soup in front of her, she was quiet long enough to slowly empty it.

They returned to the couch, this time Ramsey snuggled up close to Brooke, and found a movie on television that Brooke thought might be kid-appropriate. The flick was a sequel to one Ramsey had already seen so she filled Brooke in on the story from the first. Brooke was amazed at her recollection of the details.

❖

Addison slipped her shoes off and crossed the living room as quietly as possible. Brooke sat slumped on the sofa, her head angled awkwardly to the side. Her soft snores were the only sound in the shadowed room. Ramsey lay on Brooke's lap, one hand curled beneath her cheek and the other holding Brooke's. They looked so peaceful that Addison considered leaving them there, but Brooke would probably have a stiff neck if she didn't wake her.

"Brooke," she whispered, touching her shoulder gently. Brooke started slightly and opened her eyes. Addison pressed her index finger to her lips, then pointed down at Ramsey. "You don't look very comfortable. Let me take her."

Addison settled on the sofa next to her and shifted Ramsey onto her own lap. Ramsey stirred for only a second, then tucked herself against Addison's chest without opening her eyes. Brooke straightened and stretched.

"How's she doing?" Addison asked, stroking Ramsey's head. Her hair clung damply to her forehead, but her skin didn't feel as warm as it had that morning.

Still a bit groggy, Brooke glanced at her watch. "She's feeling better. We ate some soup a few hours ago."

"She bounces back quickly. She'll be running around like usual by tomorrow. Thanks again for staying with her. I hate not being here when she's sick." Addison brushed her fingers over Brooke's forearm. Then, because it felt good to touch her, she left her hand there.

"It was no problem. She's a great kid." Brooke met Addison's eyes, but it was too dark for Addison to read the expression in them. "She's very affectionate." Brooke glanced down at Addison's hand still resting on her arm. "Like you."

"I'm sorry." Addison began to remove her hand, but Brooke covered it with hers.

"That wasn't a complaint."

"No, then what was it?"

"An observation, I guess. You're a very touchy-feely person. Is that a maternal thing?"

"No. I've always been this way." Addison stroked her fingers along Brooke's forearm. Brooke pressed on her hand more firmly, as if trying to still the movement, but she didn't pull away. Brooke stared at their hands and Addison felt Brooke's forearm twitch beneath her palm.

"Tell me something I don't know about you," Addison said, attempting to distract Brooke from their physical contact.

"Like what?"

"Anything. Don't think about it. Just blurt out the first thing that comes to mind."

"I want to write something amazing," Brooke answered quickly, then looked surprised at what she'd said.

Addison remained silent, stifling her questions, and waited for Brooke to continue.

"Until recently, I'd convinced myself that I'm satisfied with the course of my career—that maybe I'll get my big break someday, but until then what little success I've had will suffice. But Diane's death has made me reexamine where I'm at."

"How so?"

"I look at her life and the impact she's made. Do you remember how many people came to that damn party she threw for herself? And then to her funeral? She touched so many lives. I wasn't very close to my parents, I barely have any friends now that Diane is gone, no family of my own. What's my legacy? What can I leave behind that will matter?"

"What do you want to leave?"

"An amazing song. More than one, really, but I'll start there. I want to write the kind of song that inspires someone, or breaks their heart, or fills them up, as long as it makes them feel something. Anything. I just don't want to wait around for it to happen to me."

Addison nodded. "I went through some similar emotions during treatment. Not so much professionally as personally."

"Obviously." Brooke glanced down at Ramsey.

"But it's not that far off, is it? You want to create something that will leave a reminder of who you were when you're gone." Addison touched Ramsey's cheek. She'd been so afraid of doing the wrong thing when she decided to get pregnant, but every day she spent with Ramsey affirmed her choice. She was scared of leaving Ramsey's life too early, of missing her milestones, but it was worth the risk for the ones she did get to share. "That's what I've done here."

Brooke turned her hand over and grasped Addison's. Their fingers interlaced naturally and Addison rubbed her thumb against the back of Brooke's. Brooke's expression was softer and more vulnerable than Addison had seen it. Her eyes, usually unreadable, were open and filled with need that echoed in Addison's body. Addison lifted her hand, about to touch Brooke's face, but Ramsey sighed in her sleep and burrowed farther into Addison's lap.

"Excuse me while I tuck her in." Though she hated to disturb the moment of intimacy between them, she gathered Ramsey in her arms.

"It's late. I should go. You've had a long day and are probably tired." Brooke started to rise.

"Wait, please," Addison said quickly. "I'll be up for a while winding down. I can never go right to bed—er, to sleep, when I get home." Addison blushed, feeling ridiculous. Brooke probably wouldn't have noticed had she not so obviously stumbled over the word. "I'll be right back." Addison hurried toward Ramsey's bedroom, hoping Brooke would still be there when she returned.

CHAPTER ELEVEN

B rooke sat down on the couch, shifting uncomfortably. Addison looked exhausted. Brooke thought she should leave, but the plea in Addison's voice kept her there. She'd stay only a few more minutes, though, then say good-bye so Addison could go to bed. Remembering how flustered Addison had become, Brooke smiled.

Despite her apprehension about getting closer to Addison, she couldn't help herself. She admired Addison for having endured what she had and come out so strong. Addison was confident and not afraid to be vulnerable. At times she appeared almost fearless, then sometimes she seemed to drop her guard completely and expose her fears and uncertainty. Her ability to be open and affectionate both enticed Brooke and made her want to run.

A week ago she could have told herself not to think about Addison this way—that Addison wasn't interested in her. But tonight she couldn't delude herself about the desire in Addison's eyes. Brooke couldn't guess where things between them might go, but if she decided to give in to the pull of attraction, Addison would probably be willing. Brooke pressed her thighs together to control the exquisite ache building between them. The swell of arousal intoxicated her, and she wanted to abandon her misgivings.

"I thought maybe I'd scared you off," Addison said as she reentered the room. She'd shed her business attire in favor of sweatpants and a T-shirt.

"You did." Everything about Addison scared her. From the tender way she was looking at her now to the voice Brooke couldn't shake that reminded her of Addison's past.

"You're still here."

"I know."

Addison settled on the sofa next to Brooke, folding one leg beneath her. "Thanks again for looking after Ramsey tonight. It was extremely helpful."

"No problem. She slept most of the afternoon, then we watched movies until she fell asleep again."

"I don't normally let just anyone look after my child. But she likes you." Addison stretched her arm along the back of the sofa behind Brooke. "And I trust you."

"She's a great kid."

"Come to the zoo with us Wednesday afternoon."

"The zoo?"

"I'm celebrating closing this deal by taking the afternoon off. Charles, Ramsey, and I are going to the zoo. Come with us."

Brooke wanted to spend more time with Addison and Ramsey, but she wasn't sure how she felt about tagging along as the fourth wheel to their family outing.

"Charles has Ramsey that night. After the zoo, you can come back here and I'll make you dinner as a thank-you for stepping in today."

"You don't have to."

"I want to," Addison said softly. Her eyes implored Brooke to accept the invitation, not only on their field trip, but also to dinner later.

"Okay." Brooke couldn't refuse. Addison had moved closer to her—close enough to catch the clean scent of her perfume—close enough for Brooke to imagine how her full lips would feel against her own.

"Good." Addison's hand brushed the back of Brooke's neck. As Brooke told herself it was an accidental contact, she did it again, her fingers lightly stroking the sensitive skin at the edge of her T-shirt.

Brooke barely held back a moan when Addison slipped her fingers into her hair and massaged her scalp. She should stop this before it went too far, but Addison's touch rippled pleasure through Brooke's body and she didn't want it to end. Addison moved closer and her breath feathered against Brooke's cheek.

"I'm sorry. I can't help myself," Addison whispered, then she grasped Brooke's chin, turned her head, and kissed her.

Addison's lips were soft, but commanding, and Brooke responded without hesitation. Addison's tentative exploration deepened and she slid her tongue along the inside of Brooke's upper lip. Brooke's body exploded with sensations, her heart seemed to pummel the inside of her ribs, and her stomach fluttered as if on a roller coaster. Addison's touch gentled against her chin, and she caressed Brooke's jaw and the side of her neck.

Brooke wrapped her arm around Addison and pulled her closer. When she rested her hand against the small of Addison's back and felt the hem of her shirt, she naturally slipped it underneath to touch bare skin.

Addison eased back, searching Brooke's face as if trying to gauge her reaction. Brooke pulled in a slow, deliberate breath, in an attempt to abate her light-headed response to Addison's kiss.

"I'm not sure I've ever had anyone apologize before kissing me."

"Should I apologize again?"

"No. I'm as much at fault for not stopping it." She should have, but Addison's mouth was simply too intoxicating. Even now, Brooke wanted to do it again. Realizing she still had her hand under Addison's shirt, she stifled the urge to slide it higher up her ribs and instead jerked it free.

"At fault? That was a pretty amazing first kiss, if I do say so myself. You don't do it justice by saying it that way."

It *was* amazing, but it needed to be their last if Brooke hoped to keep her sanity. The part of her that wanted to keep kissing Addison could too easily win against the part that knew it wasn't a good idea. Panic began to replace the hot sizzle in her blood, but the taste of Addison lingered on her lips.

Whenever she thought about letting down her guard with Addison, she immediately remembered how helpless she felt when she lost Diane. The memory of impotently watching death claim Diane bit by bit until she was unrecognizable as the strong woman she'd once been was too fresh. She would never again sit by the bedside of someone she loved while they waged a losing battle.

"Brooke?" Addison watched the shutters come down in Brooke's eyes, replacing the haze of arousal that had consumed them only seconds ago. That kiss had just rocked her world, and she was sure Brooke had felt it, too. But now Brooke was pulling away. She kept her hand on the back of Brooke's neck, needing to maintain the physical connection. "Talk to me, Brooke."

"I can't do this."

"Which part? You're a very competent kisser, so I don't think that's what you're having trouble with." Addison tried to defuse the serious mood Brooke had slipped into. Suddenly Addison needed to downplay their kiss just as much as Brooke probably did. No kiss had ever felt more natural and exciting at the same time. She'd been concerned about her growing attraction to Brooke, but she now knew that was the least of her worries. Brooke would break her heart if she let her.

"Addison, I can't." Brooke's voice was rough, and it seemed an effort for her to get the words out.

Brooke pulled away and scooted forward to the edge of the sofa. She'd put mere inches between them, but the separation took them much farther apart. She cradled her head in her hands.

"It was just a kiss." Addison had never made a bigger understatement in her life. There was nothing simple about what they'd just shared.

Brooke lifted her head, and when their eyes met, the pain reflected in Brooke's shook Addison. Losing Diane had been hard on Brooke, Addison understood that. She'd lived the other side of Brooke's hell and, though she'd survived, she tried to imagine how Charles might have felt if she hadn't. Or how she might feel if, God forbid, something happened to take Charles out of her life. How difficult would it be to get over that devastation? Did Brooke just need more time to heal?

"I should go." Brooke stood.

"Hold on." By the time Addison rose, Brooke was halfway across the room. "Brooke, wait. At least say you'll still go with us on Wednesday."

"Addison—"

"Please." Addison caught her just as she opened the front door. "I promise I'll behave. Ramsey would love it if you go."

"Oh, you can't use the kid."

"Come over at one o'clock. We'll all ride together. What could happen with Charles and Ramsey along?" Addison purposely didn't mention their original plans for dinner after Charles left with Ramsey. "You can't just avoid me. We aren't done with the fundraiser yet."

After a second of deliberation, Brooke nodded. "I'll see you Wednesday."

"Thanks again for helping with Ramsey today."

Brooke waved over her shoulder as she left. Addison closed the door behind her, then collapsed against it. Her legs felt weak and her fingers still tingled where she'd touched Brooke. She shook her head, recalling the line of her thoughts a moment ago. Had she really been contemplating whether Brooke might someday soon be willing to take a chance in a relationship?

Aside from Brooke's issues, Addison had her own reasons for hesitating. Her first instinct was to use Ramsey as an excuse. She had to be careful about who she brought in and out of her daughter's life. She and Charles had made that deal when Ramsey was born. Ramsey had never seen her with another woman. No one had interested her enough for a second date in such a long time, let alone bringing them home to meet Ramsey.

But, she admitted, Ramsey was young and would adapt. In fact, she already had a classmate who had two dads, so the concept wasn't foreign to her. Another, perhaps stronger, reason for her hesitation was vanity. She could handle kissing Brooke, if that's as far as it went. But the thought of getting naked in front of anyone, especially

Brooke, nearly sent her into a full-blown panic attack. She had no problem imagining what it might be like to undress Brooke. If she pulled Brooke's T-shirt over her head would she find the expected sensible white bra or be surprised by silk or lace? But Addison's fantasy fog dissolved in a cheesy, '80s television manner when Brooke reached for the buttons on her shirt.

❖

"Would you like a cupcake?"

Addison turned, already formulating a polite refusal. Stacey held a tray of cupcakes frosted the same teal blue as the blouse she wore. Addison swallowed the impulse to ask if the coordination was on purpose.

"No, thank you."

"It's good to see you back. We've missed you at these meetings." She stepped around Addison and set the tray in the only empty space on the table behind her. A coffee urn, bottles of water, ham sandwiches on dinner rolls, and an assortment of chips covered the rest of the surface.

"I've missed the spread at these meetings," Addison said, picking up a bottle of water. Stacey gave a half smile as if she wasn't sure if Addison was joking, so Addison gave her rehearsed excuse for missing a few support-group meetings. "Work has just been crazy. Between that and the fund-raiser—"

"Do you need me to put someone else on your committee? I mean, I just assumed you and Brooke could handle it, but she probably doesn't know the first thing about organizing a fund-raiser."

"No, actually she—"

"You poor thing." She touched Addison's shoulder sympathetically. "You're probably doing all the work by yourself. I think Mr. Poole has the catering organized. I'll ask him to give you a call."

"No," Addison blurted, nearly choking at the thought of Mr. Poole and Brooke working together. "We have it covered. It's going to be great."

"Okay, I was simply trying to ease your considerable burden. If you don't even have time to make a meeting, you must be overwhelmed." Stacey's tone let her know that Addison had hurt her feelings.

Addison sighed. "Thank you, Stacey. I know you want to help. But I promise, Brooke and I have things under control. And, hey, here I am at a meeting."

Stacey smiled, then, distracted by a newcomer in the doorway, she excused herself. The man had barely stepped inside when Stacey met him, shaking his hand vigorously and ushering him farther into the room. He looked relieved.

Addison remembered how nervous she was when she arrived for her first meeting. She didn't know anyone, cancer was new to her, and her treatment was making her sick. She nearly left before she got out of the car that night, but Stacey happened to pull into the parking lot just as Addison shifted her car into reverse. She'd escorted her inside and made her feel like one of the group. Stacey's kind heart and generous nature had been a light in the storm for Addison and for many others in this room.

As the moderator called everyone together, Addison picked one of many empty chairs. Their group attendance fluctuated and tonight the crowd was sparse. When she was new, Addison had tried to keep up with who was missing and why. But counting the number of people who had died depressed her. Immersed in her own treatment, she hadn't had the luxury of focusing on negative things. She spent what little energy she had trying to will her cancer away.

Brooke wasn't the first person to question her participation in a support group. After her surgery, Addison's friends and family expected she would stop attending. Even Charles had admitted a few years ago that he didn't understand why she'd continued. While she didn't go as religiously as she used to, for Addison this group was a touchstone to her past. She wanted the reminder of how lucky she was and that she should stay involved in working toward a cure for all types of cancers. And after what she'd gone through, she hoped she could provide needed support to someone else who was just beginning their difficult journey.

Addison suspected some of Brooke's disdain for the group stemmed from jealousy. Diane had found comfort and support among people who understood her situation in a way that Brooke couldn't. From everything Addison had gathered, Brooke had no other close friends. Diane was her world, and she would expect Diane to be the same. So, naturally, she thought Diane would depend on her during her treatment.

But Addison had gotten to know a little about Diane during her time in the group. Diane was protective of Brooke. Addison suspected that was generally a dynamic of their relationship, not only related to Diane's cancer. Diane cared for her and probably thought it best to spare her as much pain as she could. Addison had seen others do the same with their family members.

Realizing once again just how solitary Brooke was, Addison wished she could comfort her. When she thought about what losing Diane must have done to Brooke, Addison wanted to find her and gather her in her arms and hold her.

CHAPTER TWELVE

Monkeys!" Ramsey exclaimed as she released Addison's hand and ran ahead. She practically skidded to a stop at the fence around the large enclosure. Inside, three big orangutans sat on the L-shaped limbs of thick trees.

Addison scanned the map in her hand as she strolled toward the exhibit. Ahead of her Charles and Brooke walked together, engrossed in conversation. Brooke said something she couldn't hear and Charles laughed. Addison had been nervous about the outing for two days, ever since extending the invitation to Brooke. She didn't realize until now how much she wanted Charles and Brooke to like each other. However, it shouldn't matter because as soon as the fund-raiser was over Brooke would probably run away from her as fast as she could.

Addison caught up with them at the exhibit. Ramsey talked to the orangutans and pretended their chattering meant they were responding to her.

"What's next, Mommy?" Ramsey turned around, squinting against the sun as she looked up at Addison.

Addison consulted the map. "The meerkats are on the corner over there."

"They have cats in the zoo?"

"Well, yes, they do. But not the kind you're used to seeing. The lions and tigers are a kind of cat. But meerkats are different. Let's go look at them." Addison took her hand and led her around the path until they reached a large Plexiglas wall. Inside, what looked to Addison like large rodents poked their heads out of holes in the ground.

"Look, babies."

In one corner of the exhibit, two larger meerkats huddled close to five tiny ones. Ramsey pressed her hands against the glass and angled as close as she could. "Aren't they cute?" she asked.

"Yeah, they are." Brooke squatted down next to her to look inside. Ramsey stood on her tiptoes, trying to get a better view.

Addison watched the two of them cooing over the babies, their faces close together, Ramsey resting her hand on Brooke's bent leg for balance. This was what she'd always had in mind when she was younger and thought about having a family. She'd done things the way she had because she'd felt time was running short, and she didn't regret it. Her arrangement with Charles worked out wonderfully. But, sometimes, Addison missed the intimacy of having a partner in every sense of the word.

Brooke and Ramsey took off toward the next exhibit, although neither was excited when Addison told them it was the reptile house. She wasn't sure if they would actually get Ramsey inside, given her fear of snakes.

"You okay?" Charles asked, as he fell into step beside Addison.

"What? Yeah, why?"

"You seemed a little far away back there."

"I was just lost in thought for a moment." Up ahead, Brooke and Ramsey stopped to peer over the side of a bridge into the stream running below it. Brooke rested against the top rail while Ramsey ducked under the lower one. Ramsey leaned a little too far over for Addison's liking, but before she could call out, Brooke reached down and grabbed the back of Ramsey's jeans, holding her up.

"Whatever it was, it looked pretty serious." Charles glanced at Brooke and Ramsey. "Want to tell me what's going on between you two?"

"Not really." Addison sighed. "I kissed her."

"Yeah? Shouldn't that be a good thing? You said it as if you gave her some kind of communicable disease."

"She doesn't want to be with me."

"She's here now."

"Only because she agreed before the kiss, and I used Ramsey to guilt her into keeping her commitment."

Charles shook his head. "Did she kiss you back?"

"Yes."

"I'm having a hard time understanding what the problem is so far."

"It's not that simple. Remember when I told you that I met her at a funeral for a woman in my group. Diane was Brooke's friend, and I don't think she's close to anyone else the way she was with her."

"Diane had cancer." Charles raised his eyebrows in understanding. "And Brooke's the quiet, broody type who thinks she can avoid being hurt by avoiding any connection to the disease that took her friend."

"Exactly."

"That's ridiculous. She's still a child. Is she even thirty yet? Chances are she'll come in contact with cancer again in her lifetime."

"I know. But she won't do it voluntarily." Addison realized she'd been twisting the map in her hands and tried to smooth out the creases she'd created.

"So, what are you looking for with her?"

"I don't know."

"Something casual?"

"No."

"Then it's something serious?"

"Do I have to know right now? It was an incredible kiss. And I guess I just don't like being told I can't do it again."

"Now that sounds like the Addison I know and love." Charles laughed.

"Shut up." Addison pushed his shoulder and he exaggerated a stumbling walk away from her.

Did she want a serious relationship with Brooke? She felt ridiculous even thinking about the future with a woman she wasn't dating and had known for only a few weeks. Brooke kept herself so guarded that sometimes it seemed impossible for anyone to get close. So, maybe that did make Addison all the more determined to get inside Brooke's walls.

❖

"I wanna see the giraffes," Ramsey yelled as she ran along the dirt road that led to the Savannah exhibit. Addison and Charles followed and Brooke brought up the rear.

"Why are the damn giraffes so far away from the rest of the animals?" Brooke grumbled to herself. The path they were on now cut through a large open field, and in the distance, she could see the signs for the next exhibit. She felt like they'd walked for miles in the blazing sun, when actually it had been only minutes since they'd left the shaded area that housed the big cats. "Apparently we have to cross the desert to see the giraffes."

Addison laughed and lagged back until Brooke caught her. "Here." She held out a bottle of water she'd bought at the snack bar as they passed.

"Thanks." Brooke took it and swallowed several big gulps.

"The elephants are over here, too. But the giraffes are my favorite and totally worth the trip."

"Yeah? Why's that?"

"I don't know. They're beautiful in an awkward way."

They finally reached the treed area surrounding the giraffe enclosure. Three of the lanky animals stood near the fence on the far side of the large open area. Ramsey called to them, giving them made-up names and summoning them with a series of kissing noises and whistles, but they showed no interest in her. One of the giraffes turned its head and looked at them insolently. Its lower jaw moved in a slow circle as it chewed whatever it had just pulled off a nearby tree. After staring at them with big round eyes rimmed with long lashes, it turned away, having apparently deemed them unworthy of its time.

"Well, that's just insulting," Brooke said. "Damn anti-social giraffes."

"Damn anti-social giraffes," Ramsey repeated.

"Ramsey, you don't say 'damn,'" Addison chided, trying not to laugh at the matching pouty looks on Brooke and Ramsey's faces.

"Brooke said it."

"Well, she shouldn't have." Addison gave Brooke a pointed look and a flush crept up her neck.

"Sorry," Brooke said. Unfazed, Ramsey went back to trying to attract the giraffes' attention. "Sorry," Brooke repeated.

"It's okay. Around her, you have to be careful. She's a little sponge, soaking up everything."

"I'll remember that."

"I don't want to talk to these giraffes anymore," Ramsey declared, shoving her hands on her hips in frustration.

"Okay, let's get moving then." Charles took her hand and they headed back onto the path.

They stopped briefly at the elephant exhibit, but they weren't interested in interacting with Ramsey either. They trekked back across the field toward the main part of the zoo, meeting several families pushing strollers and trailing kids of various ages.

"Doesn't that make you want a few more?" Charles asked after they passed a ridiculously large family.

"Lord, no. I'm not one of those women who can handle a gaggle of children."

"A gaggle?" Brooke laughed. "I think that's geese."

"What about you, Brooke?" Charles asked. "Do you want kids?"

"No."

Addison gave her a curious look, but Charles pressed for more. "None?"

"I've never felt a strong urge to be pregnant. In fact, I'm a little afraid of childbirth."

"Sure, but that's the beauty of being a lesbian. You don't necessarily have to be the one to bear the child."

"I guess not. But I've never been in a relationship where talk of children as a real possibility has come up. And I don't hear my clock ticking loudly enough to make me want to go it alone."

"Well, you certainly have some time to decide."

Brooke nodded. She'd known women in college who were baby-crazy, always talking about graduating and settling down with their husbands and having kids. But, already, she'd known she was different from her classmates. As an only child, she didn't have any nieces or nephews to attach herself to. Brooke tended to overlook children after a cursory glance, never feeling the pull of maternal instincts.

Even now, though she'd been okay with watching Ramsey the other day and had to admit how cute the kid was as she ran around the zoo, she didn't yearn to raise one of her own.

"Critter Encounter?" Brooke read the sign pointing to the fork in the trail that Ramsey had taken. "That doesn't sound promising."

Addison smiled. "It's the petting zoo. We'll have to drag Ramsey out. She could spend hours in there."

When they reached the entrance to the fenced-off area, Ramsey stood waiting, practically bouncing out of her shoes with excitement.

"Now, Mommy?"

"Go ahead." Addison barely had the words out of her mouth before Ramsey scurried through the gate.

"Be gentle with the animals," Charles said, as he followed her inside.

"I'm surprised that in her excitement she remembered she couldn't go in until we said so." Addison laid her forearms across the top of the fence and rested her chin on the back of her hand.

A llama, a donkey, and some pigs occupied stalls lining the open paddock area where a dozen or so small goats roamed freely. Ramsey wove between the goats, touching them as she passed. Only the bravest among them didn't shy away when she darted toward them. She tried to imitate their bleating, but hers came out more like a grunt.

Brooke leaned against the fence next to Addison. Comforted by the sound of a gentle breeze rustling the leaves overhead and the smell of hay and feed that teased her nose, she couldn't remember feeling more at peace since Diane died. Even thinking about her now didn't bring the same sharp stab of pain. Instead, she registered a dull ache and the echo of emptiness.

Ramsey had found one particularly affectionate goat that bumped her shoulder and nuzzled her hand.

"I think he's hungry." Charles shoved his hand inside his pocket and dug out several coins. "Do you want to feed them?"

Ramsey nodded and hurried over to what at first glance looked like a bubblegum machine. Charles put a quarter in the dispenser and cupped his hands under the chute while Ramsey turned the dial. Seeds and grains flooded his hands, and Ramsey immediately dipped in for a fistful.

"Are you okay? We're not boring you to death, are we?" Addison nudged Brooke's arm with her elbow.

"No. Of course not."

"I wasn't sure how exciting a life you're used to. But I know a day at the zoo isn't that thrilling, especially if you don't like kids."

"I didn't say I didn't like them. You know how you sometimes have this vision of what your life is going to be. Well, mine never included kids."

"I understand." Addison smiled. Brooke enjoyed the sparkle in her eyes when she was teasing.

"Besides, I'm not very high-maintenance. Spending time with you has been more socialization than I've had in months."

"Yeah?" Addison canted her weight to her left, bringing her closer to Brooke—close enough for Brooke to see her pupils constrict against the shaft of sunlight that poked through the canopy and fell directly on her face.

"Yeah. It really helps take my mind off things. I know we've had a bit of a rocky start, Addison, but I appreciate the friendship you've extended to me. It's definitely helped me deal with some tough times."

"Friendship? Is that what we have going here?"

The sun lit up Addison's auburn hair, making streaks of it shine like copper. Brooke's skin tingled where Addison's bare arm rested against hers. "Friendly" didn't often describe what Brooke felt toward Addison. Today, the casual atmosphere of their zoo trip kept the usual flares of arousal down to a slow burn of awareness. But throughout the day, Brooke had been conscious of Addison, of the way her khaki shorts showed off her long legs, and how the gusting wind flattened her T-shirt against the swell of her breasts.

She'd tried to counteract those moments by concentrating on the interaction among Addison, Charles, and Ramsey. The three of them were a family, though not by the traditional definition, and it worked well for them. Addison had said she didn't need anything complicating her life. Despite their kiss the other night and the look in Addison's eyes right now, they'd both be better off if they didn't cross that line. So, yes, friendship was all they could have.

"Okay, Ramsey, five minutes, then we're ready to head home," Charles said as he stepped outside the paddock.

"That's not going to work," Addison said as he rested against the fence next to her.

"I know. The warning was for me, not for her."

"Ramsey, come wash your hands," Addison called, walking over to the hand-washing station just outside the fence.

"Not yet."

"Let's go."

"No, Mommy."

"Now, Ramsey." Addison's tone left no more room for argument.

"She's better at playing the bad guy than I am," Charles told Brooke. "I know I need to be tougher on her sometimes, but I just want her to be Daddy's girl forever."

Brooke didn't speak, letting Charles interpret her polite smile however he wanted.

Ramsey took her time getting across the paddock. She slowed to pet every animal in her path, darting glances at Addison to see how much more she could get away with. Bravely, she met Addison's eyes, her own shining with defiance, her mouth pressed together tight.

Brooke laughed. "You guys might be in trouble when she gets older." Ramsey would be a rebellious one, and, with her looks and personality, she'd be a popular kid.

Addison shook her head. "I know."

Ramsey struggled with the metal latch on the gate, frustration making her less likely to succeed by the minute.

Charles and Brooke both reached for the latch at the same time.

"Sorry," Brooke mumbled as she pulled her hand back and stepped away.

Charles smiled and opened the gate. Ramsey stomped past him to the hand-washing station and shoved her hands under the water.

"I think it's almost nap-time," Addison said loudly as she pumped soap into her hand, then rubbed it over Ramsey's.

Ramsey pinched her eyebrows but, wisely, didn't say anything.

Brooke let Addison and Charles start out on the path before she followed, feeling awkward about the exchange with Charles a minute before.

Ramsey stepped easily between Charles and Addison and grabbed each of their hands, the tension from moments ago forgotten. She'd already forgiven her parents for not giving in to her pleas for more time.

Every few seconds she let her body drop so they supported all of her weight as she swung between them, trusting each time that her parents wouldn't let her fall. Brooke had never had anyone trust her so completely. Despite the unorthodox arrangement Charles and Addison had, it was clearly working. Today had been proof that Ramsey was well-adjusted, secure enough to venture out on her own, but also not afraid to show her affection and dependence on her parents. Despite how comfortable today had been, Brooke was reminded that she was on the outside of this little family.

CHAPTER THIRTEEN

A ddison opened the front door and flipped the switches for the foyer light as well as the porch light behind her. As they'd driven home, the clear blue sky had given way to the silver and pink tones of dusk.

"Get your backpack, sweetie. I'm taking you to preschool tomorrow," Charles said as he closed the door behind him.

Ramsey disappeared down the hall.

"She'll sleep well tonight." Addison slipped off her light jacket and hung it in the hall closet.

"Yep, she'll be out halfway through the first bedtime story," Charles said.

Ramsey returned dragging a backpack straining to contain its contents. The zipper was half open and a tuft of sandy-brown fur poked out between the teeth.

"That bag wasn't that full when I packed it earlier." Addison grabbed the strap of the bag as Ramsey passed.

"I added a couple things," Ramsey said, her tone indicating she knew better than her mother what should have been included.

"How much did you add?"

"Toddy wanted to bring his friends."

Addison smiled as she extracted a brown bear, a small yellow kitty, two Barbie dolls, and a purple monkey. "All of his friends?" Ramsey and the brown bear had been inseparable ever since she'd gotten it for her second birthday. At the time, she'd had trouble saying "Teddy" so she'd christened him "Toddy."

"It's a sleepover at Daddy's house."

Addison repacked the bag, leaving Toddy and the monkey. "I think Kitty and the Barbies will stay with me."

"Are you having a sleepover, too?" Ramsey looked at Addison then at Brooke.

Addison flashed on an image of herself pulling back the sheets and guiding Brooke into her bed. Her face flamed hot and she avoided Brooke's eyes, instead focusing on answering Ramsey. "No, honey. You're the lucky one."

Charles took Ramsey's bag and slung it over his shoulder. When his eyes met Addison's, he winked. Addison's scowl only made him grin wider.

"Bye, Mommy."

"Good-bye, sweetheart." Addison swept Ramsey up in a quick hug.

"Bye, Brooke." Ramsey headed for Brooke with open arms. Clearly caught off guard, Brooke managed to squat down in time to catch her in a swift embrace.

"Have a good night." Charles held the door for Ramsey, then followed her out.

Addison turned to Brooke. "Can I take your coat?"

"I should get going, too." Brooke pulled her jacket tighter around her.

"What about dinner?"

"I don't think it's a good idea." Brooke glanced at the closed door as if recalling Ramsey's innocent question.

"Relax, Brooke. I'm only offering to cook for you. Chicken and broccoli Alfredo, no commitment involved." Brooke didn't answer but she didn't dart toward the door either, so Addison decided to interpret that as a concession. "Throw your coat over the back of the couch and come keep me company." She headed for the kitchen, hoping Brooke would follow, but she didn't allow herself to check.

She turned on the burner and pulled out a skillet and a pot for the pasta. After she reached into the refrigerator for supplies, she was pleased when she closed the door and found Brooke propped against the opposite counter.

"Anything I can do to help?" Brooke asked.

Addison passed her a loaf of crusty bread on a bamboo cutting board. "You can slice this. Knives are over there."

Addison didn't feel the need to fill the silence as they worked, enjoying the rasp of the knife through bread and the sizzle of sautéing chicken. She'd planned the zoo outing in an attempt to make up for the time she'd been away from Ramsey lately because of work, and it had been worth it. But knowing Ramsey, she didn't envy the preschool teacher tomorrow who would have trouble getting her to focus on anything but the animals she'd seen today.

Brooke hummed softly while she arranged thick slices of bread on the cookie sheet Addison gave her. Addison recognized the tune but stopped short of humming along. She did, however, sneak quick glances at Brooke. The zoo probably wasn't normally Brooke's thing, but aside from a few times when Brooke's expression went all dark and serious, Addison thought she'd enjoyed today as well. She'd seemed more relaxed and open than Addison had seen her before. Once, Addison even thought she'd let her guard down completely, and she wondered if it could be that easy—if she and Brooke could get past Diane's death, and cancer, and everything else, and make it work. But then Charles had interrupted them, and Brooke repositioned her defenses.

Addison had once thought Brooke a closed book, but she now realized she might be written in an entirely different language.

❖

"That was delicious, so rich and cheesy." Brooke finished her last bite and groaned, a low vibration of pleasure that Addison felt to her own depths.

"Thank you. I'm glad you liked it. It's easy to make. I could write down the recipe if you want. I got the Alfredo from a magazine and added the broccoli because the only way Ramsey will eat it is if I smother it in cheese. You can make it plain or with the chicken. Or, I suppose, you could try other things in it if you wanted to."

Brooke smiled indulgently and Addison realized she'd been rambling again. She tore off a piece of bread and stuck it in her mouth. She'd spent most of the day with Brooke, but without Charles and Ramsey as chaperones the atmosphere suddenly felt more intimate. Perhaps she should have turned on a few more lights before they sat down.

"So, is your big project at work all wrapped up?" Brooke asked.

"Yes. We'll still be handling units in the complex, but the closings will be more spread out."

"Do you have to work long hours often?"

"It varies, depending on what we have going on. Usually, my schedule is somewhat flexible, which is one of the reasons I've stayed there. But despite my complaining, I've been glad for the overtime lately."

"I guess the poor real-estate market makes your job difficult."

"Even though interest rates are in the basement, we're having a harder time finding loans for buyers that wouldn't have had a problem a few years ago. Every so often we hear rumors of cutbacks. But this deal gives us some breathing room until we can put something else together."

"I certainly don't have a business mind. I'd be bored to death in an office wearing a suit."

"It's not exciting, but it's stable." Addison took Brooke's plate and stacked it on her own. "What drew you to writing?"

Brooke frowned. "I don't know that I ever made a conscious decision. I started playing the guitar when I was twelve and never put it down. I've worked odd jobs when writing didn't pay the bills."

"Like what?" Addison deposited their dishes in the sink and waved off Brooke's attempt to start cleaning them. "Leave them, I'll get them later." Addison went into the living room and settled on the sofa. Brooke glanced at the chair nearby, but Addison had dropped her briefcase in it when she came home from work. For a moment, Addison wondered if Brooke would move it, but she sat down next to Addison.

"I waited tables, though I don't know a songwriter who hasn't done that. I also worked as a roadie for a country band's tour. But probably my weirdest job was in a chicken-processing plant down in Shelbyville."

"Oh, my God, I don't want to know what you did there."

Brooke laughed.

"Seriously, we just finished eating chicken."

"Yeah, it wasn't the job for me. I didn't last three months."

"I don't think I'd last three days."

"It wasn't all that bad. When the chickens came in on the trucks, I took—"

"No. No, I don't want to know." Addison covered Brooke's mouth with her hand. Too late, she realized she'd practically flung herself in Brooke's lap in order to reach her. She froze, teetering on the edge of falling into the dark pools of Brooke's eyes. Her chest rested against Brooke's and she felt the rise and fall of her breathing.

"Addison." Brooke's voice was muffled as her soft lips moved against Addison's palm.

Addison eased back slightly and removed her hand, but she remained pressed to Brooke's side.

"Addison, you promised you'd behave." Brooke sounded like she had to force her words out.

"I know." Addison smiled. Brooke's breathing had picked up and she balled her hands into fists. "But I don't want to."

"God, how did you do this?" Brooke shifted, presumably trying to put some distance between them, but she was already against the arm of the sofa so all she did was jostle Addison closer. Addison put her hand on Brooke's thigh for balance and fought the urge to slide it higher.

"Do what?"

"How did you get me from chicken-processing to totally turned on in under a minute?"

Addison laughed softly. When she squeezed Brooke's leg, the muscles twitched. Reluctantly, she withdrew her hand and moved back to her side of the sofa. "Wow, when you put it like that it almost kills the mood."

"Almost?" Brooke flexed open her hands. She shook her head and her hair fell forward, nearly obscuring one eye.

"Yeah, almost. Because now I just want to prove that I could turn you totally on in another minute." Addison gently pushed Brooke's hair back, sliding her fingers slowly through the silken strands. She traced her thumb over the arch of her eyebrow and down her cheekbone.

"You might be right about that."

"I know I'm right." Addison was still halfway there herself. When she touched Brooke's lower lip, Brooke's tongue darted out and swiped across the pad of her thumb. A hot streak of pleasure shot through Addison. Brooke froze for a second, as if the motion had been involuntary and unexpected.

"Less than a minute," Brooke murmured. She pulled one side of her lower lip between her teeth and her eyes melted like chocolate.

Arousal raced through Addison's blood, leaving a tingling trail in its wake. Her control snapped like the recoil of a bungee cord, and she grasped Brooke's chin and kissed her, aggressively. The scrape of Brooke's teeth on her own lip told her that Brooke felt the same all-consuming need. She shoved her hands into Brooke's hair and urged her closer—kissed her harder. Brooke thrust her tongue against Addison's, claiming her.

Brooke grasped Addison's hips and pulled her into her lap. Addison broke free only long enough to slide one thigh on either side of Brooke's. She covered her mouth again, drinking in the taste of her, like warm honey, sweet and thick.

"God, I need to touch you." Brooke kissed her jaw and the side of her neck. When her lips touched Addison's earlobe, she shivered.

Brooke slipped her hand beneath Addison's shirt and stroked her skin surprisingly gently, given the force of their kiss. When Brooke's fingers brushed the bottom of her bra, panic surged through Addison. She put her hands on Brooke's shoulders and pushed back, desperate to get space between them.

"Wait."

"What's wrong?" Brooke's mouth still moved against her neck.

"I need a minute." Addison rested her forehead against Brooke's and drew in a deep breath, then slowly released it.

Brooke slid her hands down Addison's sides, but she didn't remove them from her shirt. She left them against her bare skin, the span of her hands bracketing her waist. Addison's racing heart slowed a notch.

"I'm sorry." Addison took another deep breath. "I know I started that, and I didn't expect to be the one to stop it, but—"

"It's okay." Brooke tilted her head and kissed Addison's forehead.

"I don't know what happened." Shaken, Addison eased off Brooke's lap and onto the sofa next to her. She hadn't done this in quite some time, so she expected to be nervous. But the anxiety that had swamped her had been strong enough to have her flailing for solid ground. "It's been so long, and I have to think about Ramsey. She really likes you, but I've never brought someone I was— interested in around her." She fumbled with the false excuses, trying to cover the tremor of nerves in her voice.

"Hey, it's okay." Brooke touched her shoulder and Addison let herself relax a little against her.

"You're being far too understanding."

"You don't want me to be?"

"No. It would help my ego if you were a bit more sexually frustrated."

"Maybe I just hide it well."

Addison nodded. A confusing mix of arousal and tension still muddled her ability to think.

Brooke's serious expression suddenly lightened and a slight smile touched her lips. She withdrew her hands. "Kissing you is—amazing—incredible. But I don't think I could have gone any further right now anyway."

"No?"

"No. I'd be thinking about what you said about letting strangers feel you up."

"Are you kidding me?"

Brooke chuckled. "Mostly. But now that I've said it, there might be a little truth there."

"Is this—um, permanent?"

"Lord, I hope not."

Addison recaptured Brooke's hand and lightly stroked her palm. She pressed Brooke's hand against the center of her chest and held it there. She closed her eyes briefly and concentrated on the warmth of her hand. "I'm not just reluctant because of Ramsey."

"I figured. But she's as good a reason as any to slow things down."

"So, where does this leave us?"

"Addison, I can't—"

"You said kissing me was amazing."

"I did. But—"

"Let's start there. I like kissing you, too, and I'd like to do it again." Addison angled forward and pressed her lips to Brooke's.

CHAPTER FOURTEEN

Brooke crossed from the parking lot to a bench near the playground, leaving a trail of footprints in the dew-covered grass. She was surprised at the number of people already in the park, given the early hour.

As she settled on the bench, a woman pushing a jog stroller with a heavily bundled baby inside ran by. A man followed his dog as it sniffed a meandering path through the wet grass, and when it stopped, he pulled a plastic bag from his pocket and waited.

Brooke sat completely still, opening herself to the layers of sound around her. The mingled laughter and shouts from several children on the playground came in bursts, and every so often, a bird chirped in a nearby tree. On another bench a few feet away, two women spoke Spanish, and though she didn't understand their words, the cadence of their speech was familiar. Farther away, the crunch of tires against rough pavement signaled the arrival of more people.

Listening calmed Brooke, helped her concentrate on something besides whatever was on her mind. Every so often she heard something that inspired a piece of music, a sound that evoked a feeling she wanted to capture. Sometimes she could clear her mind enough to tackle that issue and, sometimes, she just needed the distraction. Today, she felt a little of both.

She couldn't avoid thinking about Addison. In fact, she hadn't been able to stop thinking about her in the three days since they'd kissed on Addison's sofa. When she could put the taste of Addison's lips out of her mind, she thought instead about the varied shades of gray in Addison's eyes as her emotions shifted. She'd been torturing herself with instant replays of their kisses, complete with slow motion and sappy theme music. But the surge of arousal that accompanied those moments was nearly as strong as when she was immersed in Addison, and she found no relief tossing and turning alone in her bed.

Despite how far Brooke let her imagination go, in reality, she wasn't entirely comfortable with how they'd left things Wednesday night. She'd practically stumbled away from that second kiss, stuttering about what a good time she had at the zoo. Addison had walked her to the door and hugged her and kissed her again, this time a peck on the lips. Since then, she'd been avoiding Addison, answering her texts briefly, only enough to avoid a confrontation.

More than anything, she fought her own desire to see Addison. On Thursday and Friday, she'd managed by telling herself Addison was at her job. So, instead, she'd forced herself to work. She'd made some headway on the melody for a new song, but her heart wasn't really in it.

Today, she'd awakened intent on getting out of the house. Her mother had always said that fresh air could cure half of what ailed you. But since she didn't have her mother's green thumb, Brooke opted for a walk in the park. Granted, so far all she'd done was sit on a bench and daydream.

She stood and set out along the same path she'd walked with Addison just a few weeks ago. They had argued and Addison had stormed off. Brooke had been equally angry, but not entirely with Addison. She was angry with Diane, but since she wasn't around, Addison made an easier target.

As Brooke followed a bend in the path that led under a canopy of trees, the air around her felt cooler and heavier. A familiar, sick knot of loneliness tightened in Brooke's stomach. Brooke had felt the same ache often as a child. Her mother and father had already given up on becoming parents and built their own life around each other when she came along. On the surface, they had done everything right, raised her in a safe, secure home. But she'd sometimes felt she intruded on their relationship.

Then one day, when Brooke was in junior high, the new girl at school had sat down beside her in the cafeteria. Diane didn't care that Brooke wasn't popular or that she kept nearly everything crammed inside of herself. Diane sat with her every day, talking about anything and everything, while Brooke merely nodded, until, without even realizing it, Brooke began to respond. They talked about every bit of their lives up to that point, and from then on, they shared each new experience with each other as well.

When Brooke came to Diane with that same knot in her stomach, worried that she would lose Diane's friendship, and confided that she had a crush on another girl in their class, Diane just hugged her and said it would be okay. When Diane fell in love with a football player, who took her virginity and bragged about it all over school, Brooke sat with her while she cried in her bedroom the entire next weekend.

Diane had been the one to loosen the knot in Brooke's stomach all those years ago. She had given Brooke unconditional friendship and support, through her career and her relationships. But then with one word—cancer—the thread of loneliness had begun to coil again. In the three months since Diane's death, that ball of pain had become a constant for Brooke. With her parents gone, and now Diane, she was truly alone in the world. No one wondered where she was or worried if she didn't call.

Her phone buzzed against her hip, and Brooke glanced at the display—*Addison*. Brooke slowed, then stepped out of the way of an oncoming jogger as she stared at her phone. She decided not to analyze the timing of the call. Giving in to her desire to talk to Addison, she clicked the Answer button.

"Hello."

"Hey, I—uh, well, for some reason I didn't expect you to answer. But I haven't heard from you and just wanted to check in."

"I'm okay. I've been busy—catching up on things." Brooke cringed at the obvious lie. She didn't have things to catch up on, and she was certain Addison knew that.

"Oh."

Yep, Addison knew. The quiet hum of static on the line mocked Brooke as she searched for something to say. "How've you been?" she blurted, running it all together so it came out more like one long word.

"Good. We're good."

"That's good." If she thought it would help, Brooke would have smacked herself in the forehead.

"Would you like to come over?" Addison asked.

"I don't know if that's a good idea."

"Ramsey's with Charles today."

"That's not the only reason I don't think it's a good idea." Brooke sat on a large rock at the edge of the trail and pulled her knees up to her chest.

"Then what else is stopping you?"

Brooke battled with her instinct to pull back emotionally. She wanted to remain closed off, wanted to keep things from Addison. But just hearing her voice eased some of the ache inside.

"Brooke?"

"Yeah?"

"I don't know what it means when you get quiet like this."

Brooke didn't respond.

Addison sighed. "This is silly. Where are you?"

"At the park."

"Do you want me to meet you there, or are you coming over here so we can talk face-to-face?"

"I'll be there in twenty minutes."

"See you then."

Brooke hung up and headed toward her car. She wasn't more than five minutes from Addison's house, but she wanted the extra time to take the long way back to the parking lot. She wasn't entirely sure how much Addison would push her to talk once she got there, but she needed to get a grip on the emotions she'd stirred up while thinking about Diane.

❖

"Are you sure you won't come inside?"

Brooke shook her head. "This is safer."

"You can at least sit down." Addison patted the seat of the swing next to her. Brooke had knocked on her door five minutes ago, then insisted they stay outside.

"I'm good." Brooke leaned against the porch railing a few feet away.

"What's going on, Brooke? Are you that weirded out because I kissed you?"

"No."

"Well, then, why do I feel this tension between us?" Despite the uneven way they left things, Addison had expected to hear from Brooke on Thursday. She waited until Thursday night and sent an exploratory text and received a terse reply from Brooke. She didn't want to seem too eager, so she didn't text or call again, even though she hated such game-playing. But Friday afternoon she caved and sent another text and, again, got a brief response that didn't invite further conversation. She'd called this morning expecting to leave a message, but as soon as she heard Brooke's voice, she wanted to see her.

"Do we really have to discuss this?" Brooke shoved a hand through her hair, but the dark strands immediately fell back over her forehead.

"Do you just want to forget about the kiss, keep working on the fund-raiser, then go our separate ways?" Addison held her breath, steeling herself for an affirmative answer, but Brooke remained silent. Brooke wanted her to back off, Addison could feel that. And she knew she probably should.

She'd given Ramsey a stable, comfortable routine. If she left things as they had been, her own heart would be safe. But she'd learned long ago that life was too short to be less than honest. Brooke interested her more than anyone had in years, and maybe that was reason enough to take a chance.

She stood and took the three steps that she hoped would close the distance between them. She gathered Brooke's left hand between hers and stroked her thumb against the inside of her fingers.

Brooke's fingertips were callused, and Addison remembered the agile way they moved over her guitar.

"I don't want to pretend nothing is happening between us." Addison met Brooke's eyes and saw the fear there, but she held her gaze, trying to exude more confidence than she actually felt. "I need to know one thing, though. Are you attracted to me because you miss Diane and you're lonely?"

"No."

"That was a quick answer. You didn't even think about it."

"I don't need to. I'm attracted to you in spite of my loneliness."

Addison rubbed her thumb over Brooke's palm. "But you're afraid to act on that attraction."

A ghost of a smile touched Brooke's lips, then disappeared. "Why do you keep saying that?"

"Because you are. I understand why. Diane was your best friend, and I think you may even have been a little in love with her."

Brooke drew her eyebrows together and tried to pull her hand free, but Addison held on. "I wasn't in love with her. We were friends."

"You don't think you compared the women you dated to her? When was the last time you had a serious relationship?"

"What difference does that make? Just because I haven't met anyone I wanted to be with in a while, you can't say I was in love with my straight best friend. I'm not some stupid adolescent." Brooke jerked her hands free and headed for the stairs leading to the sidewalk.

"Wait, Brooke. Please, don't go." Addison took a step forward, to the edge of the porch.

Brooke stopped but still faced away from her. "Why are we even talking about this? You've been almost as resistant to anything happening between us as I have. You didn't want to complicate the life you have with Ramsey and Charles. What changed your mind?"

Addison shrugged, then realized Brooke couldn't see her. "I don't know. I like my life. But I also like spending time with you. You make me feel good. Can't that be enough for now?"

"This never works, you know." Brooke turned around and looked up at her. "People say they can get involved and not think about the future, keep it casual, whatever, but it never turns out that way. One person always gets more invested than the other."

"I know." Addison was almost certain that she would be that person. And she asked herself the same question Brooke had, why was she suddenly willing to take that chance? Brooke's eyes were soft and vulnerable, and Addison wanted more than anything to hold her.

"But you still want to do this?"

Addison descended the three steps between them and wrapped her arms around Brooke's neck. Brooke circled Addison's waist and rested her hands against the small of Addison's back. The warmth of Brooke's hands through her cotton shirt set off sparks along her spine.

"Yes, I do," she whispered, turning her face into Brooke's neck and nuzzling her soft skin. She pressed her lips just below Brooke's ear. When she gently sucked her earlobe, Brooke shivered and tilted her head to block her access.

"If this goes too much further, we should take it somewhere other than your front yard," Brooke said.

"Yeah? How much further do you want it to go?" Addison eased back and smiled.

"I'm not sure, but if your neighbor across the street keeps trimming the same shrub that gives him the perfect view of us standing here, it won't have any leaves left."

Addison grabbed Brooke's hand and pulled her toward the front door. "I knew I could get you inside somehow."

❖

Brooke sat on the couch and watched Addison practically flit around the room. She swept up a stack of mail from the coffee table and moved it to the kitchen. She straightened several coloring books and magazines on the end table. She turned on the lamp, then turned it back off.

"Was that too much light? Not enough?" When she started away again, Brooke caught her hand.

"Sit down."

Addison sank onto the couch beside her. "I really made that easy on you, you know. I practically had to beg you to sit with me out there." She nodded toward the front door.

"Are you okay?" Brooke circled her fingers around Addison's wrist and caressed her tender skin. She trailed a line lightly up the inside of her forearm to her elbow and back down.

"I—um—"Addison grabbed her hand and stilled it. "I can't think when you do that."

Addison's shy smile touched Brooke. On the porch, she'd seemed so certain about what they should do, so much so that she'd won Brooke over. With one embrace, Addison had seduced Brooke into setting aside her doubts, even if only temporarily. Things might get messy later, but when she looked at Addison right now, later seemed so far away.

"What do you need to think about?" Brooke reclaimed Addison's wrist and stroked slow circles inside her palm.

Addison angled toward Brooke. "Well, for all my openness about my treatment and teasing you about my implants, I'm feeling quite tentative with this part of it."

"This part?" Brooke raised Addison's hand and kissed the ridge of her knuckles.

"I haven't been—physical with anyone in a long time."

"How long?"

"Let's just say a *very* long time."

"Well, the mechanics of it haven't really changed." Brooke grinned.

Addison raised an eyebrow. "Really? Because I figured it had probably gone all high-tech by now."

"Probably. But I'm an old-fashioned girl. All I need is you. I'm not trying to rush you." Brooke kissed the inside of Addison's palm and smiled. "Okay, maybe I am a little. But you started it outside with that whole ear thing. Do you want to slow down?"

"It's not that. Not really." Addison drew a deep breath then released it. "Oh, hell. It's not that big a deal. I don't know why I'm having trouble getting it out."

"Whatever it is, just say it."

"Okay. Cancer and pregnancy weren't necessarily kind to my body."

Brooke ran her eyes over Addison's figure. She'd admired her curves in a wide range of attire that now included the worn blue jeans and green cotton button-down she wore today. "You have a great body."

"With clothes on, maybe. But I have scars and stretch marks that'll send you running for sure."

"You think I'm that shallow?"

Addison covered Brooke's hand. "It's not about you. It's me. I'm just not comfortable with myself."

"We all have insecurities about ourselves. I could list a handful of things I hate about my body without giving it any thought."

"Well, this might be a bit more than that."

Brooke shifted forward and rested her hands on Addison's knees. Pushing aside her own hesitance about letting things progress, she focused on making Addison comfortable. She met Addison's eyes and waited until she was certain Addison saw the sincerity in her own, then said, "You're beautiful."

Before Addison could argue, Brooke kissed her. Reminding herself to be patient, she slowly caressed Addison's lips. As Addison slipped her tongue confidently against Brooke's, a ripple of pleasure spread outward.

"I'm glad you think so." Addison rested her forehead against Brooke's and undid the top button of her shirt.

"You have to know you're gorgeous. But that's not what I mean." Brooke brushed her hands away and slipped the next button free. The verdant vee of her shirt parted to reveal a creamy wedge of skin and a hint of cleavage. Brooke moaned in appreciation and worked open the next few buttons. A pale-pink bra embraced her breasts, and Brooke traced the lacy edge, then dipped her fingertip lower. "You're beautiful."

Addison had spent the past nine years trying to tell herself that her scars didn't matter, that saving her life had been more important. While that was definitely true at first, once she was out of danger, her vanity had resurfaced.

"Sure, they look great when you dress them up." A seed of panic unfurled like the new shoots of an unwanted weed in the garden. Determined to ignore it, she slid her shirt off, then contorted her arm behind her and promptly unsnapped her bra. She shrugged her shoulders forward and let it fall into her lap.

Brooke met her eyes. "Wow, you just ruined my moment. I was going to tenderly undress you, revealing your breasts slowly."

Addison smiled. "Oh, and I messed it up."

"Yes, you did."

"Well, maybe we'll just have to try another time." Clutching her bra to her chest, Addison grinned and picked up her shirt. Before she could get her arm in the sleeve, Brooke whipped the shirt from her hand.

"I can probably get the mood back."

"Yeah?"

Brooke caressed Addison's hands until she opened them, then she lifted the bra free and set it aside. She dropped her eyes. "Oh, yes, absolutely."

Addison fought the urge to fidget as Brooke stared at her breasts. She looked down and tried to see them as Brooke might. The horizontal scar that bisected one side of her right breast had faded over the years, but the absence of a nipple was probably startling. The crease beneath her breast hid the scar from the implant on her left side. Her breasts weren't evenly weighted, and her right one was slightly misshapen, not enough to see when she had clothes on, but it was evident now.

This was a bad idea. She looked around for her shirt, but Brooke had flung it into the chair nearby. She grabbed the throw from the back of the sofa and hugged it to her chest. Brooke wrapped her hand gently around Addison's forearm, eased Addison's arm down, and took away the blanket.

Addison raised her eyes to Brooke's face, and what she saw took her breath away. When Brooke's worshipping gaze moved over her chest, Addison had never felt more cherished. For the first time in a very long time, she didn't feel broken.

Brooke cupped her breast, curving her fingers around it deliberately. She rolled Addison's nipple between her thumb and forefinger, and it puckered in response.

"Can you feel that?"

"Yes. I didn't lose any sensation in that one."

Brooke lowered her head and kissed her nipple, then pulled the tight flesh gently into her mouth. Pinpoints of pleasure radiated through Addison. She shoved her hands into Brooke's hair and pulled her closer, arching her back to give Brooke better access. While Brooke's lips and teeth worked her sensitive nipple, she cupped her hand around Addison's other breast and her thumb fell against the spot where her nipple should have been. Addison gasped and pulled back.

"Wait."

Brooke lifted her head slowly, as if fighting a haze of arousal. "What's wrong?"

"I'm sorry. I need a minute." She covered Brooke's hand and moved it aside.

"Did I do something?"

"No. I'm sorry." Addison took Brooke's hand and placed it back on her breast. "It's just, no one but my doctor and I have touched me there since the surgery."

"I don't have to—"

When Brooke started to pull back, Addison stopped her. She had areas of permanent numbness on the underside of her breast, but, where she did have feeling, Brooke's skin was warm and soft. When Brooke's thumb had brushed the scarred area where her nipple would have been, Addison had felt a swift ache for the loss of a part of her womanhood. But since she couldn't undo her past, she held Brooke's hand there, getting used to the new sensation.

"I opted not to have nipple reconstruction."

"Why?" Brooke didn't sound judgmental, only curious.

"I didn't want to be put completely back together, as if I could pretend everything was normal again."

Brooke continued looking at her, first caressing her nipple, then smoothing her finger over the top of her other breast. Addison had lived with the results of her surgery for long enough to be accustomed to the way she looked, but she'd never had anyone else's opinion to consider.

"Does it bother you?" Addison caught Brooke's hand and threaded their fingers together.

"No. But if you need more time, we can stop." Brooke swept her tongue over her lower lip, and while Addison was certain she only did so to moisten it, her body reacted in other ways. Only minutes ago, she'd felt that tongue against her own, Brooke's beautiful mouth moving with purpose over her skin.

"I don't need more time." She cradled Brooke's face in her hands and kissed her. *I only need you.* She stopped short of saying the words provisionally, despite how much of herself she'd revealed, they still felt too intimate. She already knew she wanted too much from Brooke, more than Brooke was ready to give. So, instead, she surrendered to the slow burn that the taste of Brooke's lips rekindled.

Brooke shifted over her, pressing her back into the arm of the sofa. She braced her hands on either side of Addison, holding her weight away from her. Addison wrapped her arms around Brooke's waist and pulled her closer. Her leg slipped between Brooke's thighs. Addison pressed her mouth to the side of Brooke's throat and felt her pulse against her lips.

"You should take this off. I need your skin." Addison tugged at Brooke's shirt.

Brooke straightened, kneeling, and while she pulled her shirt over her head, Addison opened the fly of her jeans. Brooke released the clasp on her bra and let it fall to the floor. Addison reached for the triangle of gray cotton she'd revealed, but before she could touch it, Brooke lowered herself back over her.

Brooke's stomach rested against hers, her upper body angled away. Thick, dark nipples tipped Brooke's small breasts. Addison dragged her hands up Brooke's ribs and cupped her breasts. She gasped when Brooke's nipples tightened before she even touched them. She skated a thumb over one, barely grazing it, and watched it knot even further.

"God, Addison, touch me, please," Brooke said through gritted teeth. She sighed, then moaned when Addison complied, squeezing her between a thumb and forefinger.

Brooke rolled her hips against Addison's and Addison pushed back, desperate to get the rest of their clothes off. Addison shoved her hands into the back of Brooke's jeans, grabbing the waistband of her panties. As she scooted down to reach more of Brooke, her neck crooked against the arm of the sofa.

"Brooke."

Brooke's mouth blazed a hot streak down the center of Addison's chest.

"Hold on."

She stopped and lifted her head, concern flooding her eyes. Addison laid her palm against her cheek. She started to sit up, and Brooke took her hands and pulled her up. Addison held onto her hand and stood, then led Brooke down the hall to her bedroom.

Brooke stood next to her bed, looking uncertain and quite gorgeous. Her bare torso tapered, then flared slightly before disappearing inside her jeans. Her fly was still open and the waistband of her panties rode low against her flat stomach.

"Making out with you on the sofa is hot, but I'm too old to do it there without needing a chiropractor tomorrow." Addison teased her, trying to put Brooke at ease.

Brooke smiled.

Addison pushed one hand inside her jeans. Brooke's panties were damp, and Addison felt a rush of moisture and a heavy throb between her own thighs. She instinctively squeezed Brooke, and Brooke gripped her elbow.

"Jesus, Addison. I won't last if you keep that up." She eased Addison's hand out of her jeans.

"Don't worry. We can do it again later."

Addison grasped Brooke's jeans and shoved them down. Brooke kicked out of them and slid her panties down as well. She helped Addison finish undressing. When they were both naked, Addison circled her arms around Brooke's waist and pulled her onto the bed.

Brooke hovered over her, stroking her stomach, her hips, her thighs, all while her mouth moved over her neck. Her teeth closed on Addison's earlobe. Addison twisted her head, seeking Brooke's mouth, then finding it and sucking her tongue into her mouth. The feel, the scent, the taste of Brooke infused her and overloaded her senses.

As they explored together, the room filled with their panting breath and soft moans. Brooke worked her way down Addison's body, her fingers drawing a map for her questing mouth. She circled her navel and detoured through the crease where her hip and thigh met.

When Brooke's fingers parted her and grazed her clitoris, suddenly Addison was the one fighting to hold out. Her heart pounded so loud she was certain Brooke must be able to hear it. Brooke kissed the inside of her thigh. She looked up and met Addison's eyes and held them for a second before lowering her head.

"Brooke," Addison whispered. Her hips lifted, almost on their own, anticipating Brooke's touch.

Brooke slid inside her, at the same time slipping her tongue into her moist folds. Addison nearly sighed in relief as that single stroke fulfilled the promise of pleasure, but a rush of need followed, overtaking her when Brooke drew her fingers back and surged forward again, slow and deep.

Brooke devoured her, licking and sucking her swollen, sensitive flesh. Addison trembled and hurtled too quickly toward release. A plea for Brooke to slow down formed in her mind but never made it to her lips. She clung to Brooke, scratching her nails against her shoulder blades.

Every thrust of Brooke's fingers created a current that threatened to sweep her away. She fisted one hand in Brooke's hair and ground against her, fighting her impending orgasm for as long as she could before letting it overtake her. Her muscles seized and jerked under the onslaught of sensations, then finally went slack, leaving Addison panting and weak.

Brooke slowed with her, easing her down. Addison lay still, unable to move, and Brooke shifted to rest against her side. When

Brooke slowly withdrew her fingers, Addison's exhausted body seemed reluctant to let them go.

Brooke moved up to lie beside her. Settling the sheet over both of them, she gathered Addison against her side.

"That was amazing." Replete, Addison closed her eyes and sighed.

CHAPTER FIFTEEN

Brooke opened her eyes to the unfamiliar sight of a brushed-nickel lamp on a cherry nightstand. She smiled, rolled onto her back, and stretched. Her muscles pulled with the pleasant echo of the previous night's exertion. After the first time, they'd napped. Then when they woke up, Addison made them grilled-cheese sandwiches for dinner. But the sight of Addison in the kitchen in only a short silk robe distracted Brooke so much that she dragged her back to the bedroom, where they stayed for the rest of the evening.

Addison lay beside her, facing the other way. The sheet draped across her torso, leaving her shoulder bare. Brooke didn't want to wake her, but she itched to trace the freckles sprinkled across her ivory skin. Unable to stop herself, she touched Addison's shoulder. Addison murmured and snuggled against her. Brooke inched closer, pressing against Addison's back, and slid her arm around Addison's waist, settling her hand against her stomach.

"Good morning," she whispered in Addison's ear.

"Morning." Addison covered her hand.

Brooke pressed her lips to Addison's neck, then her cheek. Addison shifted onto her back, wrapped her arm around Brooke, and pulled her down for a kiss.

"Did you sleep well?" Brooke asked.

Addison glanced at the clock. "Six solid hours."

"I should have let you sleep a little longer." She rose on one elbow and ran her fingers over Addison's bare stomach, watching muscles flex and jump in response. "I can't stop touching you."

"Yeah?" Addison caressed Brooke's hip. "Are you a morning person?" Her suggestive tone was enough to make Brooke wet.

"I could be. What time is Ramsey due home?"

Addison shrugged. "Charles and his mother were taking her to church. They'll probably go out for brunch afterward. Are you worried about her?"

"Are you?"

"I asked you first. I know you said you didn't want kids. Oh, God, not that I expect you to think of Ramsey as yours. But, generally, someone who doesn't want kids wouldn't want to be around other people's children either. And even if this is something casual, Ramsey and I are a package deal."

"Ah, well, I like Ramsey. So, no worries about that. Besides, all I said was, children weren't in my plan."

"They weren't in mine either when I was your age, at least not as anything more than an abstract, maybe-someday type of thing. You have time to figure it out."

"Not that much. I'm almost thirty. I should have figured some of these things out by now." Brooke rolled onto her back and folded her hands under her head. *Something casual.* That's what Addison had said. And that should have been perfect, because Brooke couldn't handle anything else right now. She shouldn't have gone to bed with Addison, but she hadn't been able to help herself. Being with Addison last night was amazing, and she didn't want to start this day with regrets. So she vowed to not get too involved and to let it run its course.

Addison lay against her shoulder, resting her hand in the center of her chest. "So what are you doing today?"

"Hmm. First I have to figure out how to drag myself out of your bed." Brooke covered Addison's hand and kissed her forehead.

"I have an idea about how to get you out of bed." Addison slipped away, clutching the sheet against her body. She took two steps toward the bathroom and let the sheet drop. "Join me in the shower," she said over her shoulder.

"Oh, hell, yes." Brooke practically leapt out of bed and followed.

Brooke could see Addison's decorating touch in the large bathroom. Like in the bedroom, modern fixtures with simple lines mixed well with feminine touches. A double vanity with white vessel sinks held a small bouquet of dried lavender and various bottles of scented lotions and perfumes. Against the far wall a bathtub stretched beneath a window. Six votive candles in glass cups lined the edge of the tub.

Addison swiped her hand across the glass of the large shower stall, clearing a swath of steam. "Are you coming?"

Brooke opened the door and stepped inside. The cubicle was twice the size of a normal shower. Sandstone tile and a built-in bench created a spa-like atmosphere. Addison pushed Brooke against the opposite wall.

"I told you I could get you out of bed," she said before she covered Brooke's mouth with hers.

"Hey, lady, I came in here to shower," Brooke teased her, pretending to push her away.

"Oh, okay. Let's do that then." Addison shoved Brooke under the hot spray.

Brooke laughed, then wrapped her arms around Addison's waist and pulled her under the water with her. Addison wiggled free. She grabbed a bottle of citrus-scented body wash and squeezed some onto a bath pouf.

She worked the soap into lather and rubbed it down the center of her chest. When she circled her breast and left a trail of suds across her fair skin, Brooke reached for her.

"No. You wanted to shower." Addison held up her hand and stepped back. She rubbed the soap over her torso, her eyes locked on Brooke's.

Brooke could practically feel Addison's wet, fragrant skin sliding under her fingers. But every time she tried to touch her, Addison batted her hands away. She continued bathing herself with a smug smile that said she knew exactly what she was doing to Brooke. She washed every inch of her body, seeming to take extra time and care, while Brooke looked on helplessly. Brooke tried to fake indifference but couldn't take her eyes off Addison.

But when Addison's hand moved down her belly and between her legs, Brooke had to act. As appealing as the idea of watching Addison touch herself was, Brooke hadn't gotten enough of Addison yet. She brushed Addison's hand aside and replaced it with her own.

"Addison," she moaned as she sank two fingers into her wet folds.

"God, Brooke." Addison slumped weakly against her, wrapping her arm around her neck.

Brooke eased her over to the tiled bench at the end of the stall. Addison sat and Brooke knelt on one knee in front of her.

"You'll hurt your knees." Addison tried to pull Brooke onto the bench with her, but Brooke stayed on the floor.

"They're fine. I need you again." Brooke kissed Addison's knee. The shower spray beat against her back as she slipped her fingers back between Addison's thighs and teased her firm clitoris. She stroked it lightly, then more firmly, then when Addison began to move her hips, she eased the pressure again. She kissed Addison's breast, warm and flushed from the hot water.

Addison responded to every touch, thrusting against Brooke's hand and grasping her shoulders desperately. Need built in Brooke, making her ache for friction against her own clit. Addison braced herself against the wall, spreading her legs in invitation. When Brooke eased her fingers inside, Addison arched her back. Her wet hair clung to her face and neck, her eyes were heavy-lidded, and her mouth parted as she gasped for breath. Brooke had never seen anything more beautiful.

Brooke bowed her back and thrust forward, shifting her weight into each stroke. Addison pushed back against her, her feet scrambling for purchase on the wet tile. She wedged her heels against Brooke's thighs, getting the leverage she needed in order to draw Brooke deeper.

Addison's cries echoed through the room, nearly incoherent sounds of encouragement that drove Brooke on. She poured herself into every stroke, silently giving Addison everything she couldn't put into words.

"I'm so close," Addison rasped. Her thighs trembled against Brooke's shoulders.

"What do you need?"

"Your mouth. Don't stop."

Still rocking her fingers in and out, Brooke spread Addison's legs wider and sucked her. She pulled Addison's clit into her mouth and flicked her tongue against it. She forced her own clawing desire aside and concentrated on reading Addison's desire. When Addison neared the summit, Brooke held on while Addison rode toward release.

Addison cried out a final time and clamped her hand on the back of Brooke's neck. When the pulsing around her fingers eased, Brooke gently removed them and laid her head on Addison's thigh.

"This bench is quite convenient."

Addison laughed. "This is exactly what I had in mind when I had it put in."

Brooke crawled onto the bench next to her and rested against the wall, the cool tile on her back contrasting with the warm mist swirling around them. "You did this?"

"Yes. I bought the house before Ramsey was born. I still want to do a lot of things to it, but this bathroom was one of my first changes."

"So, you were planning for this moment? Or maybe I'm being presumptuous."

"What do you mean?"

"I shouldn't assume I'm the first woman you've had in here—"

"You're the first. Did you really need me to say it?"

"No. That's not what this is about."

"Good." Addison stood. She grabbed Brooke's hand and pulled her up. "Now, let's finish this shower so I can take you back to bed. I'm not done with you yet." She squeezed a dab of shampoo into her palm. "Come here." She rubbed the shampoo into Brooke's hair. Despite the hot water, Addison's fingers against her scalp raised goose bumps on Brooke's skin.

Brooke tipped her head back and gave herself over to the feel of Addison's hands and the fantasy of this day. She refused to think about the consequences or the practical reasons this wasn't a good idea. God, if Addison could make her feel like this, maybe she was worth the risk.

❖

"Mommy, we're home."

Addison straightened her shoulders and tried to control her expression. Charles and Ramsey entered the kitchen, and Ramsey dropped her backpack on the floor.

"Take that to your room." When Ramsey looked like she wanted to argue, Addison gave her a stern look. Pouting, she grabbed the strap of the bag and dragged it toward the hallway.

"Pick it up," Addison called.

Charles smiled. "Did you miss her?"

"Absolutely. Coffee?" Addison pulled the carafe from the machine and poured a mug.

"No, thanks." He glanced at his watch. "Is this your first cup?" He narrowed his eyes and Addison felt him taking in her disheveled hair, oversized T-shirt, and boxer shorts.

"No, it's not." She'd had a cup with Brooke in bed.

"It looks like you just got up. Are you having a lazy day?" He sat down at the kitchen table.

"I guess I am."

"Yeah? What did you do all weekend?"

"Brooke came over yesterday and—"

"Mommy, can I watch TV?" Ramsey called as she hurried back into the room.

"Yes, sweetie. For thirty minutes." Addison waited until she heard the television come on before she spoke again. "I slept with her."

Charles raised an eyebrow. "Last night?"

Addison nodded.

"How was it?"

"Great. Pretty amazing, actually."

"Are you going to do it again?"

A hot flush crept up her neck.

"You already have." He laughed.

"She just—I don't know—she makes me feel good."

"Well, yeah, I hope so. Otherwise there would be no point in sleeping with her again. Wait, was she here this morning?"

Addison nodded.

"How much did I miss her by?"

Addison glanced at the clock. "About an hour."

"Damn, we should have skipped brunch." Charles grinned. "I'd love to have seen her face if we walked in here while you two were—"

"Okay, that's not a good idea."

"But it would have been funny."

"She would have been embarrassed. But beyond that, I really don't want to confuse Ramsey right now."

"What's confusing? She knows Brooke—knows you're friends."

"Yes." Addison dropped into the chair across from him. "But she doesn't need any more information than that. I don't want her getting attached to Brooke only to be heartbroken."

"Honey, that ship has sailed. I watched them at the zoo. Ramsey's almost as in love with Brooke as you are."

"I am not in love with her."

"No?"

"No. I just like spending time with her. Something about her, I just—she makes me feel brave."

"How so?"

"When I'm with her, I'm not as self-conscious about my scars as I thought I would be. I do things with her that—" Addison stopped, realizing what she was about to say. Charles wouldn't want to hear it, but it was the truth. This morning, she'd walked so brazenly into the shower naked without giving a thought to her scars, or the pooch on her belly that she wanted to be flatter, or how she wished her butt were higher and tighter.

"That's a good thing. It all sounds good, Addison. So why do you look worried?"

"Because it all sounds *too good*." She propelled herself out of her chair and across the room.

"Hey, don't stress about this. You've lived in this little family bubble of ours for too long." He stood and followed her, then wrapped an arm around her shoulders. "Let this be whatever it's going to be. And if that turns out to be nothing, Ramsey and I'll be here to help you through it."

He really was a good friend. He'd always been there and she'd never had to question that. But at some point, his primary identity in her eyes had changed to that of Ramsey's father.

"I haven't really seen you, Charles. I've been so wrapped up in myself for—" she shoved a hand through her hair— "Well, since I got sick, I guess. I needed you."

"I didn't mind."

"I know. But even when I was well again, I got in the habit of needing you, for myself, then for Ramsey."

"Remember the good old days, when all we had to worry about was who was buying beer that night?"

Addison sighed. "Yeah. That was a very long time ago. I got old."

"I didn't." He tossed his head and smoothed two fingers over the hair at his temple. "I'm ageless."

She twined her arms around his waist. He enfolded her in a big embrace and she inhaled his spicy scent. The comfort she found in being pressed against his solid chest had gotten her through some tough times, including chemotherapy. But she wasn't the same fragile woman he'd held while she shivered with nausea. She was stronger and could face whatever happened with Brooke. She and Brooke had come into each other's lives for a reason, and Addison was brave enough to find out what it was.

Chapter Sixteen

You've made a big mistake.

Brooke paced her living room, trying to get the thought out of her head. She'd had an amazing night and an even more incredible morning with Addison. She should be able to enjoy it before she let herself freak out.

"You're a grown woman," she muttered. "You're allowed to have a good time. You've slept with women before and didn't get all spastic about it. Sure, but those women weren't Addison. She's beautiful, and smart, and fun, and no one has ever made you feel this way."

Great. Now, in addition to talking to herself, she was answering herself. That's what happened to people with no friends. They had whole conversations with themselves until they eventually went crazy and got fifty cats and ended up on that television show about hoarders. And she didn't even like cats.

"Okay. Calm down. You're blowing this all out of proportion." She strode across the room and grabbed her guitar, then plopped down on the couch. "You like Addison. She seems to like you."

She cradled the guitar in her lap and began to play a series of chord progressions. She'd done the same warm-ups thousands of times, and the familiar routine eased her anxiety.

"I'm scared. She was right about that." Brooke nodded as if agreeing with herself. "She was wrong about me being in love with Diane. But she was right that I'm afraid of loving anyone. And why shouldn't I be?"

She worked through the chords, then moved on to picking out a new melody. She used minor chords and dramatic changes to paint the mood of the piece. She closed her eyes and let the music infuse her. Humming softly, she played the first few lines over and over until they felt right. She grabbed a notebook and pen from the end table and took notes on her progress.

She still knew how to do this. Through all that had happened with Diane, she'd stuffed her creativity deep down, but for the first time in months, she felt like she could retrieve it. She'd been holding everything balled up inside for fear that if she let her pain out, even a little, she would lose control and never get it back. At first, when Diane was still alive and fighting her cancer, Brooke forced herself to be strong for Diane; then later, she stayed frozen to keep her sanity.

But today, as she poured out her feelings of loss and loneliness, she released her anguish. Her heartbreak echoed through the loft along with the sound of her voice breaking as she tried to sing the melody. She kept writing and playing and singing until her throat was sore and her fingers cramped. Finally, she set aside her guitar and curled up in a ball on the couch, wrapped her arms around her stomach, and cried—deep, wrenching sobs.

Eventually, when she had no more tears left, she rolled onto her back and splayed her arms above her head. She stared at the ceiling and opened herself up to all the things she hadn't allowed herself to think about.

How could she go on without Diane? She'd been numb for months, but especially now, when her feelings for Addison confused her so, she needed her best friend. Diane had known Addison through their support group. Ironically, if Brooke hadn't been so obviously against the group, Diane might have talked to her about the members. Maybe they would have talked about Addison. Diane probably liked Addison. If she were here, she would tell Brooke to stop being afraid and go for it.

Brooke sat up and scrubbed her hands over her face. She would also tell her to get off her ass and start writing again. Diane had been pushing her for years to open up and write something from her heart. She'd accused Brooke of writing too many emotionless honky-tonk, cheating songs.

She'd been skating through life superficially, never feeling anything too deeply. But in the past year, she'd had her share of emotions. Maybe she could finally fulfill Diane's wishes and pour those feelings into her music.

Her phone rang as she picked up her guitar again. She answered without looking at the caller ID.

"Hey, what are you up to?" Addison's voice sounded tentative. Brooke immediately conjured her last image of Addison as she'd been when she'd left her that morning, sitting on the edge of the bed with the sheet draped loosely around her.

"Not much." Brooke wedged the phone between her ear and her shoulder. She rested her fingers against the strings of her guitar. "Actually, I've just been writing a little."

"That's great. I don't want to interrupt."

"It's okay."

"But if you're being productive—"

"No. I can get back to it later. How did you know I wanted to talk to you?" Brooke leaned back and put her feet up on the coffee table. *How did you know this was exactly what I needed right now.*

"ESP?"

"Probably not."

"Are you okay?" Addison's concerned tone made Brooke want to share what she'd been feeling while writing. She wanted to tell her she needed her and ask her to come over.

"Yeah, I'm fine," she said, instead.

"You sure? There's something in your voice I can't place."

"It's nothing."

"If you need to discuss something, I'm here."

"Did you call to tell me that Ramsey's with Charles?" Brooke ignored Addison's offer. Her emotions were raw, and though she was certain her tear ducts were empty, she wouldn't take the chance of breaking down while on the phone with Addison.

"Not tonight." Brooke thought she could hear the sexy smile in Addison's voice. "She's actually curled up asleep on the couch beside me."

Unexpectedly, Brooke wished Addison would invite her over to sit with them. She imagined the two of them next to each other, drowsy and content to look at each other by the glow of the television. Maybe she would carry Ramsey to her bed before joining Addison in their bedroom—er, her bedroom.

"Can I see you tomorrow night?" Brooke asked, still caught up in her intimate fantasy. "If Ramsey's going to be there, it can just be friendly. I could bring a movie."

"Tomorrow is parents' night at Ramsey's preschool."

"Tuesday?"

"Dinner with my boss."

"Wednesday? But that's my final offer. I don't want to appear desperate."

"I have a support-group meeting."

"Skip it. After Ramsey goes to bed, we can make it more than just friendly."

"You could come with me."

"No, thanks," Brooke said, not trying to hide her displeasure. The bubble of happiness in her head around the two women on the couch ruptured.

"They're really a great group. Can't you try to have an open mind?"

"I don't want to go."

"Will you tell me why?" Addison's soft voice reached out to her like a supportive hand.

Brooke set her guitar aside and slid to the edge of the couch, ready to jump up and move if need be.

"Brooke?" Addison asked when she didn't answer. "Why don't you want to go to my support group?"

"Drop it, Addison."

"I'll make you a deal. If you go with me, you can come back to my house afterward and I'll be as *friendly* as you want."

"Damn," Brooke muttered. Despite her resistance, Addison's sexy suggestion turned her on. "You're really trying to bribe me with sex?"

"Is it working?"

She wanted to say no. She had solid reasons for wanting to avoid the group. The last place she wanted to be was the one place Diane preferred in her waning months. So she could stick to her plan and continue to refuse, or she could go, pretend being there didn't bother her, and avoid talking to Addison about it.

"Okay."

"Pick me up at a quarter to six. Are you going to hold me to that whole sex thing?"

"Absolutely. I'm getting something out of this."

"Good. I hoped you would. See you then."

❖

"You all right?" Addison whispered

"That's the fourth time you've asked me."

"Well, I'm worried. You look like you're about to throw up." Addison covered Brooke's hand and squeezed. Brooke absorbed the warm sensation of Addison's skin, but she released her too soon.

"I'm fine." She closed her eyes and forced herself to breathe slowly. She tried not to think about Diane here, but she kept picturing her sitting in the chair next to her.

I needed to be here. These people understood the pain I couldn't share with you.

She heard Diane's voice, not weak and breathy like the last time she'd seen her, but clear and strong. She glanced around, but no one seemed to notice the empty chair that was talking to her. Shutting out Imaginary Diane, she focused on the woman leading a discussion about managing the side effects of chemotherapy.

Brooke remembered all too clearly how Diane's treatment had affected her body. Diane tried to keep from Brooke just how sick she was, but one particular day, she hadn't been able to hide the nausea and bone-deep chills.

Across the aisle, Stacey nodded along with everything the woman was saying. She'd assaulted Brooke almost as soon as they'd stepped through the door, gushing about how happy Diane would have been to see her there, and didn't she feel better being among people who knew her pain. Brooke balled her fists and nodded tightly, resisting the urge to tell Stacey to mind her own business. Addison took Brooke's arm and led her away under the pretense of introducing her to the others.

Now, Brooke listened to one man talk about how difficult it had been for him to be ill in front of his wife, let alone his children. He described the toll that his cancer, then his treatment, had taken on him. He said he had continued to fight because he didn't want that to be the way his kids remembered him. Now he'd been cancer-free for over a year and attended every one of his son's basketball games. Children have a short memory and he was happy to be their hero again. More difficult, he said, was getting his wife to regard him as a man again. She'd seen him at his weakest and most beaten and sometimes still treated him as if he were that broken man.

"If I'm still healthy after five years or ten, will she finally believe I'm strong again? How do I make her understand that I'm not someone she needs to take care of anymore? That I'm her husband, her partner in this marriage," he said, shaking his head.

Others in the group began chiming in with suggestions. He listened and nodded along with some of them. Another man told a similar story and explained that he'd started engaging in daredevil activities in order to prove to his girlfriend that he was still a man. But after skydiving, bungee jumping, and drag racing, he'd eventually had to sit her down and tell her what he was feeling.

Brooke tried to hold on to her dislike of this group, but the members slowly won her over. She could definitely understand how such a group might help someone who was dealing with cancer themselves, or that of a loved one. But, personally, she probably wouldn't be back.

❖

Addison sat silently in the passenger seat of Brooke's car. When they first left the meeting Addison had tried to engage her in conversation about the group, but had received only one-word answers. She switched topics to something safer, but Brooke wasn't any more talkative.

Brooke steered into Addison's driveway and stopped, the engine still idling.

"Aren't you coming in?" Addison asked as she reached for the door handle.

"I'm not really going to make you deliver on your bribe."

"Is that because you're being honorable? Or because you don't want to talk about the meeting?"

Brooke shrugged. "I'm just not sure I'm in the mood tonight."

Addison got out of the car. Brooke probably thought Addison should just go inside, but Addison didn't want to leave her alone. Whether they talked about it or not, she didn't want to lie in bed and think about Brooke all alone in her apartment. Addison circled the car, opened the door, and held out her hand. "Come on. No expectations and no pressure."

Brooke hesitated.

"We can sit on the porch again if you want to."

Brooke smiled faintly and took Addison's hand. Addison led her to the porch and hesitated.

"We can go inside," Brooke said.

Addison unlocked the door and waited for Brooke to enter. Her babysitter sat on the couch in front of the television.

"Any problems?" Addison asked.

"She went right to bed at seven."

Addison gave her several folded bills and walked her to the door. She waited until she'd gotten into her car and backed out before she turned off the porch light.

"Make yourself at home. I'm just going to look in on her," Addison said to Brooke as she headed for the hallway.

She stuck her head into Ramsey's room. Ramsey had kicked off her covers and lay sprawled across the middle of her bed. Addison gathered her up and turned her to rest her head on the pillow, then pulled the sheet and comforter up to her shoulders.

When she returned to the living room, Brooke had settled on the couch. Addison sat next to her and immediately took her hand, wanting the physical contact. When Brooke had picked her up earlier, they'd shared a quick kiss, but other than the quick clasp of their hands during the meeting, they hadn't touched.

Addison stretched her other arm along the back of the sofa and brushed her fingers against the back of Brooke's neck. Brooke's expression changed and she tilted her head into Addison's hand. Addison slid her hand into Brooke's hair at the base of her skull and massaged the back of Brooke's head. Her fingers brushed the curve of Brooke's ear and Brooke shivered.

"Addison." Brooke's voice was low and raspy. "I told you, I wasn't serious about the bribe."

"That's not what this is about. I missed you today. I wanted to touch you." She leaned back against the arm of the sofa and patted her chest. "Come here."

Brooke stretched out and lay half on and half next to Addison. She rested her head on Addison's shoulder and her arm across Addison's stomach.

"You may have been right about a few things," Brooke said quietly.

Addison remained silent, sensing this wasn't one of those times when Brooke needed to be pushed. Brooke didn't speak for several minutes, but Addison held her questions in.

"I wasn't in love with Diane, at least not in a romantic way. But maybe I did compare the women I dated to her. At some point, she became the kind of woman I was looking for." She lifted her head and met Addison's eyes. "But I can live with my exes not measuring up to her. I'm having a hard time living without my best friend."

Addison stroked Brooke's cheek. "I can imagine how difficult that is."

Brooke laid her head back down and slipped her hand under the hem of Addison's shirt. "I hated that she seemed to need that group so much. It's not that hard to figure out why. Your group gave her something I couldn't. And I'd have done anything for her, to help her, to save her."

"Oh, honey, she knew that. But you couldn't save her, and she knew it broke your heart. She needed to let go, and she couldn't ask you to help her do that."

Brooke took a deep, shaky breath, and Addison guessed she was trying to keep from crying. Addison held her tighter and stroked her head.

"My parents live near Philadelphia. When I was diagnosed, my mother basically moved in with me. She went crazy trying to find things she could do for me, from cleaning my house to running my errands. I knew it was hard for her to watch me go through it, but I needed to fight on my own. And it would kill me to see Ramsey get diagnosed, especially since I'm passing on my bad genes to her."

"That's not a guarantee that she'll get it, is it?"

"No, but I increased her odds."

"But don't you also increase her awareness? If she knows to be vigilant, she'll probably catch it early and have a good prognosis."

"I've never thought of it that way." She'd only felt selfish when thinking about Ramsey. Brooke's outlook didn't change Ramsey's genetics, but it did give Addison a bit of hope that while she might inadvertently make Ramsey's life more difficult, she wasn't necessarily passing on a death sentence.

CHAPTER SEVENTEEN

O h, God, Addison, don't stop." Brooke pushed her hips against Addison's thrusting fingers. "Oh, please. Don't stop."

Brooke fisted her hands in the sheet next to her hips and ground against Addison's hand, the force of her motions flexing Addison's fingers back with each push. As if realizing what she was doing, she suddenly eased up and stopped.

"I'm sorry," she said.

"Why?"

"I didn't mean to—uh, I thought I might be hurting you."

After slowly withdrawing her fingers, Addison moved up to lie next to her. "You can be a little aggressive if you want to. You aren't going to break me."

"I know."

"Do you? Because sometimes you look at me like you want to rip my clothes off, but when you touch me it's as if you're being overly careful."

"I don't want to be too rough."

Addison smiled. Physical pain was the least of her worries when it came to Brooke. She was more likely to get her heart shattered. She pressed her lips against the side of Brooke's neck and kissed her gently, then closed her teeth over the same spot. Brooke sucked in her breath sharply.

"Was that painful?" she asked against Brooke's skin.

"No."

She bit her again, this time a little harder. "How about that? Still okay?"

"Oh, yeah, that's good."

"And if I roll you over and slap your ass, would that be okay?"

Brooke flushed, but her eyes gave away the excitement Addison's words caused.

"I think we both know the lines here, and if you cross one I'll let you know. Outside of that, I don't want you holding back with me. I'm not fragile and I don't want you to treat me like I'm still sick. Okay?"

"Yes."

"Good. Now, roll over."

Brooke's brow furrowed. "Are you seriously going to slap my ass?"

"Maybe." Addison grabbed Brooke's hips and pulled her onto her stomach.

Brooke laughed, then stopped suddenly when Addison crawled over her. Addison pressed herself firmly against Brooke's ass, her breasts resting against Brooke's back. She bent her head and touched her lips to Brooke's ear.

"Do you have any lines I shouldn't cross?" She smoothed her hand down Brooke's side.

Brooke pushed back into Addison. "You could pretty much do anything you wanted to me right now."

"Mmm, you make me want to test that." Addison smiled. She'd never been quite this brazen before. She eased to Brooke's side and traced her hands along Brooke's spine, into the hollow of her lower back, and over the curve of her butt. She lifted her hand and, without giving herself time to hesitate, gave Brooke's ass an exploratory slap.

Brooke jumped. She whipped her head around and looked over her shoulder at Addison. "I didn't think you'd really do it."

Addison bit her lip and smiled. "What do you think?"

Brooke grinned. "Try again. A little harder."

Brooke held her gaze as she raised her hand. The sharp sound of Addison's second slap cut through the room. Brooke's eyes darkened and she lifted her hips. A shock of arousal shot through Addison, and the slight sting in her hand excited her.

"Did you like that?" she asked as she touched Brooke's reddened skin.

"See for yourself," Brooke challenged.

Addison moved her hand between Brooke's legs and underneath to cup her. Her fingers slid easily through Brooke's wetness and inside her. Brooke arched, pushing back into her. Addison pulled her fingers nearly all the way out and sank them deep into her again. Brooke thrust against each long, slow stroke.

Addison kissed the small of Brooke's back, then ran her tongue over the swell of Brooke's buttocks. Brooke trembled and moaned. She rose on her hands and knees.

"I love the way you feel inside me," Brooke murmured between panting breaths.

Addison braced her weight on her other arm, bowed her back over Brooke's, and pumped her fingers in and out. Brooke let her head hang between her shoulders and rocked into Addison's thrusts.

"Harder, baby." Brooke encouraged her. As she increased her pace, Addison followed.

Brooke's body tightened, beneath her and around her, hovering at the edge of release for several long seconds. The muscle in Addison's arm burned from exertion, but she kept on, stroking faster and harder until Brooke cried out and arched back with one final thrust. She went rigid, squeezing Addison's hand between her thighs, then fell forward, sprawled out on the bed.

Addison eased down beside her. She draped her arm across her back and traced a lazy figure eight on her shoulder blade. Addison drew the sheet over them both.

Brooke raised her head and kissed Addison. "You are wonderful," she murmured.

"You make me that way. I've never been like that with anyone."

Brooke rolled to her back and stretched her arms above her head. "That was almost enough to make me glad I went to that meeting."

"Almost? Do I need to try a little harder next time?"

Brooke held the back of Addison's head and kissed her forehead. "I'm sorry, I didn't mean it like that. That was perfect. And I am glad I went to the meeting. I understand a little better what Diane was feeling."

"Anytime you'd like to go back—"

"That's not necessary." Brooke sat up and rested against the headboard. "I'm glad I went tonight. But I don't think the meetings would help me. I can't process my emotions by talking to a bunch of strangers."

Addison pushed herself into a sitting position. "Well, the idea is that you go on a regular basis, then they aren't strangers anymore."

"When we met, you thought it was a good idea for me to meet these people. But now that you really know me, do you still think I could open up there?"

"No."

"That's my point."

"Okay." Addison raised her hands in surrender. "You know that you have an open invitation. But I won't bring it up again."

"Good." Brooke touched Addison's face. "These past weeks have flown by. Can you believe the benefit is this weekend? I still feel like we've missed something and we just won't know it until it falls apart on Saturday."

"That's normal. I always get that way the week before. But we've gone over the plan so many times. Every act has confirmed its attendance. Short of someone just not showing up, I don't know what could go wrong."

"Don't jinx it," Brooke said with a stern look.

"If something happens, we'll improvise. Trust me, no matter how scattered things seem, the event always comes together in the end."

Brooke nodded. "I'll admit, nothing has turned out the way I would have predicted for a while now. For example, if you'd told me the first day we met that we'd end up here, I wouldn't have believed it."

"I would have."

"What? Seriously?"

"Yes. The day we met, I said that I ramble when I'm uncomfortable."

"I remember." Brooke laced her fingers into Addison's.

"You never asked me why I was uncomfortable."

"Okay. Why were you?"

"I was attracted to you, very much, even then, and I didn't want to be."

"Why not?"

"You really have to ask? You were all surly and—"

"Surly?" Brooke laughed. "I was surly?"

"Yes." Addison lifted her chin, sticking by her opinion. "That's the best way to describe you."

"I don't think so. Regardless, I thought you were attractive, too. I was checking you out in that skirt and charcoal blouse from the street as you were going into Diane's house."

"Yeah?"

Brooke nodded.

"I didn't see you."

"I know." Brooke glanced at the bedside clock and picked up her shirt from the end of the bed. "I should get going."

"You don't have to." Addison smiled and pushed the sheet away. The sight of Addison's naked body was enough to make Brooke forget why she should leave. Addison's long, firm legs were her weakness. Brooke didn't bother trying not to stare at her trim thighs, the curve of her calf muscle, her slender ankles, and feet that were surprisingly sensitive to Brooke's touch.

"I don't want to, but you probably need to sleep before work tomorrow. You said you and Charles have an agreement about bringing people around Ramsey, and I'd rather not try to sneak out before she wakes up in the morning," Brooke said without taking her eyes off Addison's body.

"She already knows you. But you're right. I don't want to confuse her by finding you here in the morning."

Brooke nodded and slid toward the edge of the bed. But Addison grabbed her arm and pulled her back in. She lay back and guided Brooke on top of her.

"I can survive on a couple hours of sleep for one day." She slipped her thigh between Brooke's and pressed firmly. "So you can leave, right after this."

❖

"Hey, Poppi. Are you all set for the fund-raiser this weekend?" Brooke asked as she walked into the nearly empty bar.

"Yep. Keith and I are looking forward to it."

"Good. Can I have a beer?" She slid onto a stool and rested her elbows on the bar.

"Sure." Poppi uncapped a bottle and handed it to her. "But just the one, we're getting ready to close. What are you doing here so late, anyway?" Poppi propped her hands on her hips, and her breasts wiggled inside the open collar of her pink plaid shirt.

"Couldn't sleep."

She'd left Addison's house thirty minutes before and, after a short drive, had ended up here. Given how she'd spent the past few hours, she should have been exhausted, but instead she was wide-awake, driving through downtown with the windows down. Despite the late hour, small crowds of people wandered the streets, probably leaving bars and heading to whatever distant public lot they'd parked in.

"I've been working on a new song for your showcase. But would you mind if I debut it at the fund-raiser?"

"No problem. You're still planning to do the showcase, right?"

"Yeah."

"Is it any good?"

"Well, I sure hope so."

"Any chance I can get a preview?" When Poppi pointed at the guitar sitting on a stand onstage, the white satin fringe hanging from the arm of her shirt swayed wildly.

"Nope. You'll have to wait. I'm still polishing it, but it'll be ready by Saturday."

"You seem excited about this one."

"I am."

"Good. But I'd hoped your good humor might have something to do with the lady I saw you with last time you were here."

Brooke's body still hummed from Addison's touch, but she forced a casual expression. "I don't know how you even remember her. You were running around here like crazy."

"Honey, I may be straight, but I'm not blind. That woman would be hard to forget." She grabbed a cloth and wiped down the surface of the bar.

Brooke laughed. "Yeah, she is pretty unforgettable."

Poppi's eyes narrowed and her smile widened. "So, I'm right. Something going on between the two of you?"

"Come on, Poppi." Brooke had never been one for girl talk. She'd never had friends that she confided in about her latest crush. Even Diane would have to pull information about her dates out of her.

Poppi snapped her fingers. "I knew it."

"What? You didn't know anything."

"I did."

"Whatever." Brooke picked up her beer, then set it back down. "How did you figure it out?"

"It's not totally obvious. But when I saw you together I noticed a definite spark. So what's the problem?"

"Who says there's a problem?"

Poppi gave her a knowing look, but didn't say anything.

"It's complicated."

"I can handle complicated." She tossed aside the cloth in her hand and folded her arms over her chest.

"Okay." Brooke took a deep breath. Maybe she needed someone to talk to about Addison. "Addison and I met at Diane's funeral. She was in Diane's cancer support group. She had breast cancer. I can't let myself really think about a future with her."

"Because of the cancer?"

"Yes, mostly. But there's more. She's got this adorable kid, who she had with her gay best friend a couple years after her treatment. He's still in the picture, and they're basically raising her together."

"That is complicated." Poppi touched one finger to her lips. "So let's simplify it. Tell me what you like about her."

"Well, other than the obvious physical attraction, she's smart and confident. She's brave, yet not afraid to be vulnerable. When I'm with her, I feel like everything will be okay. And she gets me. She seems to understand when I need space and when I need to be pushed."

"What are you afraid of?"

"Losing her."

Poppi shook her head. "Not just that. You're afraid of loving her and losing her. But it sounds like you're already falling for her. So isn't this really a matter of losing her now or the chance that it may happen somewhere down the road?"

"It's not that simple."

"It can be. If you love someone, it's for better or worse. Keith makes me want to hurl him off a cliff at times, but I love him and I'll stand by him no matter what happens. No one has any real guarantees, Brooke."

Brooke pushed her empty bottle back across the bar and threw a ten-dollar bill down next to it. Spilling your guts to a friend was apparently overrated. *No one has any real guarantees.* She could have gotten that from a Lifetime movie.

"I'll see you Saturday," she said as she headed for the door.

CHAPTER EIGHTEEN

Saturday morning dawned crisp and clear, streaks of orange and pink coloring the horizon. Sycamore Park bustled with volunteers getting ready for the Community of Hope fund-raiser. Stacey had corralled Addison as soon as she arrived and tasked her with helping set up for registration.

Addison had checked the forecast from her phone this morning, and the predicted clear skies and seventy-five-degree weather would be perfect. Despite the slight chill in the air, in a couple hours, the morning sunshine would warm the walk participants.

Volunteers had stuffed the goody bags for the walkers the night before. Addison arranged the plastic bags, filled with advertisements, energy bars, and an assortment of donated promotional items, on the long table in front of her.

She glanced at the parking lot across the park for the sixth time in the past thirty minutes. Brooke should be here soon. She'd just seen her yesterday when they had come to the park to supervise the construction of the stage and backstage tents. But she still couldn't wait to see her again. She forced her attention back on the paperwork she sorted.

Five minutes later when she looked up again, she saw Brooke's car pulling into the lot. She gave up all pretense of work and sat back to watch Brooke lift a backpack out of her trunk, then close the lid. Dressed in jeans and hooded sweatshirt, with the bag slung over her shoulder, she looked like a college coed crossing the dew-dampened grass on her way to a class. A light breeze ruffled her hair and she pushed it back.

"Good morning," Addison said when Brooke reached her. She handed Brooke a cup of coffee.

"Are you sure it's morning?" Brooke grumbled. "My day's looking up, though, now that I'm here with you." She smiled and glanced around them at the others working nearby. She didn't make a move toward Addison, but her eyes clearly relayed her desire to touch her.

"I'm glad you are. We'll have a beautiful day for the event."

"If you're going to be chipper, you can go work with Stacey."

"Aren't you excited? Today we see the payoff for all our planning."

"I probably will be once I wake up." Brooke smiled.

"You will. When you see all of the families here, walking for themselves or their loved ones, you won't be able to help yourself. Some of them are still going through chemo, but they come out and walk as far as they can. It's inspiring."

"Okay, okay. I'm pumped." Brooke clapped her hands together with mock enthusiasm. "So what are we doing first?"

"The walkers will start arriving soon. After we finish setting up here, we can move on to our own checklist. Grab that box and start unpacking it and laying things out on that table."

"Will do." Brooke opened the box and pulled out a bag of silicone bracelets with A Community for Hope 2010 stamped into them, key chains with the same message, and name badges that read, "I walk for_____".

"Put these markers next to those so they can fill in the name of whoever inspires them."

"So they have to go through all this just to do the walk?"

Addison laughed at Brooke's perplexed expression. "It's not that bad. Walkers will come here to check in. Some will have printed all the paperwork off online, and others need to fill it out today." Addison affixed forms to a stack of clipboards and laid a handful of pens next to them. "Once they're checked in and given a number, they go past that table and pick up some of the freebies."

"There's our emcee." Brooke nodded toward the parking lot.

Poppi strode across the grass in heels far too high for the uneven ground. She had certainly dressed the part, from the pink-and-white bow in her teased hair to the pink skirt billowing around her knees.

"Hey, Poppi, thanks for coming," Brooke called when she got close enough to hear.

"Hi there, kiddo. Keith is getting his equipment from the van. Where do you want him to set up?"

"Over there." Addison pointed at the stage across the lawn. "We're almost done here. If you'll tell him to bring everything over, I'll be there in a minute to show him the diagram of our stage layout."

"No problem." She turned and headed back to the parking lot.

Brooke shook her head. "I don't know how she can walk in those things."

"Practice. When you wear them all the time, you get pretty good at it. But I'll tell you, nothing feels better than taking them off at the end of the day."

"They make your legs look sexy, especially in those little skirts you wear. But I really like it when you take your heels off and walk around in your stockings."

"My skirts are a perfectly appropriate length."

"I agree, they're perfect." Brooke dropped her eyes to Addison's legs, and Addison felt the caress as surely as if Brooke had actually stroked her.

"Okay. You should go."

"Where?"

"Anywhere else. It'll be a long day if you keep looking at me like that."

"Maybe we can sneak away behind the stage and—"

"No way. Get that idea out of your head. There are too many people around here for that." Addison shook her finger at Brooke, but her mind was filled with images of the two of them hiding in a tent backstage.

The fantasy dissolved when she glanced at the stage and saw a very tall man with gray hair and a long goatee carrying a large black case. Poppi wrapped her arms around him from behind, almost making him drop the case. "Why don't you go help Keith with his gear? I'll finish this."

❖

"Are we ready to start?" Brooke asked, holding out a microphone.

"Absolutely." Poppi grabbed the mic and sashayed out onstage. Normally Brooke wouldn't use such a term, but she couldn't think of another way to describe the swing of her hips and the prissy motion of her upper arms bent sharply at the elbow.

"Hello, everyone, and welcome to the eleventh annual fund-raiser for A Community for Hope."

Poppi waved her hand and a collection of thin gold bracelets shimmied down her wrist. "It's wonderful to see so many people coming out to help us raise awareness and money for research. My name is Poppi and I own Poppi's Cabaret down on Broadway. I'll be here all day guiding you through the fun activities we have planned. Let's give a big round of applause to the folks who volunteered so much of their time to put this event together."

The massive crowd hooted and clapped. Brooke couldn't even guess how many people pushed up in front of the stage, but she'd heard another volunteer say they had definitely exceeded the previous year's attendance.

"You've probably all been touched by cancer in one way or another. I have as well. I've had family and good friends who were lost or lost someone." She looked over, met Brooke's eyes, and nodded almost imperceptibly. "So let's make this a great day to honor them and get one step closer to a cure."

Poppi turned the microphone over to the head of the walk committee, who instructed everyone where to line up. The crowd dispersed. The walkers headed for the start line, and supportive friends and family spread blankets and lawn chairs on the grass near the stage.

After checking that everything was in order for their next scheduled segment, Brooke left the stage area and wandered toward the course laid out for the walkers. She stopped and leaned against a tree not far from the start. The path would lead them through the park, not far from the stroll she'd taken one day with Addison.

People of all ages clustered around the start line, waiting for a signal to begin. Some of them carried signs and wore T-shirts with the names and photos of loved ones, some of which had the dates they'd passed away, others with the word "Survivor" emblazoned across the front of their shirt. Brooke remembered seeing the shirt for sale in the souvenir tent.

But whether for themselves or for others, every one of them had given up their Saturday to be here, to support this cause. Brooke was suddenly ashamed that she'd only agreed to do the same after Diane had browbeaten her into it. And that she'd contemplated backing out after Diane died.

The starter gave the signal and the throng surged forward onto the marked path.

"I love the kickoff," Addison said as she came up beside Brooke.

Brooke bumped her shoulder against Addison's. "You were right. This is pretty amazing."

"It reminds me how lucky I am."

"You know, you're pretty amazing, too." Brooke touched the small of Addison's back. As she let her hand fall away, Addison grasped it and squeezed quickly before releasing it again.

"Why?"

"After everything you've been through, the fact that you can still be so positive astonishes me. I'd be so angry. Hell, I have been angry."

"It's not that hard to be positive. Sure, I could detail the pain and the fear, and the months of not knowing. But if I do that, I also have to talk about the incredible doctors and nurses who took care of me. My own family was so supportive. Charles was my rock. If I talk about the scars and the insecurities I still carry, I also have to remember that I'm cancer-free. I have a beautiful daughter who I fall more in love with every day. Life is good for me, Brooke." She waved at the crowd around them. "It's a lot more than some of these people will get a chance at."

Brooke nodded slightly. She felt bad for the plight of the participants, but she doubted she would ever truly be able to be as optimistic as Addison.

❖

"Addison," Stacey called as she hurried across the lawn. She flipped through a clipboard stuffed with papers until she apparently found what she was looking for. "Your first act is scheduled to go on in ten minutes. Are they ready?"

"I'm sure they are. Brooke is back there coordinating everything right now."

"Gee, maybe you should go check on her." Stacey's expression indicated that she thought Addison should know better than to leave Brooke alone with a task.

"She's probably got everything covered." Stacey looked as if she wanted to argue, so Addison added, "But I'll go double-check."

Stacey nodded with satisfaction. Addison plastered on a fake smile before heading for the stage. Stacey needed every event to be perfect, and micro-managing them was her way of ensuring that it was. Though Addison was confident Brooke had things moving backstage, she didn't mind the excuse to seek her out.

A large enclosed tent had been set up behind the stage and covered nearly every inch of free space back to the tree line. Addison pushed the flap open and entered. Inside, they'd used screens to form temporary dressing rooms for the various performers. The open area in the center contained tables and chairs, and one long table held an array of deli trays, fruits, beverages, and other snack items.

The members of Grove Tree Road lounged at one table, holding drinks and picking up snacks off one mutual plate in the center of the table. Addison waved as she approached.

"You guys have plenty of time before you perform. You're welcome to go out there and join the festivities." Grove Tree Road was set to close the show.

"We've been in and out," Tyler Cason said.

"Great. Have you seen Brooke?"

He hooked a thumb over his shoulder toward the dressing-room area.

As Addison made her way around the corner to the temporary enclosures, she ran directly into Brooke, who was stepping out of one of them. Brooke grabbed her by the shoulders.

"Hi," Addison said. Her breathlessness as she looked into Brooke's eyes had nothing to do with their near-collision and everything to do with the feel of Brooke's hands grasping her upper arms firmly.

"This reminds me a little of our first meeting." Brooke pulled her lower lip between her teeth.

"A little. But I don't recall seeing quite so much lust in your eyes that day."

"Well, it was a solemn occasion," Brooke reminded her, and Addison immediately felt like an ass. "Or, maybe I was just better at hiding it then," Brooke added, making her feel better.

"Are we ready with our first act?"

"Back to business, huh?" Brooke teased, trailing a finger around the collar of Addison's T-shirt and up the side of her neck. Addison raised an eyebrow and Brooke sighed. "Yeah, she's ready to go."

"Good. Let Poppi know she's on in five." Addison kissed Brooke quickly on the mouth, sliding away when Brooke tried to deepen the kiss. "Later, stagehand."

"Stagehand?" Brooke grinned and moved closer. "I like it."

"Yeah? Do you want to play the stagehand and the rock star tonight?" Addison wished she could ditch the rest of the event and take Brooke home right then.

"Why wait until tonight? We're here." She looked around. "We have all the props."

"Do props do it for you?"

"Sometimes." Brooke smiled and slipped her hand under the hem of Addison's shirt. "They can set the mood."

"I'll remember that." Addison wondered if Brooke was getting as wonderfully uncomfortable in her jeans as she was. Addison swayed toward Brooke and was about to kiss her when she heard voices behind them. She grabbed Brooke's wrist and pulled her hand away. "We have to stop."

"Stop what?"

"You know what." She nodded toward the dressing rooms. "Get your girl on the stage." She winked at Brooke, then forced herself to walk away.

❖

"So, did everyone enjoy the walk?" Poppi paused for effect and the crowd cheered as expected. "Well, we've got lots of great performers lined up, including an opportunity for *you* to entertain *us* during our karaoke contest this afternoon. See Keith over there to pick your song and sign up.

"This first young lady came to Nashville two years ago from Oklahoma just hoping to land a record deal. One year later, she did. She's been working hard on that album for the past year. Next week you'll be hearing her first single on the radio, but today she's going to give us a sneak peak. Put your hands together for Francie Collins."

The young brunette bounded onto the stage carrying a guitar that looked way too big for her petite frame. A black leather vest hugged her torso, and her knees poked out through the frayed edges of holes midway down the leg of her blue jeans.

"Hey, y'all," she drawled into the microphone.

"That's Francie Collins?" Addison asked in disbelief. The compact firecracker didn't fit the image Addison had conjured, given her old-fashioned-sounding name.

Brooke elbowed her lightly in the ribs.

"Ow, what?"

Brooke glared at her. Addison liked the hint of jealousy in Brooke's eyes.

"I just thought she'd be a little more—um—*Hee Haw*, that's all." Addison fixed an innocent expression on her face, then purposely turned to stare at the woman on the stage. "I think I've been missing out by not listening to country music."

The hint of jealousy grew and turned Brooke's smile into a smirk. "She's a little young for you, isn't she?"

"Oh, that was low." Addison smiled in spite of her words.

Brooke held up her hands in front of her. "Hey, I'm just saying, I think she's actually closer to Ramsey's age. But don't worry, she's over eighteen, so if that's what you're into—"

Brooke failed to smother her laughter when Addison buried her fingers in her ribs and tickled her.

"Okay, okay, I'm sorry."

Addison stopped, but stayed poised to start again. "You know I don't want some young hottie. I only want you."

"Yeah, thanks. I don't need reminding that I'm not young or hot anymore." Brooke's jaw tightened and flexed, but Addison wasn't sure it was because of an imagined slight about her age.

"You okay?"

"Absolutely. But I should go check on the next act."

"Brooke—"

"She'll be done soon."

"She just started," Addison said, but Brooke had already turned away.

CHAPTER NINETEEN

How are the sign-ups going?" Brooke asked, looking over Keith's shoulder at his computer. He sat on a stool in front of two small tables pushed together in an L-shape that held two laptops and a soundboard. A tabletop microphone stand sat in front of him, and two floor stands, lowered to their shortest height, stood behind him.

"Almost all the slots are full." He brought the spreadsheet of the schedule up on his screen and showed her.

"Good. I hope the competition is fierce. We had some good prizes donated."

"Like what?"

"Two nights in a cabin in Gatlinburg and a fancy dinner, tickets to a hockey game, awesome seats three rows off the ice, and a gift certificate from Home Depot."

"I heard you're going to play. Poppi says you have something new."

"Yeah, I'm up right after lunch."

"It's good that you're getting back to it," he said with a nod.

"Poppi really does tell you everything, doesn't she?"

"Pretty much." He spun on his stool and began typing on the other laptop. "And I can usually tell when she's not telling me something."

"You guys have been together for a long time, huh?"

"Yep."

"What's the secret?" Being among all of the families today had started Brooke thinking about how lonely her life had been. Even before Diane died, Brooke had essentially kept herself closed off from everyone else.

"There's no secret. Love each other. Support each other. Have a good healthy fight every now and then. That's key. Poppi and I are solid because we're honest enough with each other to fight when we need to. And we've needed that bond to get through the tough times together."

"It's that easy?" Brooke joked. She'd spent some time with Keith and Poppi, and "solid" definitely described them. At first glance, it seemed that Poppi's passionate, lively nature could overpower Keith's subdued personality, but, actually, they complemented each other. Keith supported Poppi and allowed her to be herself, and she clearly cherished him for his quiet strength.

"Nothing that's worth it is ever easy." He rubbed his goatee. "Sounds corny, I know. But it's true. Poppi wanted nothing to do with me when we first met. I had to chase her for a while before she let me catch her. Who are you trying to woo, anyway?"

"No one." Brooke instinctively sought out Addison and found her across the grass talking to a group of people all wearing purple T-shirts with someone's picture silk-screened on the front. Addison smiled and touched one woman's arm. Whatever she said to her made the woman suddenly hug her. Brooke marveled at Addison's endless compassion, and she didn't think it was entirely due to her history with cancer. Addison was a generous, social person by nature.

"You don't ask that kind of question unless you have someone in mind."

Brooke snapped her eyes back to Keith, hoping he hadn't seen her watching Addison. "Just taking stock, man. I'm not getting any younger, you know."

"Yeah, well, whoever she is, she'd be lucky to have you."

"Thanks. I'll let you get back to it. See you around." Brooke wandered off, still pondering his final words.

She appreciated the compliment, but she wasn't so sure. Addison was probably the bravest woman Brooke had ever met. Brooke, on the other hand, was afraid to take a chance—on anything. She was sleeping with Addison and spending time with her and Ramsey. She could avoid making a commitment, but she was kidding herself if she thought she could deny any feelings. Addison attracted her, on a physical level, but also on an emotional one. And she had a way of chipping apart all of Brooke's barriers.

The only way Brooke could avoid getting further caught up in whatever she and Addison had started was to avoid her altogether. Just the thought of not seeing Addison made her chest ache. But after today, they wouldn't be working on the fund-raiser together, so they wouldn't need to see each other. Then it was up to Brooke to be strong enough to stay away.

As she contemplated the idea, she glanced up and saw Addison heading right toward her. When their eyes met, Addison's smile lit Brooke up from the inside. Addison held nothing back and the emotions on her face scared Brooke. In an expression as simple as a smile, she conveyed desire, joy, and love. Addison loved her. *Addison loved her.* And because of that, Brooke would most likely end up breaking both of their hearts.

"Hey, there," Addison said as she reached Brooke. She brushed her hand down Brooke's arm.

"Hey." Brooke forced a smile and avoided eye contact. She didn't want Addison to read what had just been going through her head.

"Are you all right?"

"Sure, why?"

"Earlier, you seemed—" Addison shook her head. "Never mind. Everything okay with Keith?"

"Oh, yeah, I was just socializing."

"You? Am I rubbing off on you?"

"Apparently."

"Poppi's doing a great job. I've barely had to worry about how things are progressing onstage."

This time Brooke's smile was genuine. "Meaning, you've been watching her every move from afar instead of over her shoulder."

Addison laughed. "Yeah, maybe. Am I that controlling?"

"I wouldn't say controlling. You're very attentive to details."

"That's just a nicer way of saying the same thing."

Brooke was saved from answering when Ramsey ran up to them with Charles trailing her.

Charles put his arm around Addison and kissed her cheek.

"Brooke, I walked for a cure," Ramsey said. Her number placard covered almost the entire front of her over-sized light-pink shirt. Only a few inches of her white athletic shorts hung out the bottom of the shirt and brushed her knees.

"I see that." Brooke bent to study the number on her chest. "Two hundred twenty-two, that's a good number."

"I picked it out. Daddy got the one I didn't want."

Brooke glanced at Charles, pretending to study his chest, then back at Ramsey. "I like your number better, too," she whispered.

Ramsey giggled.

One of the badges Brooke remembered seeing on the table that morning had been half-stuck to Ramsey's sleeve. Brooke straightened the fabric and pressed the sticker on more firmly. Judging from the handwriting, Ramsey had obviously filled her badge in herself. The words "I walk for Mommy" hit Brooke harder than she expected.

She straightened, and when she glanced at Addison she thought she saw tears welling up. She held Addison's gaze, wishing she could touch her physically and hoping she could convey enough reassurance in her own eyes. The stark pain in Addison's face was more than Brooke had ever seen in her before and let her know that despite the brave front and positive attitude, Addison still bore the scars of her past.

"I have to go—check on something," Addison said, breaking eye contact.

"I want to go with you, Mommy."

"Okay, sweetie, come on." Addison held out her hand and Ramsey grabbed it.

Brooke watched them walk away, moved by what she'd just seen in Addison. The badge on Ramsey's arm had brought home to Brooke that if it weren't for Addison's treatment, not only would

Addison not be with them today, but neither would Ramsey. Brooke hadn't just fallen for Addison, she'd also come to care for Ramsey. She was a smart, funny, engaging child, and who knew what she might accomplish. Addison's successful fight against cancer might have given the world a peacekeeper, or a doctor, or a scientist. She glanced around at the children running around among adults sitting in chairs or on blankets. One of these kids could be the one who found a cure for cancer, and it was only because of efforts like this one that funds were available for research that allowed some of them to be here today.

She turned toward Charles and found him studying her intently.

"You guys make a cute couple," he said, apparently having completely mistaken the emotion of their exchange for something else.

"We're not—" Brooke stopped, not certain exactly what they were, but realizing she should probably choose her words carefully when talking to Addison's closest friend.

"Oh. My mistake, I thought—well, you must know that Addison tells me everything."

"I probably should have. I'm sorry. I just don't know exactly what I'm doing. It's been a while since I dated anyone, if that's what you want to call it."

"Well, I guess it doesn't really matter what I call it." He narrowed his eyes warily. Brooke tried not to fidget under his gaze. "I apologize if I'm being nosy, but Addison has been through a lot and I tend to want to protect her."

Brooke nodded. She'd thought she knew exactly what Addison had been through, but she hadn't—not really—until just now. "That's understandable."

"So, this is where I ask what your intentions are."

"With all due respect, that's between Addison and me." Brooke forced a more confident tone than she felt. She didn't want to talk to Charles about this at all, but certainly not here. "I will say, regarding my intentions, that I've been completely honest with Addison."

"I guess that's all I can ask."

Brooke shoved her hands in her pockets. Had she been honest? She'd thought so, but here she was with Addison, acting like nothing was wrong, when only a few minutes ago she'd tried to convince herself that she should stay as far away from Addison as possible.

Addison returned looking much more composed than she had when she'd left.

"We scoped out the line at the food tent and it seems to have gone down. Is everyone ready for lunch?" Addison asked.

"I think I'll skip it," Brooke said.

"Really? Are you okay? You're not nervous about playing afterward, are you?"

"No. But I should probably check on things backstage."

Addison waved a hand dismissively. "It's under control. After this act, there's a break before we start the open mic for the songwriters. There's nothing to check on. Come eat with us."

"That's okay, I'll catch up with you later."

"Come on," Ramsey said, taking Brooke's hand. "You can sit by me."

"Ladies first," Charles said, extending an arm to indicate they should go ahead.

Brooke gave in and let Ramsey lead her. When they reached the cluster of tables underneath the large tent, only a few people were ahead of them. They shuffled down the line, filling their plates with barbeque, beans, and potato salad. Addison fixed Ramsey's plate, while Ramsey carried plastic cutlery for all of them.

"Where should we sit?" Addison asked when she reached the end of the line.

Charles and Brooke spoke at the same time.

"There's a picnic table over there."

"Ramsey and I have a blanket over here."

Addison followed Charles as he led them toward the area in front of the stage.

"Mommy, I want pie."

"Ramsey, Mommy has her hands full." In addition to her and Ramsey's plates, Addison had two bottles of water tucked under her arm.

"I got it," Brooke said. "Lemon meringue or apple?"

"Apple."

She picked up a slice and tilted it onto a plate with a piece of lemon meringue for herself, then managed to juggle her plate, the dessert, and her own drink.

When they reached the area Charles had staked out for them, Ramsey plopped down and patted the blanket next to her.

"Sit here."

"Okay. Will you hold this for me?" Brooke handed Ramsey her unopened can of soda, which Ramsey set in the grass just outside the edge of the blanket.

"It goes right there, in case you spill," Ramsey said, obviously quoting a rule she'd been given. "Just watch you don't get ants in it."

"Ants?"

"Ants like soda," Ramsey declared. "I spilled mine on the table outside our house one day and a million ants came to drink it."

Brooke lowered herself carefully to her designated spot. She set the dessert plate on the other side of her, out of Ramsey's sightline so she wouldn't be tempted away from her lunch just yet. "A million, huh? Well, help me keep an eye out then. I don't want to share my drink with a million ants."

"They would probably drink it all and there wouldn't be any left for you."

"Exactly." Brooke parted the grass outside the blanket and bent even closer, pretending to peer down between the blades. "I don't see any ants, but we'd better watch for them anyway."

Ramsey nodded and began passing plastic forks around.

"Here's your lunch, sweetie." Addison set a plate on the blanket in front of Ramsey. "Use your napkin, please."

Ramsey spread a napkin over her knees and picked up a piece of the sandwich Addison had cut into fourths for her. Every few minutes she glanced toward Brooke's drink, keeping a vigilant watch for ant intruders.

Brooke picked up her own sandwich and took a bite. The pulled pork was tender and the barbeque sauce had a nice tangy flavor.

"This is really good."

"That barbeque place not far from our house donated it. It's my favorite," Addison said.

Soon they were all quietly clearing their plates. Brooke watched the last act of the morning, a young band with an edgy alternative feel. The lead singer was a natural entertainer, engaging the audience with his infectious energy. Soon, like many people around her, Brooke was bobbing her head along with the music.

Brooke and Addison had contacted them based on a rave review by one of Addison's co-workers. They were the only band that Brooke hadn't personally seen perform before. But she actually liked what she'd heard so far and made a mental note to check the souvenir table and see if they'd put out any of their CDs. In addition to their auction items, several of the acts had donated promo items, like music and T-shirts, to be sold for the benefit.

"They were a good call, huh?" Addison asked.

"Yeah, your friend was right. They're pretty cool."

"Can I have dessert now?" Ramsey asked as she pushed away her half-empty plate.

Brooke looked at Addison first, and she gave a small nod. Brooke moved the dessert plate between them and held up her own fork. "Let's dig in."

Ramsey sunk her fork into the wedge of apple pie and ate a mouthful. Brooke did the same with the lemon meringue.

"Mommy, try a bite."

"No, thanks."

"Yeah, Mommy," Brooke prodded. "Try a bite." She loaded up her fork and angled it toward Addison.

"That's okay."

"Come on, it's so good." Brooke purposely let a bit of flirtation leak into her voice.

"Maybe just one bite." Addison leaned forward and enveloped the fork in her mouth. She eased back, letting it withdraw slowly. She swallowed, then said, "Mmm, you're right, that's very good."

"Tease," Brooke whispered before sitting back next to Ramsey.

"Want to try mine?" Ramsey asked Brooke.

"Don't mind if I do." Brooke took a forkful. Ramsey looked expectantly at Brooke's pie, obviously waiting for her to extend the same offer. "Oh, did you want some lemon meringue?" Brooke asked innocently.

Ramsey nodded.

"Well, help yourself then."

Ramsey glanced at Addison for only a second, and when no disapproval was forthcoming, she sunk her fork into Brooke's dessert. She made a face as she chewed the tart filling.

"Good, huh?" Brooke asked.

Ramsey nodded.

"Want some more?"

"No, thank you. I'll just stick to my apple," she said politely.

"Okay, then." Brooke smiled. When she met Addison's eyes, she felt that thing again that tore her in two. Addison's emotions were there for the taking, displayed in her eyes like an enticing display in a storefront window.

Part of Brooke wanted to get away from the raw intensity of her emotions when she was with Addison. But the part of her that needed to feel alive in a way that only Addison could make her feel seemed so much stronger. She craved the inclusion she felt from Addison and Ramsey. She had no illusions about fitting in the dynamic of Addison, Charles, and Ramsey's family unit, but she wanted to pretend she had a place even if it was only for today.

CHAPTER TWENTY

A re you decent?" Addison pushed aside the flap that led to the makeshift dressing room without waiting for a reply. She half hoped Brooke wasn't, since she'd been thinking about getting her naked all day.

But when she stepped inside, Brooke sat, fully clothed, in a director's chair while a thin man applied makeup to her face. Several of the local hair stylists and makeup artists had volunteered for the event. The man's spiky, multicolored hair made Addison glad he wasn't touching Brooke's head. Brooke had refused a stylist, saying she could shove some mousse through her hair herself.

"Remember, nothing over the top," Brooke warned him, casting a quick glance at Addison that implored her to supervise.

"Honey, don't worry. You'll still be beautifully butch when I get done with you." He swept a long-bristled brush over her cheekbones.

"That's all I ask." Brooke sat back in the chair and let him work.

"Are you ready?" Addison beamed, practically vibrating with excitement. Brooke had refused to play the new song for her, so she thought it must be something special.

Brooke smiled. "You seem more excited about this than I am."

"It's a new song. Aren't you pumped to debut it?"

"I guess so."

"I think you are, but you don't want to show it in case the song isn't well received."

Brooke raised a brow, then relaxed it when the makeup guy clucked in disapproval and held another applicator poised in front of him.

"You don't know everything," Brooke said.

Addison almost laughed at her petulant tone, but she knew from dealing with Ramsey that laughing was the worst thing she could do.

"I know that you're an amazing woman." Addison moved behind Brooke, dropped her hands on her shoulders, and spoke close to her ear. "And you're going to do great out there."

The makeup guy brushed his hands together. "Okay, all done." He glanced at Addison, then back at Brooke. "Try not to smudge that lipstick," he said with a wink before he pushed through the tent flap.

Addison and Brooke both laughed after he was gone. Addison circled Brooke, slid onto her lap, and draped her arms around Brooke's neck.

"Oh, you are so going to smudge your lipstick," she said, her mouth only inches from Brooke's. Brooke leaned forward and Addison angled away, teasing her with the almost-kiss before giving in. Brooke took control immediately, cupping the back of Addison's head, and slipped her tongue against Addison's. Brooke's body was warm and solid against hers, and her mouth demanded more. Addison's heart raced, and she pressed into Brooke, trying to get closer. Brooke kissed her like nothing else mattered except this moment, this embrace, and Addison would crawl inside her if it meant holding onto that feeling.

Brooke tore her mouth free. "Ah—Addison, you have to stop."

"Stop what?"

Brooke clapped her hands onto Addison's hips and stilled them. Addison hadn't realized she'd been rotating her hips against Brooke's lap, but she now registered her need for a little friction to relieve the ache building between her thighs. If Brooke would just touch her for a minute or two, that might be enough. She grasped one of Brooke's wrists, fighting the urge to guide her hand where she needed it.

"Okay, just a second." Addison squeezed Brooke's wrist and inhaled deeply, then let her breath out slowly and eased off Brooke's lap. She rubbed her thumb over Brooke's mouth, removing the smudge of color below her lower lip. "Do you want me to fix your lipstick? He picked a great shade for you." She glanced at the table behind her and saw several different tubes of lipstick.

"No, I don't like that stuff anyway. I just let him do it because I didn't want to be rude."

"Well, that was nice of you."

Brooke stood and pulled a pinstriped vest off a hanger on the rack behind her.

"Let me." Addison took the vest and held it out while Brooke slipped her arms into it. Addison turned her around and pulled the front of the vest closed over her white T-shirt. "Very nice," Addison said, taking in the wide leather belt threaded through her blue jeans.

"Stop doing that. I have to go out there and perform the first song I've written in months, and you're looking at me like you want to throw me down right here."

"When I get my hands on you, I can't help skipping ahead to what we'll be doing later."

"You sound pretty confident."

"Confident that I can get you into bed? A little." Addison reached for Brooke, but Brooke captured her hands and folded them between them.

"Thank you for trying to distract me. But I need a minute before I go out there."

"Okay. Are you okay with me being in the audience?"

"Absolutely. I wouldn't want you anywhere else."

"I'll see you afterward?"

Brooke nodded.

Addison kissed her one more time, then forced herself through the flap in the tent. Nervousness fluttered in her stomach, but she told herself Brooke would be great. She knew Brooke had been trying to appear as if her expectations were low, but Addison sensed that this song meant more to Brooke than she let on.

❖

Brooke stood at the side of the stage and waited while Poppi introduced her. Poppi talked about how far their friendship went back, but Brooke only half listened. She'd put on a brave front for Addison, and, in truth, having Addison in the dressing room with her *had* helped distract her.

She'd tried rehearsing what she might say to introduce the song, but she couldn't get her thoughts together without feeling like she was rambling. So she decided to swallow her nerves and speak from her heart.

"…bring to the stage, Nashville songwriter Brooke Donahue." Applause followed Poppi's words.

Brooke's feet wouldn't move. Fear pounded in her chest. Last night, she'd talked to herself for a couple of hours while doing some final rehearsals. But all rational thought fled when she considered what she was about to do. This was more than just a song. She was about to go out on that stage and lay herself bare.

Poppi was looking at her as if trying to convey a message. *Get the hell out here*, she said with her eyes.

"She's a little shy, folks. Let's get a little louder and see if we can't convince her to get her butt out here to play a song for y'all." The crowd clapped and yelled in response.

"One foot in front of the other," Brooke muttered. That was how she'd gotten through the past four months, and maybe it would get her through today as well.

She walked across the stage to where Poppi stood, and Poppi hugged her before exiting on the other side. Brooke scanned the audience until she found Addison's face. She met her eyes and held them for just a second, relaxing marginally.

She adjusted the microphone, then gripped it tight as she spoke. "I want to thank you all again for coming out here. I had the good fortune to be involved in planning this event and, let me tell you, it was an eye-opening experience. I've never done anything like this before. But through it all, I've met some inspiring people. The strength, bravery, generosity, and positive thinking I've seen in the past several weeks has amazed me."

Addison's smile encouraged her to continue. Brooke was surprised by how much Addison's approval had come to mean to her in such a short time.

"Like so many people, I've seen the commercials about the importance of cancer screening and the news stories about this breakthrough or that, but didn't give them much thought. Earlier this year, though, cancer affected me in a very big way. I lost someone very dear to me. She was a great friend, and, as I watched her take on the fight of her life, she endured far more than I could have. So I want to dedicate my part in this event, and this song, to Diane."

Brooke reached behind her, grabbed her guitar, and swung it around her body. She adjusted the strap against her shoulder and wrapped her hand around the neck.

Addison wondered if Brooke was stalling when she stretched her fingers before laying them on the frets. Her hands trembled and Addison longed to go up there and hold them.

She held her breath as Brooke began to pick out a slow, achingly sad melody on her guitar. Brooke had discussed asking some local musicians to play with her but in the end had opted for an acoustic feel, and Addison knew now that was the best choice.

When Brooke began to sing, the raspy quality Addison loved in her voice carried over the crowd. Brooke's song told the story of loving someone unconditionally and receiving that love in return. When she sang about admiring the strength and courage with which that person faced adversity, she left no doubt she sang for Diane. In the end, though she knew Diane wanted to hang on, to be there for her, she had to let her go, had to set her free from her pain.

Addison listened with her heart, absorbing Brooke's grief as if she could spare Brooke from carrying it. She couldn't take her eyes off Brooke's face as it changed throughout the song. She watched her tight brows smooth out and her eyes go from stormy and dark to simply sad, shining with unshed tears.

Emotion roughened Brooke's voice, but she carried on, her fingers coaxing agonizing tones from her instrument. Her hands quickened, flying over the strings, and her voice followed, becoming more desperate as the pace of the song increased. Her melody built as if she were carelessly flinging herself toward a cliff despite knowing the pain she would find should she tumble all the way to the bottom. And with a final gasping declaration, she took that leap, flying into space with nothing to hold on to—suspended before she plummeted.

By the time Brooke finished with a haunting chord, several people around Addison dabbed their eyes. Brooke stood in the middle of the stage, alone, and as vulnerable as Addison had ever seen her. She had poured her grief out over the stage, and it puddled at her feet.

The audience exploded with applause and cheers. A small smile touched Brooke's lips and she looked up toward the sky briefly. She waved and walked off the right side of the stage.

Addison immediately began to weave her way through the crowd. She needed to see Brooke—to try to soothe her. She arrived in the backstage area as Brooke stepped down and set her guitar on a stand.

Tyler Cason stood waiting for Brooke, and he caught her before Addison could reach her. "That was an amazing song. I was back in the tent, and when I heard you starting to play it, I just had to come out and listen."

"Thanks." Brooke scanned the backstage area purposefully, and Addison's heart leapt at the thought that Brooke might be looking for her.

"Hey, listen, I know you probably have people waiting in line for your stuff, but we're getting ready to record our first album and I'd love to pitch that song to my producer."

"Seriously?"

"Oh, yeah. A lot of people can relate to that kind of loss, and you bring the emotion across perfectly."

"Don't you need to talk to the rest of your group?"

"They loved it as much as I did. Trust me, if you agree, they're on board."

"I don't know."

Addison didn't know either. The song was very personal, and she wasn't sure how she would feel hearing someone else play it, even a band she liked as much as Grove Tree Road. She knew

Brooke had no interest in being a performer, but she was born to sing that song.

"Actually, I was thinking you could make a guest appearance on the album. The song needs your voice. We'd make it a duet. Think about it and give me a call next week. You still have my card?"

"Yes."

"And, hey, I want the song. But if you need to hang onto it, I understand. Either way I'd love to do some writing with you."

"Okay. I'll get back to you," Brooke said, shaking his hand.

When Brooke turned away and saw Addison, she visibly lost her composure. Her eyes welled and she bit her trembling lower lip. Addison closed the distance between them and gathered Brooke in her arms. Brooke relaxed against her, wrapped her arms around Addison's waist, and sighed against her neck.

"Come home with me tonight," Addison said, cradling the back of Brooke's head.

"Addison, I can't."

"You can and you will. I need to hold you tighter, preferably with less clothes."

"I don't think I'll be in the mood." Brooke began to pull away, but Addison drew her back in.

"I'm not talking about sex. I just need to hold you."

"Okay," Brooke said, and, though Addison knew she was wrong, she let herself believe that Brooke was talking about more than just tonight.

❖

"Okay, y'all, I'm going to take full credit for bringing this next act to you. They've played in my bar and I think you're going to love them as much as I do. Aside from being a great bunch of guys and gals, they're impressive musicians. Give it up for Grove Tree Road."

The band spilled onstage to an onslaught of applause. Apparently they'd brought along a ton of their fans. They kicked right into an upbeat country song that soon had the crowd clapping along.

Brooke leaned on her right hip and stretched her legs out into the grass beside her. Addison sat on the blanket next to her. In front of them, despite the noise, Ramsey slept curled up under Addison's jacket with her head resting on Brooke's balled-up sweatshirt.

"The kid can sleep through anything." Brooke shook her head.

"She's exhausted," Addison said as she tucked her jacket closer around Ramsey.

"I know the feeling." Brooke glanced around. "It's been a long day, but I've enjoyed it."

"Good. We had another great year. I'm sure we raised a bunch of money, but sometimes it seems it's just as important for people to get out here and see other families going through the same things and winning, or to commiserate with the ones losing the fight. Not all of these people will make it, but none of them have to be alone."

The band switched to a slow song, and Brooke's mind wandered back to her own performance. She'd written the perfect tribute to her friendship with Diane. But she also hoped she'd captured the feeling that the friends and family of those fighting cancer went through, wanting to hang on even when the only thing left to do was let go.

Brooke wanted Diane to fight so badly that perhaps Diane hadn't felt completely comfortable talking to her about what she really felt deep inside. She'd battled until the end, or at least Brooke thought she had. If she had times when she was too exhausted to fight, when she wanted only to lie down, she never told Brooke. Maybe that's where Brooke had failed Diane a little. But she'd been so afraid to talk about it, afraid to even whisper that Diane might not make it, as if she could accidentally influence Diane's fate.

But she was here. And that was one thing Diane had wanted. She'd made Brooke commit to this event and Brooke had followed through. Had Diane foreseen any of the lessons she'd learned because of her involvement in the fund-raiser? Brooke glanced at Addison. Had Diane foreseen that as well?

For the second time that day, Brooke looked to the sky and hoped Diane was somewhere watching her. *I miss you. But I think I'll be okay.*

CHAPTER TWENTY-ONE

The flame danced around its tender, charred wick, licking the inside of the votive glass that kept it contained. Two layers of glass away, a twin glow flirted back from its own prison. The two seemed so well choreographed that Addison pretended they communicated with each other, that if only they could somehow surpass the boundaries placed between them, they could become one blaze.

"What are you thinking about?" Brooke asked, tilting her head back to look at Addison.

"Us," Addison said, but she didn't expand.

"Oh." Brooke's response was just as cryptic.

Addison let her hand drape over the edge of the tub. The bubbles clinging to her wrist reflected tiny rainbows from the candles she'd lit around the room. Brooke reclined between her legs, her back pressed to Addison's chest. Addison bent her head and kissed the wet spikes of Brooke's hair.

"I overheard you and Tyler talking. Are you going to take him up on his offer?"

"To record the song? I don't know."

"It sounds like a good opportunity. He seems willing to work with you to make sure you're comfortable. I don't know anything about the music business, though. Can you trust him?"

Brooke nodded. "I think so."

"Yes, it's a very personal song. Only you can decide what to do with it. But what would Diane want you to do? Keep it locked up? Or share it and get a big break in your career at the same time?"

"That's a good point." Brooke looked over her shoulder and smiled. "I'm thinking about it, I promise."

"Okay." Addison wanted Brooke to take a chance on this song. But this was one case where she couldn't push Brooke. She could only support her and whatever decision she made. So, instead, she lay back and enjoyed the gradual relaxation of her exhausted muscles. "I really needed a hot soak."

"Me, too." Brooke traced her fingers over Addison's arm, raising goose bumps in their wake.

"I'm glad you came home with me. I know you'd have preferred to be alone but—"

"There's no place else I'd rather be."

Addison wrapped her arms around Brooke and pressed her lips to her cheek. She let her hands wander under the water, stroking Brooke's belly and up her chest. But when her fingertips caressed Brooke's left breast she frowned, then returned to it.

"Addison, I'm sorry, I meant it when I said I wasn't really in the mood tonight. Do you mind if we just get in bed and cuddle?"

"Have you always had this?" She pressed her fingers into the swell of Brooke's breast, on the outside of her nipple.

"What?" Brooke touched herself near Addison's hand.

"Hold on." Addison continued to probe until she isolated the lump, no bigger than a marble. "Here." She put her hand over Brooke's and guided her fingers.

"I hardly feel anything. That's nothing."

"Was it there before?"

"I don't know. I guess not."

"You guess not? Or you know." Addison's heart raced and fear chased up the back of her throat.

"Jesus, Addison, what's wrong with you?" Brooke sat up quickly, sloshing water over the edge of the tub and onto the floor.

"Have you ever felt that lump before? Because I haven't noticed it, and I've been touching your breasts quite a bit lately."

"No. I haven't."

"You should make an appointment to see your doctor. It could be benign. Lots of women have lumps that turn out to be nothing.

It isn't necessarily a cause for concern, but you should go have it checked anyway just to be sure."

"Addison."

"They'll probably do a mammogram, and maybe an ultrasound, then the doctor will tell you how he wants to proceed. Even if they decide to remove the lump, I hear that's a fairly easy surgery."

"Addison," Brooke said more firmly. "If I promise to make an appointment will you stop talking about tests and surgery?"

Addison took a deep breath, then let it out slowly. Somewhere in the middle of her rambling, Brooke's lump and Addison's own treatment had blurred together.

They got out of the bathtub and dried off, neither of them speaking. For Addison, uncertainty had replaced the excitement of the day. She couldn't get a read on what Brooke was thinking and that made her anxious.

She wanted to force Brooke to talk to her, but by doing so she might only make Brooke curl more tightly into an emotional ball. So Addison moved silently around the bathroom. She took out her contacts, brushed her teeth, and washed her face. Since Ramsey was asleep in the next room, they both put on T-shirts and boxers.

They reached their respective sides of the bed at the same time and paused with the sheet in their hands, looking at each other.

"I'll make the appointment," Brooke said quietly, because she didn't know what else to say. She couldn't guess what was going on in Addison's head. She barely knew what was happening in her own. Addison's discovery had sent a bolt of panic through her, and listening to Addison go on and on about surgeries hadn't helped. She tried to focus on what Addison had said first, that lots of women got lumps that were eventually diagnosed as benign. A quick search of the Internet tomorrow morning would confirm if that was true, and then maybe she could breathe again. For now, she needed to get into this bed and close her eyes and try to sleep.

Brooke drew back the sheet and climbed in. When she felt Addison crawl into the other side, she turned toward her. Addison opened her arms and Brooke moved closer and laid her head on Addison's shoulder. The solid feel of Addison's chest beneath her cheek reassured Brooke. She rested her arm across Addison's belly and grasped her opposite hip.

Addison kissed her forehead. Brooke wanted to say something—thought she should. But she didn't know what. She'd just had her most emotionally draining day since the day Diane died. She'd run the full spectrum too, from the nerves about the song to elation when the audience and apparently Tyler Cason received it well. Not to mention tearing her own heart out for five minutes while she performed. At the end of it all, she might finally have been able to let go of a little of her guilt and grief.

Less than an hour before, she'd stripped her clothes off and stepped into the oversized tub with Addison, intent on winding down before crawling into bed. She'd submerged herself, thinking this was how she wanted to end every day. But whatever relaxation she'd been able to find had imploded with Addison's hand on her breast.

She closed her eyes and tried to force herself to sleep. But she was still awake a long time later, obsessively probing the lump as if it might go away on its own. Restlessly she turned over and shoved her arms under the pillow, trying to find a comfortable position. Beside her, Addison slept nearly as fitfully, tossing off her side of the covers, but not fully waking. After pushing the comforter to the bottom of the bed, Brooke rolled to her side, gathered Addison against her, and arranged the sheet over both of them. She stroked Addison's damp hair off her forehead.

All of the instincts that had been telling her to push Addison away were blaring full alarms now. But for tonight, she shut them out and let the slow rhythm of Addison's breathing lull her to sleep.

❖

"Mommy."

Addison woke to the sound of Ramsey's voice seconds before she flung herself onto the bed. Ramsey landed and immediately launched herself farther up. Addison caught her, almost in midair, stopping her from pouncing on Brooke.

"Lightning-fast reflexes," Brooke said, her voice still rough from sleep. She rubbed her eyes and sat up.

Ramsey crawled to the middle of the bed and lay down between them. "Can I watch cartoons in here?"

"Yes." Addison picked up the remote off the nightstand and turned on the television on the dresser.

"Not that one."

Addison flipped through the channels until she came to another animated show. Ramsey nodded in approval.

Brooke watched Ramsey as if waiting for the inevitable questions. But Addison knew she was wasting her time. If Ramsey had questions about finding Brooke in her mother's bed on Sunday morning, they'd come later, after she'd had time to digest the situation. It was just as likely that Ramsey wouldn't think it odd that Brooke had slept over. Children were intuitive, and it had been quite some time since Ramsey asked any questions about why Daddy didn't live with them like other kids' daddies.

So, the three of them lay there watching cartoons. *I could wake up like this every morning.* Addison shook her head, mentally chastising herself. If she thought Brooke was poised to run before last night, she was probably lacing her shoes about now.

"Can I have cereal for breakfast?" Ramsey asked as the credits rolled on her cartoon.

"You sure can."

"Do you want cereal?" Ramsey looked at Brooke.

"No, thanks. I need to get home soon."

"Ramsey, honey, go brush your teeth."

"Before breakfast?"

"Yes. Then you can brush them again afterward." She wanted a reason to get Ramsey out of the room for a moment before Brooke made her escape.

Ramsey shrugged and climbed off the bed. Addison waited until she'd left the room and the door closed behind her.

"Brooke, I—"

"I should get going. I have a million things to do at home." Brooke bolted off the bed. She began throwing on her clothes from last night in such a hurry that instead of removing the boxers, she pulled her jeans on over them.

"Please wait."

"I can't, Addison. I can't do this." Brooke fisted her hands at her sides. "I can't be what you want me to be."

"I haven't asked you to be anything."

"You have. You do. Every time you look at me like you don't want this to end."

"I can't deny that. I don't want this to end. Do you?"

"No. And that's the problem."

Ramsey burst through the door and said, "Mommy, I brushed my teeth."

"Okay, sweetie. Go to the kitchen, I'll be right there." When Ramsey had left, Addison spoke quietly. "Brooke, I know losing Diane messed you up. But you've made so much progress, and I hoped that if you got a chance to work through things, we could—"

"I can't."

Addison sighed. "Brooke, I love you. And I think you love me. Why is that such a problem?"

Brooke stared at her.

"What?" Addison asked, frustrated.

"You love me."

"Yeah, so what?" She hadn't meant to make the revelation, but it was true.

Brooke shook her head. "And I do love you. God, I love you so much." Hearing those words and the sincere emotion behind them made Addison's chest ache. She took a step toward her but Brooke held up a hand. "And that's why I have to leave."

"Honey, that doesn't make sense."

"It does. I wanted you from the first time I saw you. But even though I noticed you, I knew right away I shouldn't get involved with you."

"Damn it, Brooke. You being scared isn't reason enough to not take a chance on what we could have." Knowing that Brooke felt the same way made her even more determined that they should be together.

"This isn't about me and Diane anymore, Addison. I won't pretend I have all of that worked out, but I'm getting there. But this—" Brooke touched her breast. "What if this is something bad?"

"You can't jump to that."

"I certainly can. We can't hide our heads and pretend we're guaranteed a fairy tale."

"Oh, believe me, I know that as well as anyone." Addison circled the bed and took Brooke's hands. Brooke wouldn't meet her eyes, but Addison didn't need to see them to guess what was going on. "I also know that going right to the worst-case scenario and stressing yourself out about it won't help. You just need to go to the doctor and get a mammogram."

"Just go get a mammogram, is that what you did?" Brooke pulled her hands free.

"For starters. And I still do, every year. On my left breast. Because nobody has any guarantees in life."

"Next you'll be telling me if I go to your precious support group everything will be better."

Addison threw up her hands. "Just go get the test, Brooke. Whatever the results are, we'll deal with it, together."

Brooke shook her head. "I can't put you through that." Brooke crossed the bedroom and was halfway down the hall before Addison caught up with her.

"You don't even know what you're dealing with yet."

"I can't take the chance, given everything you've been through." She descended the stairs and headed for the front door.

"Damn it, Brooke. Stop." Addison grabbed her arm. Realizing they were within earshot of the kitchen Addison lowered her voice. "You're overreacting."

Brooke stopped, because the plea in Addison's voice touched her. Just a few tests and Brooke could know her fate, she realized that. But she couldn't quit superimposing the memory of a very sick Diane onto herself. If she had to go through that again, at least she could spare Addison the pain of sitting at her bedside.

"I can actually see you shutting down." Addison shook her head and the disappointment on her face broke Brooke's heart.

"I'm sorry." Brooke didn't know what else to say.

"I can help you through this if you'll let me. I've been where you are, scared out of your mind. There's no other fear in this world quite like being afraid you're going to die. That one will make you break out in a cold sweat and shiver from the inside."

A chill raised bumps on Brooke's arms when she saw the torture in Addison's eyes.

"I beat the cancer, but that terror lingers for a long time. I don't think I truly started to let it go until sometime after Ramsey was born. It would have been so easy to be angry about what I went through. But I wanted to raise my daughter to be strong and to believe that anything's possible. And I realized that the way to show her that was by example."

Brooke stood there with her hand on Addison's front door, unable to turn the knob.

"I worried about what I was passing on to her and if I would be here to help her through whatever came. But I started keeping a notebook, where I wrote down things I wanted to tell her when she was older in case I wasn't around. Then I tried to let everything else go. You can do the same thing. Trust me, trust us, and let everything else go."

"I'm sorry, Addison." Turning that knob and propelling herself through that door and out of Addison's life was one of the hardest things Brooke had ever done. But she didn't let herself cry. While she drove home on autopilot and dragged herself up the stairs to collapse on her bed, she didn't shed even one of the tears that burned her eyes.

CHAPTER TWENTY-TWO

B rooke Donahue."

Brooke stood and followed the pleasant woman in scrubs down the hallway. They stepped into an alcove where the woman recorded her height, weight, and blood pressure. Then she showed Brooke into an exam room and left her with instructions on which way to put on her gown.

Brooke undressed and pulled it on, then scooted onto the paper-covered table. She was in the wine room today. Each of her gyno's exam rooms had a theme. Brooke's favorite had a beach theme. The wallpaper had sandcastles and brightly colored lounge chairs with matching umbrellas. When she lay back for her exam, she could look up at the framed photo of a coastline on the wall and pretend she was somewhere else. It was a great idea. The beach room.

But today, she stared at pictures of grapes, with the names of each various species listed below them in flowing script. On a good day, she didn't care that much what a pinot noir grape looked like in comparison to a sauvignon. And today, she cared even less. She wanted the beach room so she could think about sipping tropical drinks under the sun and forgetting her cares.

After a warning knock, her doctor entered the room.

"What seems to be the problem today, Brooke," she asked while reading Brooke's chart.

"I found a lump. In my breast."

"Okay." She flipped through the pages for another minute, still not making eye contact. Finally, she set the folder aside and looked up. "How long ago did you find it?"

"A few days." Brooke had gone home Sunday morning, knowing she had to wait until Monday to call for an appointment. First thing Monday morning, she phoned, preparing herself to go in that day, but the receptionist offered her a slot two days away. When Brooke inquired about getting in sooner, she said she'd call if they had any cancellations. Brooke spent the next two days ignoring Addison's calls, yet sitting on her couch and listening to the messages Addison left on her machine. By the end of the second day, the phone had stopped ringing.

"Let's see what's going on." The doctor pushed the Call button on the wall nearby, then stepped over to the sink to wash her hands. The nurse came in and silenced the button. She stood quietly in the corner while the doctor asked Brooke to put her hands on her hips, then raise her arm, then the other in the air so she could examine her breasts.

Brooke glanced over and the nurse was looking around the room as if she'd rather be anywhere else. Brooke wanted to tell her to go away, that she'd be much more comfortable without her there anyway. Instead, she quietly followed the doctor's instructions.

"Okay, I feel what you're talking about. Something's definitely there." The doctor probed some more, moving the lump around with her fingertips. Brooke knew the size and shape of the lump intimately. She'd touched it obsessively, trying to gauge whether it seemed to grow each day.

Brooke tried to focus on the doctor's words as she talked about her options, but she kept hearing, "Something's definitely there." By the time she left the doctor, with an appointment for an ultrasound and a return trip to her office, she wasn't feeling any better about her situation. Her ultrasound was scheduled for Thursday, but she couldn't get back in to see her doctor until Monday. She'd assumed this would all move a bit more quickly. Instead, she now expected to wait at least a week to get her ultrasound results. Then, the doctor had said, if they needed to biopsy or remove the lump, she would mostly likely refer Brooke to a general surgeon, since she didn't do any cutting.

❖

"Stop picking at your food."

Addison dropped her fork on the table with a clatter that made the couple at the next table jump. She didn't bother with an apologetic look that wouldn't be sincere anyway.

"Addison." Charles's voice carried a note of warning.

"This was a bad idea. I shouldn't have let you talk me into it."

"You've barely left the house all week unless it was for Ramsey."

"So?"

"Moping won't do any good." Charles lifted his napkin from his lap and wiped his mouth. "She walked out on you. Now you pick yourself up and move on."

"You didn't see her face when she left. I can't get it out of my head." Addison had tortured herself with the memory of their argument, the anguish on Brooke's face, and the fact that the first time they professed their love was in the midst of all that.

"Do you think she'll just realize she made a mistake and come running back to you?"

Addison didn't have an answer. For the first day or so after Brooke left she'd hoped Brooke would answer her calls. But, eventually, Addison found her self-respect and stopped calling. Addison had been trying to act like nothing was wrong for Ramsey's sake, but she missed Brooke. Every day she'd walked by Brooke's "I'm sorry" card on the refrigerator next to the one Ramsey had made, her heart broke a little more.

"What are you going to do?" Charles asked.

"If she doesn't want to be with me, I can't make her. But I care about her and I'd like to know that she went to the doctor."

"That's crap. You haven't shied away from anything since your diagnosis. If you love her, go get her."

"Aren't you the one who said she was too butch for me?"

He shrugged. "She won me over."

"She's not answering my calls. Do you really think if I show up on her doorstep she would open the door."

"It's worth a shot, isn't it?"

Addison sighed. "I've known for a while that I was setting myself up for a fall. But I couldn't help it. Maybe it's better to respect her wishes and leave her alone."

"She's scared, of her feelings and of what this lump might mean for her, and for you. She's probably a little angry, too. You know what scared and angry feels like. If you'd pushed me away when you got sick, would you have wanted me to respect your wishes or to persist?"

His words were still ringing in Addison's ears an hour later while she knocked on Brooke's door. She didn't hear any sounds coming from the loft, but the thick steel door would probably block them out. She knocked again.

"Brooke, if you're in there I really need to talk to you," she called.

She paced the hallway outside Brooke's apartment, mentally practicing what she would say if Brooke opened the door. She would lead with "I love you." After that she wasn't certain whether to take a hard-line approach or maybe appeal to Brooke's emotions.

She stared at the door, wondering if Brooke was on the other side looking through the peephole. She pressed her hand to the cool surface, hoping that if Brooke was that close, she could somehow transmit her feelings through it. How could she make Brooke see that being apart was harder than just facing whatever happened together? Just because Brooke had severed their physical connection, Addison hadn't suddenly stopped feeling anything for her.

Five minutes later, when she'd wandered the entire length of the hall about a dozen times, she finally decided to give up. Sending one last plaintive look toward the door, she headed for the stairs. She didn't allow herself to cry until she got in her car; then her tears flowed freely until she reached her driveway. She grabbed a tissue from the glove box and cleaned up her face before she went inside.

❖

Brooke sat on the steps of the Ryman Auditorium and watched the tourists file by. She'd driven downtown and parked her car, then walked around for over an hour before settling here. The turmoil within her quieted on the steps of one of the most amazing buildings in Nashville.

The Mother Church of Country Music was sacred. In fact, the building was originally built as a church and later became a celebrated concert hall. Back in the day, before the Opry moved over to Briley Parkway, country-music careers were made on the stage just inside those heavy wooden doors.

At this hour, the building was already closed for tours, and since no one was performing tonight the doors were locked. But Brooke didn't need to go inside to see the rows of pews, the balconies, or the historic stage that a few times a season still housed the red-barn backdrop of the Grand Ole Opry. She had a clear picture of them in her head.

The spirit of this place raced through her blood, in every pulse inside her veins. For as long as she could remember, she'd dreamed of seeing an artist perform one of her songs onstage.

Now she wondered if that would happen. She'd let the years and her career get away from her, and she'd had to lose Diane to see that.

"God, seriously," she muttered. "I'm just going to sit around acting all melancholy?"

A couple walking by looked at her as if they thought she was a homeless person talking to herself on the street. She glanced down at her clothes. Her jeans and sweatshirt were clean, not high-dollar but not transient wear either.

"I have to find something else to do for the next few days." She'd had her ultrasound yesterday and now faced a weekend of sitting around waiting to go back to the doctor for the results.

She stood and, after one final glance at the building behind her, she walked down to Broadway and turned the corner. She fell in with the flow of pedestrian traffic and traveled the few blocks to Poppi's place.

Once inside she went directly to the bar and plopped down on a stool.

"What'll it be?" Poppi asked as she approached.

"I need a job."

"From what I hear, you already have one. Tyler was in and told me he offered to buy your song."

"Yeah, he did." With everything else going on, Brooke hadn't thought anymore about his offer.

"Are you planning to do it?" Poppi lifted a bottle out of the cooler and held it up in invitation, but Brooke shook her head.

"I don't know." Brooke rubbed her hands over the surface of the bar, tracing the pictures of the big-name stars who'd played here. "Are you going to give me a job? I've waited tables before, you know."

"Since when are you that hard up for income?"

"I'm that hard up for something to fill my time."

"I'll give you a job, as long as it doesn't replace your career. You seriously consider Tyler's offer, or at least making some new moves on your own, and I'll let you wait tables here."

"Great. I can start right now."

"You can start tomorrow."

"Thanks, Poppi." Brooke left before Poppi could change her mind.

Brooke stepped outside the bar and pulled out her cell phone. She called up her contacts and scrolled down to Tyler Cason's number, then connected the call.

"Is that offer still on the table?" she asked when he answered.

"Absolutely."

"You can record the song."

"Yeah? That's awesome. I'll have our producer get in touch with you."

"Okay. And if you're still interested in doing some writing, I could use the distraction."

"Anytime."

"Great. I'm—going to be tied up for a little bit, but I'll call you in a couple of weeks or so, and we'll work out a time to get together."

"That sounds great, Brooke. I'm looking forward to it."

During the walk back to her car, Brooke thought about the history of this town. She lived in the birthplace of country music and had somehow lost her passion for it.

But when she thought about how she'd felt while performing at the benefit, she realized she hadn't really lost it. She just hadn't been looking for it.

CHAPTER TWENTY-THREE

Addison fought the knot of people blocking the door and finally burst through them into the crowded bar. Saturday night at Poppi's wasn't for the timid. Loud, live music and a throng of people shouting over it made it impossible to really hear anything inside the packed room.

Addison wove her way to the bar and was relieved to see Poppi working. She was the only person Addison knew who also knew Brooke. She hoped Brooke had shared her troubles with Poppi and maybe she would be able to tell her how she was doing.

"Hey, there," Poppi said when she caught sight of Addison. She worked her way to Addison's end of the bar, putting up drinks as she went. "Can I get you anything?"

"Have you seen Brooke?" Addison wasn't interested in a drink, and she couldn't focus enough to order one out of politeness until she'd heard something about Brooke.

"Sure." At first Poppi seemed surprised that Addison was asking. But then she narrowed her eyes and Addison could tell the moment when she caught on that they'd had a falling-out. She glanced toward the back room, then at a table nearby. "Hey, Wayne, don't be rude. Get up and let the lady have your table."

"What?" The burly looking man with an overgrown beard hollered back.

"Get up and give this lady your table."

He looked like he wanted to argue, but Poppi's expression said no one argued with her. So he elbowed his two buddies and they picked up their beers and motioned to Addison.

"Sit down, honey," Poppi said.

Addison did as she was told, and in less than a minute she knew why. Brooke rushed out of the back room, stopped by the bar to pick up a drink order, then beelined for a table on the other side of the room to drop it off. Brooke barely looked up as she worked her way around to Addison's table. She was only a step away when she finally did and their eyes met.

"Addison," she whispered.

"I love you," Addison blurted.

Brooke spun around and headed toward the back room. Addison looked helplessly at Poppi, who motioned for her to go after her. She sprung out of her chair and forced her way through the crowd after Brooke.

When Addison cleared the doorway, she found Brooke in a storage room with her arm braced against the wall and her forehead pressed to the back of her forearm.

"Brooke, please talk to me."

Brooke didn't turn around. "What are you doing here?"

"I could ask you the same. You're working here now?"

"It's temporary."

"Did you go to the doctor?"

Brooke sighed, then turned around and leaned back against the wall. "Yeah. I'm waiting for test results. Depending on the ultrasound, I may have to have surgery."

"Why did you shut me out?"

"I had to."

"No. You didn't." Addison took a step closer, but Brooke still looked like she might bolt.

"I can't watch you sit by my bedside hopelessly while I wither away the way I did with Diane."

"Even after everything I've been through, I've never been without hope."

"You can spout all the platitudes you want, but we both know what could happen. Those people at the benefit, the ones who don't have a chance, I could be one of them now."

"Don't you think you're being a bit melodramatic?"

"No." Brooke sighed and her shoulders slumped. "Maybe."

"Let me be there for you right now. We'll figure out the rest later."

"We'll only get more attached. Maybe I'm being dramatic, but you can't tell me for sure that this won't get bad. I refuse to put you through that."

"This isn't easy for me either, you know."

"What?"

"I haven't been sick for many years. But the emotional scars never completely go away. I'd put that time behind me and built a life that I was happy with. Then you came along and made me want things I haven't wanted in so long. Now, knowing something could be wrong has stirred all those old fears and memories up."

"See, it's probably best if we—"

"But I love you, Brooke. I love you, and to me that means through the good and the bad. You running away doesn't change that."

Brooke shook her head.

"I love you. And you can't change that. I love you. Hell, my kid even loves you. We could have something here."

Brooke's eyes closed off and Addison saw the final wall slip into place. Brooke wouldn't let her in, and if that was ever going to change, Brooke would have to come to it on her own.

"I'm sorry things happened this way, Brooke. You warned me from the start that you didn't want to get involved, but I couldn't help myself. So, I brought this heartache on myself." Brooke flinched, but Addison continued. "If you need me, you know where to find me."

She closed the distance between them, then kissed Brooke on the cheek. Her heart screamed at her to grab Brooke and hold on, but she forced her legs to move instead, propelling herself farther away from Brooke.

As she passed through the main room, Poppi gave her a curious look. Addison shook her head and kept going, needing to clear the bar before she lost control.

❖

"You're an idiot," Poppi said to the nearly empty room. She stood behind the bar putting away trays of freshly washed glasses.

"What?" Brooke moved from table to table, wiping down the surfaces. She stopped when she reached the one where Addison had sat waiting for her. When she'd seen Addison there, she'd felt like someone had punched her in the stomach. She'd never felt so sick and yet so happy to see someone.

"I don't know what happened between the two of you, but that girl came here with her hat in her hand and you stomped on it."

Brooke tilted her head. "I'm confused, Poppi. Was her hat in her hand, or was I stomping on it? And did you mean I was stomping on her hat or her hand?"

"Okay, smart-ass. Both ways, you're an idiot who's going home alone and broken-hearted."

"You don't understand."

"I don't have to. That girl loves you."

"Good God, Poppi," Brooke flung her towel down on the table in front of her, "this isn't a country song. Love doesn't fix everything."

"No. But it makes everything worthwhile."

Brooke shook her head and silently went back to wiping down tables. She could feel Poppi casting disapproving glances her way, but Poppi didn't say another word. Brooke finished her work and left.

She drove directly home, taking a bit of satisfaction in slamming the door behind her. She strode to the bedroom, intent on steaming away the aches of the last couple of hours in a hot shower.

She stopped when she noticed a box of Diane's things that her mother had sent over. She'd set it in the corner of the room and completely forgotten about it for months. Skipping the shower, she pulled the box near the edge of the bed, sat down, and lifted the flaps. A stark white envelope sat on top of the contents. She opened it, knowing it was from Diane's mother.

Toward the end, one night very late, Diane had initiated a heart-to-heart with her. She told Brooke she refused to write the sappy, if-you're-reading-this-you-know-I've-died letter. She said she was brave enough to say everything to Brooke's face. Then she proceeded to tell her how much she loved her and how much their friendship had meant. They talked for hours, cried together, then never brought it up again.

But now as Brooke flipped open the plain white card, a part of her wished Diane had broken her own rule. The scribbled words inside weren't in Diane's handwriting, though.

The two of you were like sisters, always looking out for each other, protecting each other. Here are a few things I think she would have wanted you to have. Thank you for loving my daughter. She was lucky to have you.

Brooke set the card aside and began to lift things out of the box. Diane's photo albums. Her high-school letter from when they played on the volleyball team together. The diamond pendant she never took off, nestled in a black-velvet box. That last one was a tough one. Brooke wished Diane had been buried with it instead.

When she pulled out a yearbook from their senior year, she paused to leaf through it, smiling at the pictures of them. At the bottom of the box, she found an unmarked DVD in a plain black box.

She slid off the bed and popped open the DVD player, set the disc into the tray, and picked up the remote.

"Don't be a sex tape, don't be a sex tape, don't be a sex tape," she chanted as she waited for the picture to come up on the television.

When she heard familiar music, she knew what she was about to see. This was a copy of the video slideshow from Diane's funeral. The photos progressed through Diane's childhood and into her high-school years. Brooke began appearing in many of them, and with each one she was instantly transported back to that day—sleepovers, sports-team photos, prom night, and graduation. She relived each moment of their friendship, missing Diane even more for the times they'd never get to have together.

When the slide from that party—that final party—popped up on the screen, Brooke thought about Addison. They'd both been there, and though Brooke searched her memory, she didn't remember seeing Addison. Knowing her as she did now, she had difficulty imagining that she could be in the same room as Addison and not notice her. Her senses seemed to go on heightened alert when Addison was around. Even now, Brooke could feel the softness of her skin, the scent of her perfume, fresh and clean like soap, and the taste of her kiss.

Right now she longed for the feel of Addison's arms more than anything. How would she get through this without her?

❖

Ramsey stuck her tongue out the side of her mouth as she gripped her pencil and concentrated. She meticulously copied the sample words Addison had written for her onto the paper in front of her, referring back to Addison's paper often.

When the doorbell rang, Ramsey almost bolted out of her chair.

"Sit," Addison said. "Finish those words."

Ramsey's lower lip poked out, but she sat back down.

Addison hadn't expected to find Brooke at her door, but when she looked out the peephole that's exactly who she saw. Brooke glanced at Addison's car in the driveway, then rang the bell again.

Addison rested her forehead against the door and tried to will herself not to answer. Almost two weeks hadn't been nearly enough time for her to get over Brooke, but she would lose whatever tiny progress she'd made the second she opened the door.

She looked out again and saw Brooke hang her head and start to turn away. Unable to let her leave, Addison jerked the door open. Brooke spun around, a look of relief on her face.

"Hi," she said tentatively.

"Brooke!" Ramsey exclaimed. She jumped down from the table and ran to the door.

Addison stuck her hand out and caught Ramsey before she could get to Brooke. "Ramsey, go to your room and play."

"No, I wanna—"

"Now, Ramsey."

Obviously hearing the tone she shouldn't argue with, Ramsey headed for her bedroom. She got halfway across the living room and turned around. Glaring defiantly at Addison, she gave Brooke a big smile and a wave, then ran off before Addison could say anything to her.

Brooke chuckled. "She's her mother's daughter."

"Don't do that."

"What?"

"Don't act like we're friends." Addison was partly angry about what had happened between them, but she was also frustrated that Brooke had so thoroughly charmed Ramsey. After Addison had made repeated excuses for why Brooke hadn't been around, Ramsey had nearly stopped asking. Now, she would probably start all over.

Brooke shifted from side to side, looking uncomfortable and uncertain, and Addison was glad. When she finally did speak, her words sliced through Addison so severely that she swore she must be bleeding inside.

"So...apparently they don't let you drive yourself home from this type of surgery."

Addison gulped, but she didn't say a word for fear that she'd break down.

"Come on, Addison, I don't have anyone else to ask."

"That's why you're here? Because you don't have anyone to drive you?"

"Not entirely."

"Why else?"

Brooke leaned forward and looked around the corner into the living room. "Can I at least come in while we talk?"

"You can talk from there." If Addison let Brooke across the threshold she might not have the strength to make her leave if she needed to.

"Okay. The ultrasound showed a solid mass. I'm having it removed and a pathologist will biopsy it right away. If it's malignant, they may have to remove more tissue before closing me up." Brooke's expression was emotionless, but her eyes showed every ounce of fear.

Addison bit her lower lip, but a thick lump was growing in the back of her throat.

Brooke held her hands out in supplication and shook her head. "I'm so sorry, Addison. I never wanted to hurt you."

"When is your surgery?"

"First thing in the morning."

"Jesus," Addison whispered, her head spinning at the thought of taking Brooke to the hospital the next day. She sucked in a breath and steeled herself for the fact that maybe Brooke was only here for a ride. "Okay, I'll drive you."

A small smile touched Brooke's lips and she released a heavy breath. "Thank you."

"What time should I pick you up?" Addison told herself she could get the time, then close the door. She could.

"Six, but that's not the only reason I'm here."

Addison waited.

"I—missed you. I was wrong." Brooke paused as if expecting Addison to say something. "First, I let my feelings about Diane's death get all mixed up with my feelings about your past. Then, in the past couple of weeks, things got worse when I thought I might be in a similar situation."

"You still might."

"I know."

"So, if nothing has really changed, what are you doing here?"

"I was going through some of Diane's things and I realized I'd been looking at the situation all wrong. She and I had some great times. We also had some tough times that I wouldn't have made it through without her. If I'd known back then that our friendship would end prematurely, I wouldn't have changed a thing. I wouldn't have wanted to miss out on what she and I shared. And I wouldn't want my fear to make me miss knowing you either. Whether we have weeks, or months, or years together, I want to spend every minute of it with you."

Brooke drew in a deep breath, waiting for Addison's response. She'd thought a lot about what she might say on the way over here, but she still needed Addison to accept her apology. "Look, I know I was supposed to bring diamonds this time, but it felt like that would have been skipping a few steps. So all I can offer is an apology. But if you need more I can go knock out another card for you."

The corner of Addison's mouth twitched. "What about Ramsey?"

"What about her?"

"I won't let her get close to someone who might not stick around. We're not looking for temporary."

"Neither am I. Didn't you hear anything I just said. I love you. And I love Ramsey."

"And you'll still feel that way no matter what happens tomorrow?"

"Yes. No matter what. You're making this kind of hard on me." Was there actually a chance she might still walk away from this alone?

Addison nodded. "I know. I want it to be hard for you. No one's guaranteed good health and prosperity. I've seen how bad things can get, and I have to know you won't run if it gets tough."

Brooke took a step forward and put her hands on Addison's waist. Addison didn't stop her. She buried her face against Addison's neck and sighed.

"I'm not going anywhere," Brooke whispered. Her heart vibrated with the truth of the words, and she hoped Addison could trust her. When Addison wrapped her arms around her, Brooke relaxed a little. Maybe she hadn't completely screwed this up.

Brooke eased back. "Now can I come in?"

Addison nodded, then stepped back. They moved to the couch together and sat down.

"Mommy," Ramsey called from the hallway.

"Yes?"

"I wanna say hi to Brooke."

"Okay."

Ramsey ran into the room and flung herself onto the couch. She sprawled across their laps, draping her legs over Addison's and laying her head on Brooke's thighs.

"Sure you want to sign up for this?" Addison asked quietly.

Brooke smiled. "Absolutely." She pushed Ramsey's disheveled curls out of her eyes and listened as she began talking about learning to write her letters.

Sitting there with Addison, Brooke was the most peaceful she'd been since Diane died. She only prayed she could hold onto that feeling until the morning. She touched Addison's cheek. How had she ever doubted that this was where she belonged?

CHAPTER TWENTY-FOUR

Honey, I'll be home in a couple of hours…Yes…Yes, I'll bring Brooke home with me…No, she can't come to the phone…Brooke isn't feeling well right now, so she's going to need to rest for a little while…I'm sure she would like that."

Addison's words reached Brooke through a thick fog as she forced open her eyes. Addison sat in a chair pulled up close to Brooke's hospital bed, and her hand cradled Brooke's.

"I would like what?" Brooke's voice was rough, her throat dry.

"Hey, sweetie, how are you?"

Testing, Brooke moved a little. She was groggy still, but felt no pain. "I'm okay. What would I like?"

Addison pressed her lips together as if trying not to show her true emotions. "Ramsey wants to help take care of you like you took care of her when she was sick."

"Did the doctor say anything?" Brooke's heart thudded. Was Addison trying to figure out how to deliver the bad news?

"Not yet. The nurse said the surgery went fine and the doctor would come and talk to you once you woke up."

Brooke nodded and squeezed Addison's hand. She lifted the sheet, pulled out the neck of her hospital gown, and looked down at her chest. The bandages there offered little clue as to what the doctors had found underneath.

"Do you still have two of them?" Addison asked, craning to look as well. Her strained voice didn't match the lightheartedness of her words.

"Yes." Brooke pulled Addison's hand into her lap and stroked up her forearm. "Are you still in, no matter what?"

"You know, at some point we're going to have to stop asking each other that."

"How about right now?" Brooke looked into Addison's eyes and realized she didn't need the reassurance. She saw it all right there.

"Okay." Addison smiled. "I'm here for you. But you should also know that if you need more support—"

"I'm not going back to your group."

"Just think about it. You don't know how difficult things may get."

"Let's take this one step at a time." She squeezed Addison's hand. She couldn't totally discount the collection of people who'd meant so much to Diane and Addison. Since attending the meeting she viewed them as people with real fears and concerns instead of a villainous group. "I promise that no matter what the doctor says today, I'll always be honest with you about what I feel. And if I become overwhelmed or need help, we'll figure out the best way to proceed together. Is that good enough for now?"

Addison nodded.

"I love you so much."

"I love you, too." Addison angled forward and captured Brooke's mouth in a gentle kiss. Her lips caressed Brooke's in a way that let her know it didn't matter what the future held. As long as they had love and hope they could face it all.

"Brooke," the doctor called as he knocked once and came into the room. "Oh, I'm sorry." He took a step back.

Addison pulled back, but when she started to slip her hand out of Brooke's, Brooke held on. She enfolded Addison's hand in hers.

"It's okay," she said.

"Are you ready for me?" he asked.

Brooke met Addison's eyes and said, "Yes, we are."

About the Author

Erin Dutton is the author of seven romance novels: *Sequestered Hearts*, *Fully Involved*, *A Place to Rest*, *Designed for Love*, *Point of Ignition*, *A Perfect Match*, and *Reluctant Hope*. She is also a contributor to *Erotic Interludes 5: Road Games* and *Romantic Interludes 1 & 2* from Bold Strokes Books. She revisited two characters from one of her novels in *Breathless: Tales of Celebration*. She is a 2011 recipient of the Alice B. Readers' Appreciation Award for her body of work.

Erin lives near Nashville, Tennessee, with her amazing partner and often draws inspiration from both her adopted hometown and places she's traveled. When not working or writing, she enjoys playing golf and spending time with friends and family.

Books Available From Bold Strokes Books

Wild by Meghan O'Brien. Shapeshifter Selene Rhodes dreads the full moon and the loss of control it brings, but when she rescues forensic pathologist Eve Thomas from a vicious attack by a masked man, she discovers that she isn't the scariest monster in San Francisco. (978-1-60282-227-6)

Reluctant Hope by Erin Dutton. Cancer survivor Addison Hunt knows she can't offer any guarantees, in love or in life, and after experiencing a loss of her own, Brooke Donahue isn't willing to risk her heart. (978-1-60282-228-3)

Conquest by Ronica Black. When Mary Brunelle stumbles into the arms of Jude Jaeger, a gorgeous dominatrix at a private night club, Mary is smitten, but she soon finds out Jude is her professor, and Professor Jaeger doesn't date her students…or her conquests. (978-1-60282-229-0)

The Affair of the Porcelain Dog by Jess Farady. What darkness stalks the London streets at night? Ira Adler, present plaything of crime lord Cain Goddard, will soon find out. (978-1-60282-230-6)

365 Days by KE Payne. What do you do when you're fifteen years old, confused about your sexuality, and the girl of your dreams doesn't even know you exist? Clemmie has 365 days to discover for herself, and she's going to have a blast doing it! (978-1-60282-540-6)

Darkness Embraced by Winter Pennington. Surrounded by harsh vampire politics and secret ambitions, Epiphany learns that an old enemy is plotting treason against the woman she once loved, and to save all she holds dear, she must embrace and form an alliance with the dark. (978-1-60282-221-4)

78 Keys by Kristin Marra. When the cosmic powers choose Devorah Rosten to be their next gladiator, she must use her unique skills to try to save her lover, herself, and even humankind. (978-1-60282-222-1)

Playing Passion's Game by Lesley Davis. Trent Williams's only passion in life is gaming—until Juliet Sullivan makes her realize that love can be a whole different game to play. (978-1-60282-223-8)

Retirement Plan by Martha Miller. A modern morality tale of justice, retribution, and women who refuse to be politely invisible. (978-1-60282-224-5)

Who Dat Whodunnit by Greg Herren. Popular New Orleans detective Scotty Bradley investigates the murder of a dethroned beauty queen to clear the name of his pro football–playing cousin. (978-1-60282-225-2)

The Company He Keeps by Dale Chase. A riotously erotic collection of stories set in the sexually repressed and therefore sexually rampant Victorian era. (978-1-60282-226-9)

Cursebusters! by Julie Smith. Budding-psychic Reeno is the most accomplished teenage burglar in California, but one tiny screw-up and poof!—she's sentenced to Bad Girl School. And that isn't even her worst problem. Her sister Haley's dying of an illness no one can diagnose, and now she can't even help. (978-1-60282-559-8)

True Confessions by PJ Trebelhorn. Lynn Patrick finally has a chance with the only woman she's ever loved, her lifelong friend Jessica Greenfield, but Jessie is still tormented by an abusive past. (978-1-60282-216-0)

Jane Doe by Lisa Girolami. On a getaway trip to Las Vegas, Emily Carver gambles on a chance for true love and discovers that sometimes in order to find yourself, you have to start from scratch. (978-1-60282-217-7)

Ghosts of Winter by Rebecca S. Buck. Can Ros Wynne, who has lost everything she thought defined her, find her true life—and her true love—surrounded by the lingering history of the once-grand Winter Manor? (978-1-60282-219-1)

Who I Am by M.L. Rice. Devin Kelly's senior year is a disaster. She's in a new school in a new town, and the school bully is making her life miserable—but then she meets his sister Melanie and realizes her feelings for her are more than platonic. (978-1-60282-231-3)

Call Me Softly by D. Jackson Leigh. Polo pony trainer Swain Butler finds that neither her heart nor her secret are safe when beautiful British heiress Lillie Wetherington arrives to bury her grandmother, Swain's employer. (978-1-60282-215-3)

Split by Mel Bossa. Weeks before Derek O'Reilly's engagement party, a chance meeting with Nick Lund, his teenage first love, catapults him into the past, where he relives that powerful relationship revealing what he and Nick were, still are, and might yet be to each other. (978-1-60282-220-7)

Blood Hunt by L.L. Raand. In the second Midnight Hunters Novel, Detective Jody Gates, heir to a powerful Vampire clan, forges an uneasy alliance with Sylvan, the wolf Were Alpha, to battle a shadow army of humans and rogue Weres, while fighting her growing hunger for human reporter Becca Land. (978-1-60282-209-2)

Loving Liz by Bobbi Marolt. When theater actor Marty Jamison turns diva and Liz Chandler walks out on her, Marty must confront a cheating lover from the past to understand why life is crumbling around her. (978-1-60282-210-8)

Kiss the Rain by Larkin Rose. How will successful fashion designer Eve Harris react when she discovers the new woman in her life, Jodi, and her secret fantasy phone date, Lexi, are one and the same? (978-1-60282-211-5)

Sarah, Son of God by Justine Saracen. In a story within a story within a story, a transgendered beauty takes us through Stonewall-rioting New York, Venice under the Inquisition, and Nero's Rome. (978-1-60282-212-2)

Sleeping Angel by Greg Herren. Eric Matthews survives a terrible car accident only to find out everyone in town thinks he's a murderer—and he has to clear his name even though he has no memories of what happened. (978-1-60282-214-6)